Denise Robertson has worked extensively television and radio and as a national newspa journalist. Starting with *The Land of Lost Content* 1984, which won the Constable Trophy for Fiction, sl as published twelve previous successful novel Denise lives in Sunderland with her husband, one five sons and an assortment of dogs.

Also by Denise Robertson

THE LAND OF LOST CONTENT
A YEAR OF WINTER
BLUE REMEMBERED HILLS
THE LAND OF LOST CONTENT: THE BELGATE
TRILOGY
THE SECOND WIFE
NONE TO MAKE YOU CRY
REMEMBER THE MOMENT
THE STARS BURN ON
THE ANXIOUS HEART
THE BELOVED PEOPLE
STRENGTH FOR THE MORNING
TOWARDS JERUSALEM
A RELATIVE FREEDOM
ACT OF OBLIVION
WAIT FOR THE DAY

"780863"185779"

009181

CBS	25/03/2002
F	5.99
AFF	D

CANCELLED

DAYBREAK

DENISE ROBERTSON

POCKET BOOKS

LONDON · SYDNEY · NEW YORK · TOKYO · SINGAPORE · TORONTO

First published in Great Britain by Simon & Schuster, 1996
This edition first published by Pocket Books, 1997
An imprint of Simon & Schuster Ltd
A Viacom Company

Copyright © Denise Robertson, 1996

The right of Denise Robertson to be identified as author of this work has
been asserted in accordance with sections 77 and 78 of the Copyright,
Designs and Patents Act 1988.

This book is copyright under the Berne Convention
No reproduction without permission
All rights reserved

Simon & Schuster Ltd
West Garden Place
Kendal Street
London
W2 2AQ

SIMON & SCHUSTER AUSTRALIA
SYDNEY

A CIP catalogue record for this book is available from the British Library.

ISBN 0-671 85263 9

Printed and bound in Great Britain by Caledonian International Book
Manufacturing, Glasgow

This book is a work of fiction. Names, characters, places and incidents
are either the product of the author's imagination or are used fictitiously.
Any resemblance to actual events or locales or persons, living or dead, is
entirely coincidental.

Prologue

In each twenty-four hours there is a moment when night relinquishes its hold on a city. Sometimes it is marked by lights springing up in a darkened tower block, sometimes by the flutter of birds taking flight from their rooftop perches. Before that moment the city is still. A single noise echoes eerily in a quiet street. A car starting up is an intrusion. Afterwards, each separate noise is drowned in the hubbub of a city waking and going about its business.

1

Monday 4.00 a.m.

Liz heard her alarm through layers of sleep and put out a hand to stop it. She was still unused to the vastness of the double bed without Dave's comforting bulk beside her. Now she left her arm lying across the empty space and calculated how long she and David had been apart. She liked doing sums in her head and the exercise soothed her. It would be thirteen months, one week and two days she concluded, because he had gone on a Saturday and today was Monday. They had hardly spoken for the preceding twelve months, never made love and, in their last three months, not even had the energy to argue. She was glad he was gone so why did she still miss his physical presence in the mornings?

After a moment she gave up wondering and threw back the duvet. It was four o'clock and her cab would come at four-thirty. If she wanted to look halfway decent she hadn't a moment to spare and appearance mattered to her nowadays, now that Simon was there, at the studio, looking tired and rumpled at five a.m. but infinitely – *infinitely* – desirable.

In the shower she tried to picture the photographs on Simon's desk – wife, children and family dog. Family photographs were as good as a 'Keep Off The Grass' sign. Except that she hadn't kept off the grass and walking on it barefoot had been wonderful . . . or *would* have been wonderful if it had not been for the guilty anguish on her lover's face. 'He's taken,' she told her reflection as she cleaned her teeth. It didn't work. She still wanted him.

As she dressed she thought of the moment she had realised she loved Simon. They had spent hours editing and re-editing a piece of film, trying to cover the shortcomings of the young researcher who had directed it. They had snipped and patched, run and rerun, jigged and rejigged until they had made something comprehensible from a meaningless jumble. 'That's it,' Simon had said in triumph, and put out an arm to hug her. She had leaned against him, sensing his gratitude, suddenly wishing that what he felt for her was something more, much more.

She had drawn away then, frightened by her own feelings, until he had reached for her jacket and draped it over her shoulders. 'Come on,' he'd said. 'We need a drink.' And in the bar she had leaned weary shoulders against the side of the booth and realised Simon was the love of her life.

In the cab she put aside personal and randy thoughts and went through today's running order in her mind. The night editor would brief them at five and if something momentous had happened they might have to junk half the prepared items. Even if it was a quiet news day, they still had a good line-up. She leaned her head against the cab's upholstery but her hair was still damp from the shower so she sat upright again.

They had a good consumer item – a petrol price war – and today's cook was Ben Ho, the top expert on Chinese cuisine. There was a hearts-and-flowers item on the new quintuplets and the fashion item was particularly strong: wonderful work-into-leisure wear. With Germaine Greer as guest of the day that was a strong programme by anyone's standards. Which was just as well when there was a journalist snooping around.

She leaned her cheek against the side window and thought about Simon. I'll always love him, she thought and was at once cheered and defeated by the thought. She had always despised women who had affairs with married men. What about sisterhood? She had never thought of herself as a feminist but there were limits.

Through the front windscreen, she could see edges of buildings emerging from the night sky. It was summer and dawn came early. She would be entering the Daybreak Television studios at daybreak. She smiled in the safe darkness of the cab and tried not to think of how long it would be before she and Simon would be alone together once more.

The time they had alone together could be measured in minutes, seconds even. But it was enough that their eyes could meet across a desk, a table, even a crowded studio. Even in a lift hands could touch briefly while eyes remained fixed on the floor signs flashing by. And now and again, when they met at her flat, it was heaven. Useless to tell herself it was a one-way street, a cul-de-sac whose end would be rejection.

I can't think ahead, she told herself firmly. Not now. Not today.

Not until some miracle made the way clear for them to be together for always.

Simon silenced the alarm with a minute to spare and extricated himself from the bed with exquisite care but it was in vain. 'Don't forget you're meeting me at three. Three, Simon! I won't be made a fool of, standing around on my own.' He moved towards the bathroom but Jane's anxious voice followed him. 'Answer me! I said I won't be left there on my own – not again. Do you hear me?'

'I hear you.' He switched on the light and turned in the doorway, trying to keep the irritation out of his voice. 'I'll be there if it's humanly possible, but I work, Jane. I have a job. You know, the thing that pays the bills? And it's only a furniture shop, for God's sake. If you did have to brave it on your own it wouldn't be the end of the world. Unless you're afraid of being violated by a bed-settee.'

'Oh yes . . .' She had struggled up on the pillows to put on the bedside lamp. 'Make a joke of it, Simon. All I'm asking is for you to be a husband for a change. A partner. I could do it on my own — I've done most things on my own in the last ten years, God knows — but for once, just once, I want some cooperation. I want to choose things for our home like our friends do — together. Is that too much to ask?' Her dark hair was rumpled on her forehead, shadowing hostile eyes and a turned-down mouth.

He didn't answer although he was tempted to point out that her choice would prevail, whether or not he was there. Instead he tried to let the shower's flow wash it all away, the mess that was his marriage, the hell on earth that was his job — even Liz, for his relationship with her too was angst-ridden.

What happened to people when they entered into relationships? Before marriage, Jane had been a bright-eyed, laughing child. Now she could govern Parkhurst. And Liz had been a cool, almost detached, certainly elusive, professional woman. Now her eyes were haunted, she was losing weight and it was all his fault.

The bathroom was newly refurbished — pale-green Italian tiles blended with an eau-de-Nil suite. Even the towels were coordinated with the white cabinets, which were stencilled in green and peach. Jane loved home-making. If she put half the effort into understanding their marriage that she put into colour-matching paint they might have fewer rows, he thought bitterly.

But as he switched off the shower and stepped out onto the pale green rubber-tiled floor he acknowledged that it was his neglect of her in the early days of their marriage that had created her obsession with nest-building. That the neglect had been born out of a desire to succeed and be a good provider went some way to mitigating his offence, but it didn't excuse him altogether.

He looked in on his children before he left the house. Nine-year-old Jake lay face down, an opened copy of *Viz* on the pillow beside him. If Jane saw that all hell would break loose. He closed the magazine and slipped it into the bedside drawer. The boy was growing up, growing up well, in spite of everything. He touched the short bristling hair and then went next door to see his daughter, Rosie, asleep in her Care Bear boudoir. She had been asleep when he got home last night. She too was growing up and he hardly ever saw her except in sleep. He bent to kiss the brow beneath the fair fringe and tucked her duvet around her.

In the light from the landing he could see the fan of lashes on her cheek. Rosie would be beautiful, like her mother, when she was grown. Please God, she would be happier! Nowadays Jane was almost a third child, always making demands. He pulled the door to and tiptoed down the stairs, trying to rid himself of bad vibes and think of the day ahead. At least work was a diversion.

His cab was waiting, its engine idling, ready to bear

him to the studio. There would be activity there already, cleaners wafting polish and dusters, coffee dripping into pots, commissionaires changing shifts, putting on a morning face to greet sleepy guests, half of them unwilling, others, the amateurs, dazed with the wonder of actually being on TV. The schmucks, to think there was even the smallest grain of magic in one of the grubbiest industries on earth. But today they must be careful. A *Herald* journo was there to observe, so anything untoward must be kept under wraps. He groaned, thinking of one extra straw. Would it be the one that broke the camel's back?

Daphne Bedford was awake long before her alarm shrilled. She had woken at half-hour intervals throughout the night, terrified of sleeping in and missing her cab. Now her eyes burned in their sockets and her mouth was dry. She had often envied TV presenters, but if this was what it entailed – getting up in the middle of the night – she would never do so again.

She looked at her reflection in the mirror as she cleaned her teeth, seeing herself for the tired old hack she was. In twenty years with the same paper she had written every feature ten times over, explored every angle of human relationships, every fault of modern living. She lifted her lip and looked searchingly at her porcelain crowns. Two thousand pounds but worth it. Ageing teeth were a turn-off in the morning.

Actually, she didn't look too bad today. She sucked

in her cheeks and lifted her chin to tauten the skin underneath. On a dark night she could pass for forty. Well, forty-five. She grinned at her own foolishness and got on with the wash that would have to substitute for her usual leisurely bath. The things you gave up for your job!

As she dressed she tried to remember how often she had written about television. It was depressing to think how many of the stars she had profiled had fallen from favour. Nothing lasted, not even journalists. Especially not journalists! She had survived eleven features editors at the *Herald* but she had an uneasy feeling that the twelfth, Lou Bryan, all five feet of her, would see her off.

She thought of Lou Bryan's face, pretty but implacable beneath the patterned bandanna. 'I want the *whole* picture at Daybreak, Daphne. Not one of your "let's be fair to the subject" jobs. There's dirt there, everyone knows it. You find it! They've promised us total access. Use it! To be honest, I'd rather Mike did it but he's not free and Daybreak might renege if we don't get in quick, so it'll have to be you.'

At that moment, Daphne had felt every one of her fifty-one years, knowing Lou would get rid of her soon, whatever she made of the Daybreak job. Still, she had five days in which to profile the life of a breakfast TV station, which meant five days comparatively free from Lou.

At first she had admired Lou, reluctantly admitting

that she had that killer instinct that you needed in
Fleet Street. If Daphne had had that ability to divorce
sentiment from story, to pursue truth ruthlessly, she
might have been features editor now instead of just
another journo. But she had not had the luck, either,
that gift of being in the right place at the right time
so that you got a scoop that made you for life. It was
unlikely that her chance would come now, not when she
was assigned to things like the Daybreak profile. With
luck, she would turn in a decent feature, a balanced
account of what it was like behind the camera as well
as in front. But there would be no scoop, no chance of
her byline on the front page, her dream ever since her
apprenticeship on a provincial paper.

She grimaced as she used blusher to give herself
cheekbones, grinned as she first outlined her lips then
filled in the colour. *C'est la vie!* She wasn't meant to be
famous. She was meant to fill pages so that advertisers
had an attractive showcase for their wares. She took
a last look at herself and then hurried downstairs.
Mustn't be late on the first day.

She settled back in the cab and closed her eyes,
reopening them quickly as they burned even more
intensely. Lack of sleep, that was the trouble. She
had meant to have an early night but, like most of
her good resolutions, it had come to nothing. Perhaps
there would be coffee at the studios, and croissants
and delightful young researchers to serve her every
whim. The woman who had liaised with her had
been nice. Liz. The surname escaped her but it was

there in her contacts book. Liz Something, Features Editor. She had sounded quite telly-ish but human. If they were all like that, it would be OK. She pictured a young, very handsome male researcher plying her with cappuccino and a smile formed on her lips. 'I wish,' she said aloud. 'In your dreams, Daphne. In your dreams.'

'God!' Chris Springer looked at the clock in disbelief and shook it. The alarm had gone off − the spring was unwound − and he had slept right through it. He leaped from the bed, reached for his jeans and extracted yesterday's boxer shorts. Where were clean ones? He looked around at the piles of clean and dirty clothing, the shoes and sports bags, old copies of *Private Eye* and general clutter that covered the floor. He would do something about this room tonight. This afternoon if he got home! He lived in squalor. Everyone who worked at Daybreak lived in squalor, shagged out by overwork. It had been eleven o'clock when he'd got home last night and then they'd sat around drinking. Never again!

As he crossed the hall he pounded on Dilly's door and then on Clifford's just in case, although they would undoubtedly be sharing a bed. 'We're late. Get up.' He could hear their mingled groanings and protestations. 'Don't blame me. I'm not a bloody wake-up call.'

He turned the shower to cold and took it as a punishment. If he could get there ahead of his guests it would be OK. Just. Unless Barry or Carol didn't like the brief, in which case he would already have been summoned and it would be curtains.

He stepped out, shivering, stroking back his wet hair. When he and Vera, the studios' cleaner, won the lottery he would retire to the Canaries to write a best-seller, and sod telly.

Three minutes later he was outside, apologising to the patient cabbie and wishing, with all his heart, that he had taken time out to find some underpants, clean or dirty. Anything to intercede between his tenderest parts and the denim that was sawing them in two.

It had seemed like a gift from heaven when he landed the job at Daybreak after two years as a runner for Red Box. Runners were the lowest form of life in television. As a researcher he was reasonably well paid and did have a chance to initiate ideas and see them come to fruition. But he was still a member of the lower orders and left in no doubt about it.

There was a strict heirarchy in television and no one was allowed to forget it. 'Do as I say, not as I do' should be embroidered and hung on the walls of management offices. He had come into television thinking it would be a forcing-house for ideas, a place where you could quite literally make your dreams come true. Now he knew that to put forward an idea was to invite disappointment.

If he could get out of breakfast telly things might improve. The mid-morning programmes were less hack-neyed and they didn't employ cartoons. The *Daybreak* programme's running cartoon featured a dog detective, a labrador called Sherlock, which made Chris want to puke every time it padded across the screen, meerschaum pipe clenched between doggy jaws.

Periodically he thought about giving it all up and doing something else. Anything as long as it dealt with real life. TV was virtual reality made flesh and *Daybreak* its apogee. Everyone who worked on it was barking!

'Ta,' he said as the cab decanted him at the studio door. He scribbled on the driver's chit, clutching his briefcase under his arm. 'Ta,' he said again and fled for the revolving door.

Vera was emptying the baskets in reception. She stood up and looked at the clock. 'Good afternoon,' she said pointedly and then – taking pity – 'They haven't missed you. Well, nobody's shouted. So get some breakfast down you. You can't think on an empty stomach.'

He put up a finger to push his glasses onto the bridge of his nose. 'Are you sure, Vee? It's bloody late!'

'Language!' Beneath her fair finger-waves Vera's brows arched. 'It *is* bloody late as you call it so don't stand there looking like a wet weekend. Get something hot into you and get cracking!'

'OK, don't go ballistic, Vee.' He turned towards the lift, tugging at his jeans as he did so. There was a woman sitting in the corner. His woman for the cut-price petrol item, probably. 'Mrs Banford?' he said but the woman shook her head.

'I'm Daphne Bedford . . . from the *Herald*. I'm here

to do a profile. I think someone's coming for me. They're seeing to it at the desk.'

As Chris smiled and withdrew he remembered the editor's warning. 'She musn't see anything untoward. Anything. You know what journos are like. They can see round corners so don't give them an inch. Heads will roll otherwise.' He had popped two of his bloody vitamin pills then and repeated the threat: 'Heads will roll.'

Safe in the loo Chris grimaced at himself in the mirror. 'Nice work, Stringer. Half an hour late . . . You're off to a great start.' Except that the journo wouldn't be gunning for humble researchers. She was after bigger game.

He sluiced his face in the basin to wake himself up and imagined the headlines that might accompany a piece on Daybreak. Barry and Carol, the main presenters, were two egomaniacs who loathed each other. Dilly, who had been with Daybreak six months before Chris, swore she had once seen Carol stick out her foot at the head of the stairs, in an effort to tumble Barry head first down a flight. Dilly was prone to exaggerate but he wouldn't put anything past Carol, who could double for Cruella de Ville any day.

As for Barry, he would sell his grandmother down the river. 'I'm on your side,' he would tell a producer and then stay silent in a production meeting while that producer's idea was hacked to pieces. If the headlines ever read TOP TV PRESENTERS IN MURDER TRIANGLE, any one of ten could've bumped them off. According to Dilly, Simon, the deputy editor, was screwing Liz, who was in charge of features. You couldn't believe everything you heard. Still, the *Herald* piece could make interesting reading.

He looked at himself in the mirror when he had dried his face. He looked bright-eyed and bushy-tailed now, like someone who'd been up and working for an hour or more. Satisfied, he let himself out into the corridor and went in search of breakfast. It was twenty past five: forty minutes to transmission and an hour and twenty minutes before his item. As he neared the canteen his producer appeared in a doorway. 'Where the hell have you been?'

'Around,' Chris said, hating how easily he lied nowadays. 'I looked for you but they said you were in the edit suite.' Once his scalp had prickled when he lied. Now it barely stirred.

Daphne had been sitting in reception for five minutes and was beginning to get impatient when a Sharon Stone lookalike appeared.

Everything about her was perfect, from her sculpted hair to her gold-kid-shod feet. Her skin was pale gold, her double-breasted suit was apricot, her nails, prominently displayed on upraised hands, were square-cut and white-rimmed. She halted in front of Daphne and pursed apricot-hued lips in what was meant to be a smile of welcome. 'Daphne?' It was said with all the warmth of a lifelong friend but the girl's eyes were cold and already flicking towards the door. 'Sorry about that . . . mild crisis . . . you know what it's like with a news-oriented programme. Well, of course you do . . . silly of me to ask.' She could obviously carry on a long conversation without any help, so Daphne let her get on with it. They moved through a door and then along a corridor until they reached a small office, which seemed to be filled with TV sets and rows of video tape.

A man rose from behind a desk. 'Daphne? Good to see you.' He held out his hand. 'I'm Simon Drake, deputy editor.' He was thin and dark and looked like Al Pacino. He gestured to the woman standing beside him. 'This is Liz Fenton . . . Liz really runs this programme.' Liz was tall and blonde and looked tired.

'We've talked on the phone. Nice to meet you.' Daphne held out a hand to Simon. 'Good of you to let me snoop like this.'

Simon smiled. He had good teeth and the smile was engaging but his eyes were wary. 'Not at all — as long as you show us in a good light.'

'Would I do other?' Daphne said. She shook hands with Liz then, and they all smiled until their teeth ached and they could fall upon the coffee the Sharon Stone clone produced.

'Liz will be your contact and general mother figure,' Simon said. 'She's in charge of features.' The women smiled at each other as he continued, 'I'll be available as and when you need me and you'll meet our editor and the presenters in due course. Feel free to ask for anything you need. We want you to see everything.'

'You are being nice,' Daphne said and hoped her tones were not too ironic. 'I hope you've got something hidden in the attic. I can't go back empty-handed.'

'Don't.' Liz was holding up a hand. 'We spent last week hiding all our skeletons and swearing the troops to silence. Don't tell me it was in vain.' They smiled again but this time with more warmth, silently acknowledging that there would have to be compromise, that both sides needed a good article, revealing enough of the truth for credibility, but not too much.

'That's fine, then,' Simon said, and there was relief in his voice. 'Today we have Germaine Greer on the papers and discussing her new book. There's an interview with the mother of the new quintuplets, the usual homes-and-gardens items and a look at fashion. What is it, Liz, some American . . .?'

'Donna Karan.' Liz had produced a thick wad of green paper. 'This is the final script. It's white for draft scripts, pink for provisional and green for the one we go to bed with. You'll see the news inserts. They're on grey. We have a new newsreader. She's come to us from the regions. You'll like her. And of course we have weather every day and the stars and cookery. It's Chinese today. Wonderful. I could smell it as I came past the studio. Our top-note is a guest of the day. Germaine today, as Simon said. We have Billy St Angelo, the film actress, on Tuesday, Hester Claire, the soap queen, on Wednesday and then – big scoop – we have Vincent.'

Daphne's eyes had widened at the name of the pop

idol. 'You may well goggle,' Liz said, gratified. 'Don't ask me how we did it. You know how elusive he is normally. But we've got him for two days. He's plugging a charity for homeless kids and we're letting him have his head as long as he stays within ITC rules.'

'Vincent,' Daphne said. 'I'm impressed.' Lou Bryan would be more than impressed. She was always talking about the elusive pop millionaire who was that most interesting thing in media terms: an enigma. He had come to stardom without a hint of scandal. There was no particular woman in his life but a sufficiency of glamorous female escorts to make him overtly hetero-sexual. He had never been seen the worse for drink or substances, never raised voice or hand in anger and was known for his efforts for charity. There must be a chink somewhere, Daphne thought. No one's *that* perfect.

'Any chance of an interview as part of the piece?' she asked. If they said yes – if they could fix it – she might even be able to expand it. Half a page on Vincent would do her no harm at all.

'If you promise to mention his charity thing,' Simon said, 'I should think he'd do handstands. He's OK by all accounts.'

Daphne could tell the deputy editor wanted rid of her now. His eyes were straying to the monitor in the corner. Something was going on in the studio but there was no sound, only his distracted expression to show that, whatever it was, it wasn't good.

'Would you excuse me?' He rose to his feet as the door was flung open to reveal a wide-eyed and white-faced girl with a headset on and a clipboard in her hands.

'Sorry,' the girl said, glancing wildly around the office. 'But they want you down there, Simon. Now! It's the intro again. She says it's her turn . . .' There was obviously more but Liz had silenced the girl with a warning look.

'Sorry.' Simon had moved round the desk. 'Just a hiccup but I must go. Ten minutes to transmission . . . You know how it is.'

'Trouble?' Daphne asked, when he had left the room.

'That depends on whether or not this is on the record.' Liz's eyes were steady on Daphne's face.

'Off,' Daphne said. 'God's honour.'

'Unless it's too, too juicy?' Liz was grinning wryly. 'Actually, it's what we call creative tension. Carol and Barry both like to do the intro – be seen first on screen. We go in on a wide shot but that's not enough. They both want to be the first to speak so they take turns.'

'And occasionally there's a small local dispute over whose turn it is?' Daphne said.

'I'm afraid so. We'll let it blow over and then I'll take you onto the studio floor. They know you're coming so you can be sure of a welcome.'

Daphne nodded but something was intriguing her. 'I've met you before, haven't I?' She wrinkled her forehead. 'Did you work as a journalist?'

'I'm still a journalist.' Liz was grinning ruefully. 'This *is* a news-oriented programme in spite of the feature items. And you *have* met me. I was married to a former colleague of yours. David Redman. He's at the *Globe* now but he was with the *Herald* when I met him. We're separated.'

'I'm sorry,' Daphne said automatically but Liz was shaking her head. 'We're over it. We're going through the legal process – no aggro. Now . . .' Her tone changed. 'Let's get you some action.'

She shepherded Daphne out into the corridor leading to the studio. 'Simon will have sorted everything out by now.' There was a note of pride in her voice as she spoke of the deputy editor, an almost proprietorial tone as she mentioned his name.

I wonder if it's hero-worship or something more, Daphne mused as they moved into the outer darkness of the studio, the well of light in the centre almost blinding to the eye. Lou Bryan would not be interested in unknowns but if there was a bit of romance around it might add warmth to the piece. Every little helped in profiling a place – an institution – rather than a personality. Love between editor and assistant and agro between presenters? That would be a potent mix. She looked at Carol and Barry, still as statues now on their leather settee.

'One minute to On-Air,' the floor-manager's voice rang out. 'Quiet everybody!' And then again. 'Quiet please!' Somewhere music was gathering pace, the familiar treacly music that accompanied the bursting buds and hatching chicks of the titles. *Daybreak* was taking to the airwaves.

Monday, 8.15 a.m.

'Thank you so much,' Chris said when they reached reception. 'That was a smashing item.' The herbalist looked like something out of *Camberwick Green* with his wispy white beard and sideboards. He glowed as Chris praised him and even more when a further programme was hinted at. 'We'll be in touch,' Chris promised, and then the taxi was drawing away with the traffic and Chris turned back into the building.

He gravitated towards the studio, knowing it would be almost impossible to work at his desk with the monitors in the office displaying whatever was going on during the programme.

In front of the camera the presenters were cooing over baby pictures as the mother of quins was displayed on a large screen, down the line from her hospital ward. 'So when will you get home?' Carol said and answered her own question. 'Very soon.'

Barry was about to launch into detail on the difficulties of neonatal care in the case of multiple births but Carol cut across him. 'I expect you've been besieged with offers of sponsorship.' Barry glowered. What was the point of mugging up on things if you never got a chance to demonstrate your knowledge? He had read every volume of *Medicine for the Common Man* and still the cow cut him out.

'I expect they're worried about anoxia and apnea,' he said, leaning forward and looking as earnest as he could. So far the mother had not been allowed to utter a word.

Carol trilled. 'Barry's so knowledgeable . . . he sometimes forgets we mere mortals aren't so well-informed. I love your bedjacket.' She leaned forward too, making sure her designer jacket was displayed to advantage. 'I really take my hat off to you, sitting up in that lovely bedjacket. When I had my son I trailed around like a lost weekend.' She smiled at camera to demonstrate the sheer impossibility of her ever looking anything but bandbox, and Barry flailed desperately for a line to get the director's attention.

'Tell me,' he said desperately. 'Tell me, how do you bond with five at once?' There had been a full page on bonding and he had read the lot. Let the bitch cap that! He was up there on the monitor now and only a minute to news time. As the mother stammered out her incomprehension he tried to look wise and

compassionate and paediatric and it worked: he held
the screen until it was time to say thank you to the
guest and hand over to the newsreader. 'Well done,'
he said to the mother as she faded from the screen.
'You'd think you were a pro.'

One up to Barry, Chris thought from his vantage
point behind the cameras. He shifted his weight to
his other foot and thought longingly of lunchtime.
He would have soup and nan bread and something hot
with chips. His item on herb gardens had gone well.
Even the director had praised the piece. He deserved
his food. He might even have a glass of wine, except
that this afternoon he had to get to grips with antique
porcelain and he didn't have all the time in the world to
read it up, as he suspected Barry had done with babies.
He put his hands in the waist of his jeans and pushed
downwards to free his crotch.

Tonight – this very night – he would establish order
in his room, fill his drawers with clean underwear and
cart his old newspapers to the tip.

I live like a slob, he thought. I *am* a slob.

It was all so different from his dreams of moving the
nation with the brilliance of his feature films. With
luck he'd be a producer one day. He might even make
head of features but he would go no further. He knew
that now.

'You're not political enough to get on,' Amy had
told him once, and it was true. Thinking of Amy
led to thoughts of Dilly and thinking of Dilly led to
thoughts of her and Clifford shagging. He thought

he'd come to terms with it but obviously not. He stood, wriggling in his jeans and trying not to think of Dilly, until the credits started rolling and the fade-out music began. It was nine a.m. and *Daybreak* was over until tomorrow.

'I'm sorry, Jane,' Simon said, shifting the phone to his other ear. 'I'd come if I could but I know I won't get away. I thought it only fair to tell you now. No, Jane. I can't 'just leave it all'. Not and keep my job. I suppose you do *want* me to stay in work?' There was a squawk from the other end of the line. 'I'm not being sarcastic. I *am* being realistic. I only wish *you* would.'

Liz had come into the room, closing the door softly behind her. 'Jane?' she mouthed and he nodded. She went to stand behind him, moving her hands up his back, widening them to grip him between neck and shoulder. She squeezed gently and rythmically and he felt himself relax. 'I'm sorry, Jane,' he said again. 'I know you'll choose well. I'll try and get home early. Yes. See you.'

He turned as he put down the phone and took Liz in his arms. 'Difficult?' she asked.

He rested his chin on the crown of her head but he didn't answer. 'How much longer?' he asked instead. How much longer could he endure a loveless marriage? How much longer could he ask Liz to take the crumbs of his life? And, equally, how could he leave his children? There would be no amicable separation from Jane, no attempt to pull together for the children's sake. It would be war, with Jake and Rosie caught in the crossfire.

'How much longer what?' Liz said, her lips against his cheek.

'Us,' Simon said gloomily. He meant, 'How much longer can we go on like this?' but Liz had arched her neck to look up at him.

'For ever, I hope. Or at least for the foreseeable future. Are you going off me?'

'Silly!' He put up a hand to press her head against him once more. 'I meant how much longer can I ask you to take all this . . . the secrecy, the fact that we're together once in a blue moon . . .'

'It's better than nothing.' She put up a hand to touch his cheek with gentle fingertips. 'Don't worry. I'm not grumbling, am I?'

'That makes it worse.' His conscience was in full flow now and not to be pacified. 'What sort of life do *you* have? I feel . . .'

There was only one thing to do. She silenced his protestations with her mouth, pressing against him in her urgency to console.

They sprang apart as a knock came at the door. It was Simon's secretary, ushering in the journalist. 'Come in,' Simon said, trying to sound welcoming. 'Did you find this morning interesting?'

'Very.' Daphne smiled as she spoke but there was an inflection in her voice that set him wondering.

'I'll organise coffee,' Liz said, moving to the door. 'Do sit down.' She moved a chair and motioned Daphne into it. 'Simon will have to go to a production meeting soon but I'm sure he'll appreciate some coffee too.' She smiled at Simon and there was a look in her eyes that said, 'Trust me. I'll make sure you're not cornered for long.'

He had a sudden surge of longing for a life with Liz, being protected instead of harried, being able to talk about work with someone who understood, making love without the constant fear of a childish wail interrupting. Except that Jane had been protective once – and understanding – and no one had interrupted their torrid sessions in the back of his father's car. It was marriage that spoiled things – even, he supposed, to a woman like Liz!

He cleared his throat and looked at Daphne with what he hoped was an encouraging smile. 'Now,' he said. 'Before we're interrupted . . . fire your questions.'

By the time the team assembled for the post-mortem the green room had emptied of guests. On the centre table plates were littered with the remnants of the toast and croissants and jams and jellies that had done service as breakfast. Half-empty cups held cold and yellowing coffee. 'Ugh!' Dilly said and pushed everything to one end of the table with a disdainful finger.

Chris flung himself onto a leather sofa and stretched out his legs. 'What did you think?'

Dilly pursed her lips. 'So-so. Greer was all right, I suppose. And your herb item was brill. Barry made a mess of the consumer item. I slaved over that. He had everything on cue cards and not a single piece of info was put out. God, why do we bother?'

Chris leaned forward to grab an unchewed piece of toast. 'They never read the briefs,' he said, cramming it into his mouth. He had still not recovered from the day's bad start. He was wiping crumbs from his mouth when Sarah Gillespie came in. She was one of three features producers. Chris liked working for her.

'Well done,' she said in his direction. The item on herb gardens had been hers to oversee but she had not been responsible for Dilly's item so she made no comment. 'We need to talk about Friday,' she said.

Dilly stood up, trying to subdue a yawn. 'I'll leave you two in peace and see if I can find something edible. See you later.' Sarah opened the folder on her knee and smiled dismissively at the other researcher.

'Right,' she said to Chris. 'Now, everyone is incandescent about having Vincent for two days. But no one — not even a megastar — can fill six hours of live TV. We still need the odd item and this one' — she waved a sheet of briefing paper — 'God likes! It's an elderly couple . . . childhood sweethearts separated by the war. He married, she married. Thought of one another from time to time. Both partners die and other two end up in an old folks' home. The same home. Love at second sight — and now it's wedding bells.'

'So we've got them live?'

'Yes. Barry asked — quite seriously suggested — we have the ceremony on the show. In between weather and news.'

Chris grimaced. 'With him and Carol as bridesmaids, no doubt?'

'We didn't get as far as that, thank God. Simon still has some remnants of decency. Anyway, they're both around the eighty mark, I gather. Our contact's the matron at the home. The old lady's fragile and he's a tad deaf but both good talkers. I've spoken to them on the phone. We're giving them the works – the bridal suite at the Imperial, outfits, the lot. Sharon has the details. But . . . I want them carefully handled, Chris. Getting them up at dead of night won't be easy.' She ran a hand down her bare brown shins and grimaced. 'I'm not sure about it but "God", our esteemed editor, wants it so who am I to argue. Anyway, I want you to nanny them. You can stay at the Imperial if you want to . . . in fact, I'd like you to do that. Be there to see them in on Thursday night, give them dinner, be on hand in the morning. They want them at the top of the show so it'll have to be a three-forty-five wake-up.'

'That's a bit savage,' Chris said. 'I mean, at their age —'

'That's why I want *you* to do it, Chris.' Sarah was getting impatient now and he knew why. She knew the sweethearts would be subject to hassle and didn't like it, but the editor had spoken and what God wanted, he got.

As if she had read his thoughts she sighed. 'I've talked it over with Simon. He had a go but God's adamant. We don't do enough for the older segment of the audience, he says. Never mind that *he* is the

one who axes every item that isn't puerile. He wants
eighty-year-old romance and he's going to have it. So
let's stop arsing about and make the best of it. If they
drop dead on air — which they might — Vincent can
always give us one of his standards by way of a
requiem.'

Chris shook his head. 'This is a bizarre business
we're in. Geriatric romance and a pop-music icon. God
help us.'

'So what are we getting out of it?' Vincent swung his
chair round to face his manager. In the background
there was the faint but unmistakeable sound of John
Lee Hooker.

'Nice that,' Dave Behan said as he shuffled papers.
'Not bad being on a comeback at his age. 'Right . . .'
He extricated a single sheet. 'You do four spots each
day, two directly on the project, two to fit in with
their programme. But — and it's a big but — they plug
the project every day next week and at least twice
in each week until the end of September. They'd like
exclusive coverage of the opening but that's still up for
grabs. I'm talking with the *Richard and Judy* people
and the Beeb. We'll decide nearer the time.'

The project was a derelict warehouse south of the
river. Vincent had seen it one day, unglazed windows
like dead eyes, only half a roof. There had been a boy,
rolled in rags like a mummified corpse, sleeping in the
boarded-up doorway and in that instant, overcome with
painful memories, he had conceived the idea. Resuscitate

the building as a halfway house for young homeless, somewhere they could get shelter, medical treatment and advice on how to get themselves off the street.

He had contacted colleagues in the music business and they had been generous. Already the building was alive with the sound of drilling and hammering. All that remained was to obtain public backing to refurbish it and keep it running. For this he would expose himself on the breakfast couch for the first and – God willing – the only time in his career. Thereafter the hostel would exist on royalties from his new album and public subscription.

He stood up now and moved across to the huge window and its breathtaking view of the Thames.

'Have we got a date for the opening?' he asked. 'I want the place up and running before winter sets in.'

'You can move the kids in before the official opening.' Dave's tone was casual. He didn't share Vincent's passion for the project: he simply went along with it because Vincent was his client and merited his attention. They had come together at the start of Vincent's rise to stardom. And to wealth, for Dave was more interested in finance than music.

At the beginning he had represented a stable of mid-level stars but, as Vincent's reputation – and earning capacity – had soared, he had dropped his other clients one by one and now gave Vincent's affairs his undivided attention. He had even cultivated an ear for a good sound and Vincent respected him for that.

'They'd like a bit of background,' Dave said tenta-
tively, knowing what Vincent's reaction would be.

'Give them the handout.'

'They've had that. They don't want a lot more, Vin.
Just the odd new detail. Everyone knows the stock stuff
. . . Christ, you're better known than Jesus. They want
something *they* can reveal . . . winkle out of you to make
them look clever. You know how these things work.
We can make something up if you like.'

'I was a teenage trainspotter?' Vincent asked bitterly. 'I won't have them digging. They've got the
basics.'

'We could say you washed dishes in Soho.'

'It says that − not in so many words, but it says I
bummed around.'

'Embroider it − anything'll do. Say you broke more
dishes than you dried. Give 'em a nice quote. They're
chuffed about getting you − they'll settle for anything.
And something like that makes the press. It's you that
wants publicity this time, Vince. Get that straight. It's
not them after us, like usual. It's us using them. Quid
pro quo.'

'All right,' Vincent said. 'I get the message. But what
can we say?'

As if on cue, the dog who had been lying quietly
at Vincent's feet raised a mournful head. Vincent put
out a hand to fondle the Great Dane and Dave's face
brightened. 'You could talk about Juno? Give them
some pics.'

'I'm not exploiting the dog, Dave.' The great head

33

came to rest on Vincent's knee but the eyes rolled reproachfully towards the manager.

'OK, OK. I'll give them the dishes story and if it's not enough . . . tough.'

'I hope I'm not going to regret this,' Vincent said, but Dave was moving on.

'We're getting overtures from the *Herald*. Lou . . . Lou Whatsername? Bryan. I've had her on twice. They want an in-depth interview – she's the features editor. She sounds OK. And they'd like some pics of this place.'

'It's all the same, Dave. The answer's no. I had to bend to interviewers once. I don't have to do it now. What else? I'd like to get over to Bermondsey when we're done.'

The manager sighed. They'd had this conversation so often before. 'I'm only doing my job, Vince. I wish you'd realise that.'

It was a time for compromise. 'I know,' Vincent said contritely. 'And I do want this Daybreak thing to work. It's just that sometimes you feel as if they're out to devour you.'

Dave shook a rueful head. 'They *are* out to devour you, Vince. Face it. And that's their job, like you've got yours and I've got mine. So the answer is not to starve them of info – it's to feed them. Give them what you want them to have, send them away happy.'

'OK, OK. I get the point. I was a choirboy. St Benedict's, Chapeltown, Leeds. I sang solo once – only once. The priest said I was NBG. I kept gerbils when I was five, Bubble and Squeak, we called them.'

'All right,' Dave said ironically. 'That's the earth-shattering stuff. Now give me some nitty-gritty.'

'Make it up.' Vince turned back to the window. 'Say anything you like, just brief me on it before I go on. Happy?'

'Estatic.' The John Lee Hooker came to an end and the room fell silent, like the river below, ten floors down.

Vera Pierce flicked her duster across the mirror and switched on the lights that surrounded it. All the bulbs glowed satisfactorily and she switched them off again. Woe betide her if one of them was lifeless and she didn't get Sparks to replace it before Carol noticed. There would be a right tantrum then and no mistake. Carol Cusack loved tantrums. They cheered her up no end.

When I win the lottery, Vera thought, I'll tell her to put her light bulbs up her arse.

She was grinning as she took a last look round the dressing room. Everything was in place and spotless and she moved next door to perform the same routine.

Barry, Carol's co-presenter, never made a scene about his light bulbs. 'Never mind, darling,' he would say. 'What's a light bulb between friends.' But he'd report you to maintenance just the same. Sly sod! She switched on his lights and found them all correct.

She leafed through his waste basket before she emptied it. You could tell a lot from waste baskets but today's was disappointing. Sweet wrappers, a cardboard book cover and an empty tube of haemorrhoid cream. Not that Barry had piles. His bum was too tight to give a haemorrhoid room! He used it on the bags beneath his eyes. Theo, the wardrobe master, had told her about that trick. And a few others!

I could write a book, Vera thought.

She chuckled as she dusted, thinking this explained why Barry had a face like a backside! If she'd been on speaking terms with Fred, her husband, she'd have told him that joke tonight, but she wasn't, so she'd keep it to herself. It didn't do to tell anything to people here, not even jokes. If it got back to the presenters you were for it. The researchers were OK – some of them. They were still bairns, most of them, so they hadn't got side. If they survived in telly – and she'd seen a lot who didn't – they got the smit. 'Arrogance', someone had called it once but 'side' was a better word. It got them all in the end. Once they started believing life on the box was more real than life itself.

'You work in telly,' she told herself in Barry's mirror before she switched off the lights, 'and you're normal.' But she had a life outside. 'More's the pity,' she said out loud, with Fred as much use as a Buddha. And mean! 'Buy it yourself,' he'd said when she'd suggested a new three-piece. As if she didn't pay for everything out of her wages. Well, nearly everything. 'Tight sod,' she said aloud. And then again, because she liked talking at the mirror, 'Tight sod.' She smiled and sucked in her cheeks, trying to look from under her eyelids as

Carol did. But Carol had enormous eyelids, set right back. She was good-looking, you had to admit.

According to Theo she was always trying to look like Audrey Hepburn but Audrey Hepburn had class, which was something Carol Cusack would never have. 'Common bitch,' Vera said aloud. She gave one last smile at the mirror before she switched off the light, but it was a wry smile. Hers was a very ordinary face.

If she and Fred had had kids . . .

'When I win the lottery,' she thought.

She was in a syndicate with Chris, the nice young researcher, who wouldn't last because he *was* a nice lad. A pound each and she bought the tickets every week. She watched the lottery drawn every Saturday night but Chris never checked the numbers. She could do him blind, not that she would. Not him. Most of the rest she would, without losing a moment's sleep but not Chris. When they won she'd adopt an orphan from Bosnia, chuck out Fred and live happily ever after. Vera closed the door on Barry's room and moved on to make-up.

The make-up artist was tidying her kit, gathering up brushes and eyeliners, capping lipsticks and putting sponges to soak free of foundation. She looked up and smiled as Vera entered. 'Hi.'

'Did you hear what Carol called Barry this morning?' Vera said, knowing that hot news never came amiss. 'She called him a sexist pig and he said she was pure bitch.'

'Not on air?' The make-up artist could only be half

37

aware of Vera's words for she had not registered shock-horror.

'No,' Vera said regretfully. 'They never row on air. Too sweet for words in front of the camera, those two. They had a punch-up over who went first, like they always do, and that's when it turned nasty.'

A figure had appeared in the doorway, frail and silver-haired and sporting a velvet jacket the colour of autumn leaves. This was Theo, who was in charge of wardrobe.

'Would you like a coffee, Theo?' Vera asked solicitously. Theo had once dressed Donald Wolfit and was a legend. Moreover, he knew it. He rolled a cigarette between thumb and middle finger and drew on it without taking his eyes from the monitor.

'I'd kill for a coffee, Vee.' His voice was treacle mixed with dynamite and years of abusing his lungs. 'Sweet as battleships, they were, this morning. There was more kindness in Belsen than there is in those two.'

The women regarded him enviously. He had a pension and could afford to speak his mind. He ruled wardrobe like a king and even Barry and Carol deferred to him. He could make remarks and not feel the need to lower his voice, which was a real privilege.

For a moment, watching him, Vera was consumed with hope that Theo would get his comeuppance one day. Why should he be the only one to get away with things? Still, they could do worse. The one who had replaced him when he'd gone to Como had run her finger along every ledge and crevice in the hope of finding dust in her precious wardrobe room and expected to be waited on hand and foot. At least Theo was grateful.

She brought him coffee in a china mug decorated with poinsettias. You couldn't give a paper cup to someone who had worked with stars. He sipped it gratefully without ever taking his eyes off the screen. 'She looks good,' the make-up artist said grudgingly. 'How old do you think she is?'

'Sixty,' Vera said firmly. 'Her bum's dropped.'

'Your bum drops at twenty-five,' Theo said. 'Our Carol's past the change but she's on HRT. So's he for that matter.'

'Men don't take hormone replacement,' the make-up girl said scornfully.

'Who mentioned hormones?' Theo was still regarding the screen, feeling with his left hand for an ashtray in which to dump his fag-end.

'You said they were both on HRT.'

'So they are.' For a second he removed his gaze from the screen. 'Humanity Replacement Therapy, that's what they're on. Only in their case, it isn't working!'

The women chuckled dutifully, knowing Theo liked an appreciative audience. 'It's true,' he said. 'They're neither of them human. They don't have blood in their veins. She has vitriol, he's got chlorine.' This puzzled Vera for a moment until she remembered that Barry had been a swimming champion.

'Does anyone know where her husband is?' the

make-up artist said. 'I know she's got a son — he's sixteen. I saw it in a magazine.'

'And some!' Theo lit another cigarette. 'He's twenty-one. She had him when she was sixteen, or so she says.'

'Was she a single mum?' Vera was still shocked by single mums. They'd always existed but they'd had the grace to be ashamed once. Now they were blatant.

Theo shrugged. 'Hard to tell. There must've been a father somewhere — and she wears a wedding ring. Maybe she ate him up after the event.'

The make-up artist chuckled. 'Like a black widow?'

Vera struggled to make sense of the exchange and Theo must have picked up on her confusion. 'A black widow spider, Vee. They eat their mates once they've had their leg over. Mate and die. That's heterosexuality for you.'

'Was he an actor?' Vera was not going to be drawn into discussing the merits of homosexuality, which she knew to be the opposite of the hetero thing.

'He can't've been anyone famous,' the make-up artist said. 'She'd've shouted it from the rooftops if that'd been the case.'

'I'll ask her one of these days,' Theo said. 'Just give me time and a drop of Dutch courage and I'll fathom it out. In the meantime, Vee, make us another coffee. My blood sugar's at an all-time low at the moment. I need some sun.'

As Vee went off to boil the kettle she counted the

weeks since Theo had returned from Como. Telly people were always having holidays, skiing, surfing, loafing around on the Costa Plenty. And Fred wouldn't take her further than Margate.

Liz sifted through the memos on her desk. Requisitions from make-up and the canteen, travel warrants, a plea from the cook for a higher clothes allowance. Were all TV cooks greedy? Perhaps it came with the job. She resisted the impulse to write 'You're here to cook, not catwalk' across the top and read on.

Carol wanted a new fridge-freezer in her dressing room, one with a cold-drinks facility. A new fridge for Carol would mean a new one for Barry. For a moment Liz considered the delicious possibility of Carol's indenting for breast enhancement while Barry demanded, 'Me too'. Conversely, of course, if he wanted penis extension . . . It had often been suggested that Carol had balls so perhaps . . .!

'What are you smiling at?' Simon was leaning against her door post, regarding her with raised brows.

'Don't ask,' Liz said. 'You really wouldn't like to know. What can I do for you?'

He advanced into the room. 'I could tell you.'

'Don't start,' she said, but she didn't mean it. She wanted him to tell her he wanted to take her to bed there and then, needed to know she was indispensable, a vital part of his life. She wanted him to abandon wife and children and home and job and take her to a desert island. Except that neither of them could live with the fallout.

'Any chance of a coffee later?' he asked. 'God wants a conference at four. You, me, him and Derek. It shouldn't take long.'

'I wish!' she said fervently. 'We'll be in there for hours.'

Simon put out a hand and covered hers, where it lay on the desk. 'Cheer up. Maybe we can snatch a few hours to ourselves this week.'

Liz tried to smile hopefully, but the bitter words still escaped from her lips. 'I won't hold my breath. Something will stop us – this place . . . or . . .'

'Jane!' he finished for her. 'I know. She's difficult at the moment . . . and I feel guilty. She does have to take a lot of the strain.'

'Do you think she suspects anything?' Liz tried not to sound hopeful. If Jane knew about them it might precipitate something – and an ending of any sort would be better than the limbo in which she presently existed.

Simon shook his head. 'No, not for a second. That's what makes it so hard. She trusts me, Liz. Implicitly. Always has done. Still . . .' He straightened up and then leaned to kiss her cheek. 'We'll make it work somehow. I promise you. And we'll get together soon, I promise.' He grimaced at Liz's small sigh. 'I know. Promises, promises.'

She put out a hand to comfort him, unable to bear his rueful expression. 'It's not your fault,' she said.

'We didn't intend this to happen. I know you're doing your best.' But as she spoke she was aware that something was happening to their relationship, an almost imperceptible slide into gloom. Once, they had seized every chance to meet for a second so that they could exchange smiles, make eye contact, hold out the prospect of love. Now, they still seized upon each chance encounter but they used it to commiserate or to apologise.

When he quit her office Liz gathered up one or two papers and set off in search of the relevant people. She needed to knock the idea of the new fridge on the head before Carol locked onto it or Barry heard about it. She was about to knock on Carol's dressing-room door when she heard a male voice from inside. It was Theo and from the sound of things he and Carol were already half-seas-over.

'I saw him, Carol darling. Not much I miss. Took up his little stance so he'd mask you. As if he could! Amazes me how the gallery let him get away with it. Still, they're a jealous lot. I shouldn't let it hurt if I were you.'

'It accumulates though, Theo. That's the trouble. Pinpricks. Constant pinpricks. Even to pros like you and I they mount up in the end.' Carol's voice was full of the unshed tears that were her trademark. 'He's not professional, that's his trouble.' She sighed heavily.

Oh no, Liz thought. Not Barry's antecedents again. He had been an athlete in his youth, a swimmer of Olympic standard. After that a commentator for the

BBC until he had lost touch with his sport. It had been game shows then and guest appearances until he had found his niche on *Daybreak*, but Carol could not forget that her co-presenter had entered the profession through the back door while she came from the legitimate theatre.

'You mustn't let them get to you, Carol.' Theo was dripping bogus sympathy. 'My god, he sits there, a reject from the corporation baths, trying to outshine a star like you. He can't even busk an autocue, let alone ad-lib. I'd like to see him get a sound stage at Elstree in the palm of his hand like you used to do.'

Not the 'You were Britain's Shirley Temple' bit, Liz thought. Not that. She lifted a hand and rapped on the door. Someone would have to do something about Theo before he poisoned the well still further.

Monday, 2.15 p.m.

The *Herald's* huge open-plan office was steeped in lunchtime torpor when Daphne emerged from the lift. One or two heads lifted as she passed. A guy at the sports desk raised a cup of coffee in salute and Nikki on fashion said, 'Nice jacket.'

'Oliver James,' Daphne said. 'Old as the hills.' Old like me, she thought. Her legs felt heavy and the early-morning start was making itself felt. Outside Lou Bryan's office Irene, her secretary, was sifting through black-and-white prints, occasionally spinning one into an adjacent waste basket.

'Is she free?'

The girl turned to look through the glass partition. 'On the phone. She won't be long. She's ringing Bienvenida Buck so she'll try and keep it short.' Her eyes rolled expressively as she patted the last photograph into line and put them aside. 'Can I get you a coffee?'

'Please. I got up at four this morning. Mark that . . . four. I'm totally disoriented.'

The secretary was rummaging in her drawer, producing at last a half-bottle of Courvoisier. 'I'll give you a *Herald* special. Guaranteed to pick you up no matter what.'

Daphne sipped the doctored coffee gratefully. It was half past one in the afternoon and she wanted her bed. Her clothes were sawing into her at waist and midriff; she was hot and tired and desperately in need of sleep. For a moment she felt frightened, old and frightened and not up to the pace of a busy newspaper office . . . and then she glanced through the partition and saw Lou Bryan waving an imperious hand.

'She want's you,' Irene said 'Make a noise as you go in – then she can cut the call short.' She made a great show of opening the door and announcing Daphne's presence. There was a burst of 'Soon, darling, you ring me, I'll ring you, of course, me too, brilliant' – and then the phone was down and the features editor was tipping back her chair and flexing her telephone arm to restore the blood supply.

'Well?' she said. 'How did it go?'

'OK. I got there for the opening. I've got reams of notes – factual stuff. There's a lot to take in. I'm doing the main interviews tomorrow – Carol and Barry – possibly one or two of the others. Wednesday and Thursday I'll get the back-room people and Friday I'll tie up loose ends. I should deliver Wednesday week. I have got a photographer on Thursday, haven't I?'

There was a pile of photographs on Lou Bryan's desk and even upside down she could see they were of Vincent, glossy four-by-tens, black-and-white and coloured. The guy got everywhere. There was one photograph, smaller than the rest and frayed at the edges inside its clear plastic cover. As she looked at it Lou Bryan's hand snaked out and tucked it away beneath the rest.

'You've got Gerry Malone on Thursday. The best. Will they give him a free hand?' She was sifting through papers as she spoke, gradually covering the photographs.

'As long as he waits until they're off air.' Daphne decided to plunge. 'They've got Vincent as a guest on Thursday. And Friday! Unheard of – you know how reclusive he is. And he certainly doesn't need money – or publicity. Still, they've got him. He's plugging some pet charity apparently.'

'The Bermondsey project,' Lou said. She didn't meet Daphne's eye. 'I've heard about it. We might do a piece eventually. Still, I don't want your piece to make too much of Vincent. Keep it on the Daybreak team – programme content, production team, you know the sort of thing. Anything else?'

I am dismissed, Daphne thought, and made her exit. She collected one or two things she needed from her desk and exchanged pleasantries with colleagues but all the while she was thinking about Lou's desk. Seeing the tiny determined little hands with their perfect, white, trimmed nails edging the photographs out of sight. Something was up, that was for sure. Why on earth hadn't Lou referred to the photographs while they were discussing Vincent?

On her way out she crossed to Irene's desk. 'Thanks for the coffee,' she said. 'And the extra ingredient. It was a lifesaver. Lou seems busy – I see she has some pics of Vincent. Funny, because he's doing this thing with Daybreak. Any idea what she's planning? I didn't have time to ask when I was in there?' Another pair of eyes were dropping, another voice was feigning nonchalance.

'I don't know,' Irene said. 'I think she's planning something for later in the year. A retrospective or something. She may do Elton or Sting instead. There's nothing concrete.'

Daphne smiled and nodded. 'I just wondered. Well, thanks again. See you later.' She went on her way cogitating. Ten-by-fours and old pics. That was a profile. But why the reluctance to talk about it? Every paper was afraid of a spoiler, its lead story picked up by a rival and imitated so as to devalue its scoop. Secrecy was part of the game – but not within the office. Perhaps I'm not cleared for security, she thought. Shades of John le bloody Carré.

She called in at Marks and Spencer on her way home and shopped for food, buying precooked one-person meals with a low-calorie sign and precooked pasties and pies. As she queued at the checkout she felt a sudden stab of nostalgia. Her mother had baked her own bread, kneading and pulling the dough, slapping and turning it, tearing the rounded, floured lumps apart to expose the raw, yeasty mixture, and then, with a few deft slaps, shaping it into perfect rounds once more. And now her daughter bought bread that had probably never been touched by human hands and came wrapped in cellophane.

She quelled her feelings of inadequacy by returning to the problem of Lou Bryan. What was she up to? She could be putting the freeze on. Daphne had seen it done before, to other staff writers and reporters who had passed their sell-by date. A slow withdrawal of confidences, a starving of information or story lines, until it could be said, with truth, that the writer had nothing to offer and would be well advised to take the severance package and go.

But, if that was all it was, why the business with the Vincent photographs? Daphne's perplexity was such that when she reached home she devoured a whole chicken-and-mushroom pasty without even warming it in the microwave.

Simon sat down as he was bidden and gazed across the vast expanse of the editor's desk, comparing its pristine gloss with the cluttered wilderness that was his own. 'God', alias Colin Frost, the editor, was regarding him with wild eyes. 'I can't stand it much longer, Simon. The strain is getting to me. I daren't take my sodding blood pressure ... I don't know why I bought that thing.' He gestured towards the do-it-yourself sphygmomanometer that lurked beside his desk. 'They're on about ratings again – we dip badly at half-eight. I thought I asked Liz to be here?'

'She's on her way,' Simon said soothingly. The editor was rummaging in his desk drawer, choosing and discarding pills until he found a bottle of orange capsules. He threw what appeared to be a handful into his open mouth and gulped, reminding Simon of the seals at feeding time so beloved of his daughter, Rosie, on the rare occasion he could take her to the zoo.

There was a knock at the door and a canteen assistant appeared with a tray of snacks. Simon looked hopefully for a tempting morsel but it was the usual carrot-and-muesli collection. 'Help yourself,' his host said, pouncing on a sliver of celery like a starving man. 'How was the cow?'

'Carol was her usual self,' Simon said carefully. 'She didn't like much on the show but she saved her finest invective for her co-presenter.'

'I hate them both.' God had settled in his chair to crack peanuts and throw them into his open mouth. 'What does she expect? I said we had Sir Cyril Fane for one show and she said, 'He's not a celebrity'. So I said, 'He won a Nobel prize', and she said, 'Last year.' Last year! As though a Nobel passes its sell-by date. How does she feel about Vincent?'

'She's very pleased about Vincent,' Simon said. 'In fact she's bloody buoyant about it. I can hardly believe it myself.' He turned as Liz appeared.

'Sorry I'm late,' she said, sliding into a seat.

'Never mind.' God shrugged and pushed the carrots towards her. 'Get some carotene into you. We need all the help we can get here. We're talking about Vincent. Is everything in hand?' Behind the desk Liz felt Simon's foot touch her own, a gentle reassuring pressure.

'Everything's fine,' she said and returned the gesture by aligning her leg against her lover's. It was little enough but it was better than nothing.

'What've we got for Monday?' God was morose. 'Not that I'll live that long. Still, it pays to look ahead. We'll add audience with Vincent . . . don't want too big a drop on Monday.

'We've got Jeffrey Archer,' Simon said proudly. 'And Bjork. And a nice piece of VT on Chinese adoption. The baby's a poppet.'

His voice has gone soft, Liz thought. The way it always does when he mentions children, especially his own. She felt a wave of anguish, thinking of her biological clock ticking away. She could give him a child – children – if she ever got the chance. Why not now and sod marriage? I could support a child, she thought, and at least he'd come to see me then.

But having a child in order to snare a man wasn't fair on anyone, especially the child itself. Suddenly she realised God's eyes were on her, awaiting an answer. 'Can you just say that again?' she said and tried to sound calm and in control. That was her role, after all: a facilitator, not a mother. Not even a lover, really, except in a subsidiary role. God was asking about facts and figures and she closed her mind to pain and concentrated on mathematics.

'I can't believe it.' Dilly was whirling between desks, awash with euphoria. 'I never thought I'd get Vincent! My God. I'll be holding the hand of Vincent. *The* Vincent! No one will believe it.' She stretched her arms above her head causing her cropped white top to rise almost to the level of her breasts. As far as Chris could see she wore no bra and the outline of her erect nipples through the thin fabric confirmed it. He shifted uneasily in his seat, wishing for the hundredth time that he was wearing underpants.

'OK,' he said. 'It's not that big a deal.'

'Wash your mouth out, Chris. This man had three number ones in a row. But you wouldn't know that, you're such a sad.'

She moved to perch on Chris's knee and twine her arms around his neck. 'But I still love you, you funny old thing. Want to come to the Grapes tonight? Clifford's playing squash.'

'Not if I'm going to hear nothing but Vincent,' he said. But he would go and they both knew it. For the umpteenth time he tried to work out if he loved Dilly. He fancied her but was it pure lust or something more? Up close she smelled wonderful, not particularly scented but warm and animal-like and faintly, faintly soapy. He pushed her away before she sensed his arousal. 'I've got to get on,' he said, 'or there'll be no going anywhere tonight.'

'Yes!' She was off his knee with a bound and pulling down her skimpy top. 'Must get on. I want to pick Amy's brains. She usually handles celeb bookings so she'll know what to do with Vincent.'

'Stand on your own two feet,' Chris said disapprovingly. 'I know you – you'll get Amy to do all the work.' Even as she nodded agreement he wondered why, when he saw Dilly so clearly, he still wanted her so much.

'I'm a bad, bad lot,' she was saying cheerily. 'And you are too upright for your own good, my son. Loosen up, Chris. And keep your nose out of my business. You have to make use of your friends in this game – if you want to get on, that is, and I do.' Her eyes were raking the room, looking for Amy, who worked twice as hard as any of them and was good at the job. At last she found her quarry and was moving away.

'See you tonight,' Chris said sheepishly and bent his head to his work.

He was working on a piece on 'attitude', which according to the tabloids, was what every teenager wanted. They should have given it to Dilly, who had attitude in spades, but they had given it to him. He bent his head to the cuttings and tried to concentrate on how you defined girlies as opposed to babes or laddettes. What a load of tripe, he thought and groaned.

'That bad?' Amy had come up behind him and laid a sympathetic hand on his shoulder.

'Not bad,' Chris said reprovingly. 'Sad, Amy. That's the buzz word for out of touch, which is what I am, an old square.'

Amy grimaced. 'So you drew the short straw! Thank God it wasn't me. They should've given it to Dilly. She'd've been —'

'Stoked?' Chris finished.

'Totally stoked,' Amy said, 'or, in English, thrilled to bits.'

'Oh, sod it,' Chris said, closing the file. 'It's not till next week. I'll think about it later.'

'Want a brew?' Amy asked. Beneath the dark hair her eyes were liquid. He had always found Asian girls attractive — now all he could think of was a blonde who was half babe, half bimbo.

'Coffee,' he said. 'Milk, no sugar. And thanks, Amy, you're a pal.' For once she didn't smile and briefly he wondered why, until he caught sight of Dilly, swinging her legs as she sat on someone's desk and everything else went out of his head.

It was twenty to four, too late to embark on anything substantial, too early to don her coat and make for home. Vera dragged an idle duster over the chairs in make-up and tried not to look too often at the clock. She was seriously considering the possibility that it was going backwards when the girl who read the news appeared in the doorway.

'Have they locked up the slap? No? Thank God — I need some blusher.' She brushed furiously at cheeks almost concave in their thinness. Skinny, Vera thought, although she looks all right on the screen. Telly does that to you, makes you put on pounds.

The newsreader had applied a hectic flush to cheeks and forehead and was dusting under her chin. 'That's better. I've got a pre-record. Ta!' She was gone in a flash of yard-long legs, passing Theo in the doorway.

He turned to watch her passage down the corridor. 'She wants some sugar on those ankles,' he said, turning back towards Vera.

'Sugar?' Vera leaned on the back of the make-up chair, frowning in incomprehension.

'To 'tice her skirt down a bit,' Theo said.

Vera chuckled. 'Good job she's behind a desk or they'd see more than's good for them.'

'I shouldn't think she keeps it secret . . .' Theo said. 'Not that one. I don't know what the country's coming to, skirts up to their ha'pennies. They'll rue it, you mark my words.'

'Have they gone yet?' Vera asked. No need to amplify 'they'. It meant only two people, Old Fifty Faces, as Barry was known, and the Iron Butterfly, which had been Carol's nickname since time began.

'Not yet. Never mind that they're keeping me here. Oh no. They've got nowhere special to go so I mustn't. I don't know why I stand it actually – its not what I'm used to.'

'Would you like a coffee?' Vera eyed the clock. He'd have to have what was in the machine. No time for a fresh brew or else she'd miss her bus. To her relief he shook his head.

'I've got the kettle on for lemon tea.' He paused in the doorway, holding both jambs for dramatic effect.

'See you in the morning . . . *if* I haven't run away from it all. And I'm not joking.'

'You might win the lottery,' Vera said, 'and then you can retire.'

Theo bristled. 'I don't come here for the money, Vee. I come to give them the benefit of my fucking expertise, fool that I am. And I never, *never* gamble. Life's a bloody gamble, darling. Heart in the mouth the whole time. I don't need a lottery.'

She waited until he had padded away in his scuffed slippers and then she advanced on the mirror. The discarded brush, still loaded with blusher, lay on the bench. On the pretext of tidying she picked it up and dabbed first at one cheek and then at the other. Beneath the lights that girded the mirror her face suddenly came alive, reminding her of the girl she once had been, wide-eyed and bonny and sure that what lay ahead was good. Now her hair was pepper and salt and her chin sagged.

In the mirror her mouth drooped, her eyes ceased to shine. It never turned out like you thought. That was the disease of youth, too much hope. She put the brush back in place and switched off the lights. Time to go home to Fred. She could hardly wait!

She was making her way along the corridor when she heard the voices from Barry's dressing room. The temptation to eavesdrop was too great. She had always hoped to see Barry without his toupee, lost in admiration of his own reflection in spite of a head as bare as a badger's bum, but so far she had been unlucky.

She peered through the crack now and saw that it was Theo to whom Barry was talking.

'She's up to something, Theo. Too sweet by half . . . I don't like that.'

'I don't know, Barry.' Theo's tone was silky-smooth and Vera grimaced. He was a smarmy bugger and no mistake. There was the sound of liquid decanting from one receptacle to another. 'There,' Theo said. 'Just a touch of the hard stuff . . . the rest's tonic.'

Lemon tea! Vera thought. Gin and tonic more like!

Theo was continuing. 'She might've had a change of heart. I live in hope.'

Barry's tone was bitter. 'I'm all for change, Theo. But there has to be something there that's capable of change. Carol's immovable, Theo. She's steel. Iron Butterfly? That's not the half of it. And did you hear that today – just before the headlines? "When I'm as old as you," she said, as if I was older than her. She's been around longer than the flood. Child star! She played Bella Lugosi's mother before the war.'

'Now, now,' Theo said. 'No need to exaggerate. The truth's enough.' He gave a wicked chuckle. 'I liked the bit in the run-through.'

There was the chink of glasses. 'What was that?'

'You weren't there – you'd gone to the loo. She stood by the columns and said, "I'll stand here . . ."' He was faking Carol's voice to perfection, dropping now to the downtrodden tones of the much put-upon. '"Unless Barry doesn't like it, and then I'll move."'

'Bitch!' Barry said with venom. 'Making it look like

I'm the one who's a prima donna. God, I can't stand much more. Does she bad-mouth me, Theo? You're my friend. You have to tell me.'

'I'm not saying a word,' Theo said. 'Pass your glass and shut your gob. She's not worth it.'

In the corridor Vera shook a disbelieving head and went on her way, her own troubles forgotten until she was seated in the bus and once more had time to brood. She had worn short skirts once, in the sixties. The swinging sixties. She had been a teenager then, the image of Mandy Rice-Davies, or so everyone said, and she could have had any man she wanted.

So *could* I, Vera thought defiantly. So why had she settled for Fred? She searched her memory, trying to remember. Had she been popular? There had been Colin Charlton from next door, and the boy with glasses who had a car and sounded his horn when he came to pick her up. And there had been Fred. Always Fred.

Suddenly she remembered Beatlemania, screaming girls and pictures of the Fab Four smiling, always smiling. She had danced close to Fred in crowded ballrooms, both of them just shifting from foot to foot, content to let 'The Long and Winding Road' wash over them and work its magic. She had leaned her backcombed head against his chest and thought she would die for love of him. Because other girls had fancied him and made it plain. He was a sharp dresser then and nipping clean, and now he hardly ever got washed.

The bus lurched round a corner and she saw that

she was nearly home. Her eyes were playing her up and she blinked furiously. It didn't do to look back. And at least he'd been faithful. Some women didn't even have that.

For a moment she was content until she realised that it wasn't fidelity that had kept him by her side. The bugger was too lazy for a bit on the side. That was the truth of it.

Monday 5.00 p.m.

Vincent stood at the window of his penthouse, looking down on the Thames. He loved the river, every bend and turn of it, especially at night when it was strung with jewelled lights and looked like fairyland, all squalor hidden away. He had lived on the South Bank for two years now, atop a mansion block with some of the most magnificent views of London.

Across the river he could see the Savoy Hotel, looking for all the world like a 1930s cinema organ. To his left was Waterloo Bridge and beyond it King's Reach and the Palace of Westminster. To his right were Blackfriars Bridge and the majestic bulk of St Paul's, not so noticeable now, in daylight, but standing proud and illuminated against the night sky.

He stood there, sipping his coffee, wishing it was cooler so he could finish it and get away to Bermondsey.

He half-closed his eyes, imagining the scene as the huge and echoing warehouse was transformed into a home – or, rather, a warren. A place where each street kid could put down a marker on his or her own space. Most of them would be boys. Boys fared worst on the streets. He shivered slightly, the picture in his mind changing to cobblestones wet with rain, the sleeve of his coat wet against his eyes and shame blotting out almost every other sensation. He had found a roof all those years ago but it had not been a haven.

The cup went down to the saucer with a clatter as he turned back into the room, and in spite of himself he grinned. Must be careful with Anneka's precious porcelain. He owned it but, like everything else in this place, it had been carefully chosen by London's hottest and most expensive young designer. He looked around him. Black and charcoal, relieved here and there with splashes of turquoise, yellow and pink. Except that they weren't yellow and pink: they were ochre and cerise. And turquoise wasn't the *turk-oys* he had always known, it was *turk-wahz*. Still, it looked good in the glossies, on the carefully stage-managed pictures Dave let out from time to time.

He was about to pick up a phone and ask for a car to be brought round when it rang. Only a select few had the number of that particular phone. He picked it up and his heart sank as he heard his mother's voice.

'Sammy?' To the world he was Vincent, the surname he had inherited from his dead father. To his mother he was Sammy, from his Christian names of Samuel

Joseph. He tried to inject a welcoming note into his voice.

'Hullo . . . nice to hear you.' A wave of longing for his mother — for every remnant of his past — to dematerialise came and went. His mother was weak, that was all. And life had never given her a chance. It hadn't been her fault — not all of it. And, anyway, it was in the past now, safely buried long ago.

'Sammy, I thought I'd ring you — seeing as you never come home.' She was using tactic number two today: reproach. He sank onto the leather couch, hoping that whatever she wanted he could supply in the next few minutes and do what he had been wanting to do all day: get down the river to the project that was gradually taking over his life.

'Things are a bit hectic, Mum. Maybe when they quieten down . . .' But he would never again go home often — not more often than he had to — and he was fairly sure his mother knew that. The trouble was that there was too much to hide, too much that could never be acknowledged, much less spoken about. 'Still,' he said, trying to sound encouraging. 'What can I do for you?'

'Oh, I didn't ring for anything special.' Vincent relaxed at the tone of her voice. That particular modulation meant she needed money and that he could supply. 'I get lonely, Sammy. You don't know what it's like . . . a life like yours, people coming and going, always somewhere to go. I sometimes wonder what I did wrong when I was a girl . . .'

As her voice droned on he pictured her. She would be curled up on the settee, the phone balanced on the arm beside her, the receiver clutched in one thin hand, a rolled-up tissue in the other. If she was going out later there would be rollers in her hair; if not, it would be matted and wispy, just as it had left the pillow.

'I do understand, Mum. I just don't know what I can do about it. Can't you join something? Dave could find out about places, something you'd enjoy.'

Her voice took on a note of impatience now. He was going down a side-road. 'I'm not well enough, Sammy. Not at the moment. And I have so much on my mind . . .'

They were coming to the point now and he had to resist the impulse to cut it all short and say, 'How much?' Instead he said, 'I'm sorry to hear that, Mum. Is there anything I can do to help?'

'So what do we know about him?' Dilly asked cheerfully.

'Well, judging by the bumf you've got there, everything including his neck size,' Chris said. The adjoining desk was piled with fanzines, glossies, newsprint cuttings and a pile of Vincent's publicity handouts.

'I'm going to put my heart and soul into this brief. My guts, my all.' Dilly's hand fluttered heavenwards. 'I can't believe it. If I can't land dinner, at least, in two whole days, I'm losing my touch. And he's so . . . so . . .'

'Rich?' Chris said.

'Gorgeous. And sexy. That aloof look is a real turn-on.'

Chris smiled, trying not to show his desire to wring the pop star's neck. The guy made good music but his private life was in all probability a sewer. Whereas Dilly, for all the bravado, was about as streetwise as Minnie Mouse. 'Get on with it then,' he said, 'and let me get on with this. I know childhood sweethearts can't compete with megastars but God wants them so who am I to argue.'

'OK,' Dilly said. 'Well, the basics are . . . Vincent is twenty-nine, born in Leeds, came to London to join Frame and then went solo.'

'Since when he's made several fortunes, written a few passable songs and been spread across half the trees in the western hemisphere.'

'What do you mean . . . trees?' Dilly said, fearful she had missed a salient point.

'Trees, wood pulp, newsprint . . . give me strength,' Chris said and ducked as her London A–Z sailed past his ear.

'Stop being clever and help me,' Dilly said plaintively. 'This is my big chance.' Across the aisle, Amy pushed back her chair.

'Leave Chris alone, Dil. I'll help you. It's all there . . . go through everything as I told you to and list the points you want to put in the brief and then select what you've got room for.'

Chris smiled his gratitude. Amy was a good sort and according to everyone had a soft spot for him. He hoped she hadn't because he liked her a lot but didn't fancy her . . . well, hardly. Not like you should if you were going to get involved.

'I've done that. I've got heaps of his achievements and a list of his girlfriends a mile long but there's not much about how he got started.'

'He joined Frame.' Chris couldn't resist joining in. 'Everyone knows he joined Frame. He *was* Frame.'

'From where, dickhead? He's at school in Leeds then he's on *Top of the Pops*.'

Amy was riffling through the handouts. 'Look, it says here he played in a school orchestra and met Chas Louvaine and the others when he came to London.'

Dilly pored over the sheet. 'I saw that but it's not much.'

'Ring his agent,' Chris said. 'Ring the *NME*! Ring Mystic Meg if you have to but per-*leese* shut up and get on with it.' He bent to his task as Amy moved past him, freezing as she bent to whisper in his ear.

'I'll buy you a pint after work, if you like.'

'Ta,' he said. 'If I get finished, that is.' He tried to smile, unwilling to hurt her feelings, uneasy that he was appearing to accept an invitation he had no intention of taking up.

'I've got a good story for you,' Amy said, perching on the edge of his desk. 'Lisa's doing that piece on the Moors Murders — should Hindley be released et cetera. We've got a crusading barrister and some of the victims' families. Anyway, she's wading through all this bumf about dark deeds and God sends her a memo saying, 'Whatever you do, keep it light!"'

'I don't believe it,' Chris said, genuinely astonished.

'It's true. Ask Lisa. I ask you . . . keep a thing like that light!'

Chris shook his head. 'It gets worse. One day I'll put it in a book and no one will believe it.'

'You should write,' Amy said, getting to her feet. 'Your briefs are so good. You could do a really analytical look at a subject.'

'God!' They turned to look at Dilly, who was leaning back in her chair and regarding them scornfully. 'You two are so sad. No one wants analysis any more, Amy. They want bonk-busters or action. Look at *Bravo One Zero* – or was it *Two Zero* – anyway, that guy made a fortune. Write one of them!'

'There you are, Chris,' Amy said drily. 'All you've got to do is join the SAS and you're made for life. Give me strength!'

'Lovely,' Simon said as Liz put coffee and a piece of carrot cake in front of him. She sank into the opposite seat and lifted her cup. 'Look deep in strategic planning,' Simon said. 'It might keep everyone away.'

Around them the canteen heaved and bubbled with whispered confidences and raucous laughter where a particularly juicy bit of gossip was being shared. 'I love you,' he said.

'Just because I give you carrot cake.' She was being flippant because, if she didn't, she might cry.

'No,' he said, moving his hand so that their fingertips touched. 'No. Because I love you and I want you and the thought that I'm screwing up your life makes me feel like a turd.'

'You're not . . . don't. I knew what I was doing. And if you think you had anything to do with David and I breaking up, I've told you . . . it hadn't worked for years. Anyway, don't talk here. Someone will see.'

'No one will pay attention. If they do, they'll think we're agonising over work.'

'They wouldn't be too far off.' She was trying to change the subject but what she said was true. 'We have a problem.'

'Oh God . . .' He pushed the carrot cake away and then retrieved it and crammed it into his mouth. 'They are not − *not* − putting me off my food. Who's done what?'

'It's Carol. Well, Theo actually.'

'Has he been pulling her strings again?'

'As only he can, apparently. It's Birgitta. He's told Carol that Birgitta is her mirror-image − only twenty years younger, of course. So Carol wants rid.'

'You're joking. I mean, you *are* joking. It took three months to find someone who could do the weather without looking like Andy Pandy on speed!'

'Wish I was. Not that I've ever thought Birgitta was our answer to Michael Fish − but she does at least give some semblance of knowing a nimbus from a cumulus.'

'She eats her words,' Simon said gloomily. 'Chews

them before she spits them out, I mean. Watch her eyes. Still, she's passable and we can't go through all that again. Besides which, that cow is not hiring and firing staff.'

'Are you going to tell her that?' Liz asked sweetly.

'No,' Simon said firmly. 'That's the editor's job. I'm just his sidekick. Let him earn his corn for a change.'

'Was that a bad pun?' Liz asked, miming God's cereal eating. 'We both know he won't cross Carol. He'll promise her anything and everything and then dump the whole thing in our lap.'

'I'll have to get round her somehow,' Simon said. 'Leave it with me.' He put out his hand. 'I want you.' Suddenly his eyes dropped. 'God, I can't believe I'm saying this. I say that to you then I go home to Jane.'

'You can't help it . . . I understand.' She was covering his hand now, trying to comfort.

'No . . . it's wrong. It's as though I'm putting my marker on you – and all the time there's nothing I can offer you. We sit here pretending we're in conference when I'd really like to stand up and shout that you're the most important thing in my life.'

'I'm not,' Liz said quietly. 'Your kids are the most important thing in your life.'

They both went quiet, looking first at each other and then away. 'Which brings us back to the sixty-four-thousand-dollar question . . .' Simon said at last. 'Are kids better off with two parents in an environment which has everything in it but love or are they better off living with a mother who loves them and seeing their father once a week at the zoo?'

'Don't expect me to give you an answer,' Liz said. 'And don't think about it now. We see one another every day, we're together when we can be. It's enough.' But even to her own ears her words were unconvincing.

It was almost a relief when the producer of the motoring strand advanced on them with a problem that was capable of solution.

The men working on the site had grown accustomed to seeing Vincent in his hard hat. One or two still stared searchingly at the face they were used to seeing in newsprint or on hoardings or the TV screen. One or two of the more forward ones shouted, 'Hi, Vince,' as though claiming aquaintance. He smiled right and left but his attention was given to the progress of their work. It was six o'clock and they were on overtime while the light lasted.

He had conceived the project but from the beginning he had employed architects to transmit his dream to paper. On the ground floor, communal living areas, a canteen, counselling rooms, a sports hall and one open-plan reception dormitory. On the second floor, cubicled dormitories so that each resident had his or her own space, furnished with the basics and a huge pegboard for them to pin up the few fragments of their former lives. On the top floor there would eventually be ten self-contained apartments whose tenants would be completely independent, running their own lives until eventually they could move out to other accommodation and allow someone to move up from the floor below. In his mind's eye he saw it as a shaft leading upwards from the squalor of the streets towards the clean bright air of the upper atmosphere.

Dave had tried to discourage him at first. 'If it was that easy, Vin, it'd've been done before. You can't help these kids . . . well, most of them. They're no-hopers. Bung them a few quid by all means but don't get tied in. They go down and you go down with them . . . and they *will* go down. They're drek. If they weren't, they wouldn't be there. Would you or I be street dwellers? Twenty-four hours, maybe. Forty-eight tops. If they've been there any longer, they like it.'

He had wanted to tell Dave about the cold that dulled your wits and fogged your brain so that all you could think of, when daybreak came, was soaking in the warmth. He had wanted to speak of the hunger that gnawed at your guts and sent acid boiling up into your throat. He had wanted to describe the fear that meant you would do anything – anything – just to get warm, to get peace. But it would have been useless. Instead, he had said, 'I'm doing it, Dave. Better go along with it – it's on its way.'

Now, as the hoist descended, he gazed at Tower Bridge above Upper Pool, remembering his first sight of it, when he had still known wonder. If they could get to the kids as soon as they reached London, get them in here where it was safe . . . He inclined his head to the contractor. 'It looks good. Do your best. The more time you can save, the better.'

The man nodded. 'We should be OK. Not that you can ever tell in this business. Once the founds are in, though, I heave a sigh of relief. That's where most of your snags crop up, in the founds.'

The words lingered in Vincent's mind as he said his goodbyes and climbed into the car for the home-ward journey. It was true that the foundations were important, in life as in building. Could you surmount those early obstacles, forget those childhood traumas? He thought of what a psychiatrist would make of his life if ever he bared his soul.

I'm a text-book case, he thought, for there was not a single moment of his life – not even during the ecstacy of making music and knowing it was good – there was not a second when he did not look back and wince at the memory.

He looked out now at London streets gentled by late sun. Too late to go to Notting Hill and browse the antique shops; too early for the Ivy, even if he had an appetite. He leaned forward towards the driver. 'Make for Hampstead,' he said. 'I fancy a walk on the heath.' And then, remembering the Great Dane languishing at home, 'On second thoughts let's go home first.' He settled back, suddenly content at the thought of the welcome waiting there for him.

Daphne poured herself a tumbler of tomato juice and anointed it with Worcester sauce. It was too early for

72

alcohol but she needed a drink. On some evenings she could be good and sip it like alcohol but tonight she didn't feel like being good. It was gone in a second. For some reason she felt frazzled and tomato juice was not enough. She opened the fridge and looked at the open bottle of Piesporter but her condition warranted something more, something rich and potent and utterly, utterly comforting. It was only a quarter to six but what the hell! She collected the bottle of Cointreau from the drinks cupboard and a glass from the sideboard and carried them through to her desk.

She had made copious notes during her time at the studios. She wanted to make sense of them now while everything was fresh in her mind. Tomorrow, for the interviews, she would use a tape recorder but there had been too much going on today, and too much hubbub, for that aide-mémoire. She had been looking, listening, absorbing, jotting down what she could. She poured a generous measure of the liqueur, put her feet on a pouffe and began to transcribe.

The set-up at Daybreak was pyramid-shaped. At the top, the editor, responsible only to a board of directors and the ITC. Beneath him the deputy editor, Simon — who seemed to do all the work. Below him a raft of people yet to be identified, except for Liz.

There's something going on there, Daphne thought. Unless she was losing her nose for intrigue and subject to senile imaginings . . .

The thought, meant to be flippant, depressed her. Everything went with age. I'm fifty-one, she thought.

She was definitely the oldest journo on the *Herald*, unless you counted freelancers hired for their reputations. I'm just a run-of-the-mill journo, she thought, and Lou Bryan means to put me out to grass.

If she didn't make a success of this assignment it would happen.

She could always marry Brian. Except that Brian was much too nice to be married for any reason other than love and she didn't think she loved him. Well, she did a bit, but not enough. Besides which, she would make a lousy landlord's wife and her pay-off from the *Herald* wouldn't last for ever.

She stopped up her glass and went back to her notes. There was a section dealing only with news, with an editor and sub-editors as in the print media. Liz was head of features with a handful of producers below her. She reported to Simon and had access to a pool of researchers and directors. There was another technical section which allotted crews and editing space, and myriad secretaries and PAs.

She would have to interview the editor – or God, as he was known – unless, like the Wizard of Oz, he was hiding. She had not glimpsed him all day. Then she'd need the main presenters, Carol and Barry. The other known faces, the weather girl who resembled Carol and the male cook . . . or was he a chef? She'd have to ask. Then there was the fashion expert with the four-inch waist . . . and she'd need at least one producer and researcher. The boy with the specs and the soulful eyes probably. Chris, that was his name. She tapped her teeth with her pen. The dresser would bear cross-examination. Today she had heard him remark on Carol's propensity for pessimism. 'Oh, don't mind her,' he had told someone. 'She could see the black side of a neon light.'

She was still chuckling when the phone rang. 'Brian . . . nice to hear from you.' Her hand was halfway to the Cointreau when she thought better of it. One of the things she admired about Brian was his ability to use drink to advantage but never to excess. 'It *is* ages . . . I'll try and make it this week. I'm at the Daybreak studios . . . yes, you do . . . the breakfast television station. With Barry Kenna . . . that's right . . . Did you?'

She listened as Brian reminisced about Barry's heyday as a swimmer. Brian had been quite an athlete himself in his youth: Metropolitan Police diving champion, a javelin thrower. He still had a good body. She moved in her chair, thinking how nice it was to share a bed with him. It *had* been ages, he was right about that.

'Your libido's still young, my girl,' she told herself when she had put down the phone. She did love Brian. She could take him or leave him, though. That was the trouble. He was a big jolly man and her head came only as high as his chest. As his heart, he had said once. But if she moved in with him it would be the end of her career. She would settle into the nice, dull routine of relationship and lose her edge and Lou Bryan would have won. 'Over my dead body,' Daphne said aloud and poured herself a large drink before she went back to her notes on Daybreak.

There was a celebrity guest each day and daily regulars such as news and horoscopes and weather. There was cooking Monday, Wednesday and Friday and home and fashion items scattered liberally throughout the week. The agony uncle had a regular spot and there was a fitness guru to wake everyone at seven, Japanese style.

Daphne began to flex her ankles. She couldn't bear it if she stiffened up with age. Suddenly she was depressed again. She reached for the bottle and topped up her glass. She had known Brian for years and years but if anything the relationship had diminished, not progressed. In the first few weeks they had been at it like knives. Now they went to bed only when she was too tired to go home from his pub. She shivered, finding the thought chilling.

She still liked sex with him . . . but not enough to make an effort to get it. She pursed her lips to emit a soundless whistle. Much more of that line of thought and she'd be sobbing her eyes out. She poured out a generous tot of Cointreau and went back to work, but, even as she scribbled and deciphered and considered her priorities, thoughts of Brian intruded.

He was solid. That was the number-one thing about him. She had never seen him flap, not even in the moment of their meeting, outside the scene of a seige, when there had been noise and confusion and shouting all around them. He resembled Brian Dennehy, the

American film star, big and unflappable and very endearing — except that when Dennehy played villians his eyes were like stones and she had never seen Brian's eyes without a twinkle.

Suddenly she realised she was daydreaming. 'Daphne,' she said aloud. 'Think about Lou Bryan.' It worked. Brian was forgotten and her pen began to race across the paper.

5

Monday, 7.00 *p.m.*

Liz had made a list of urgent tasks before she left
her office and headed it 'Action This Day', but by
the time she reached home her desire to restore order
to her life had abated. All she really wanted to do, if
she couldn't be with Simon, was curl up in her oldest
robe, drink wine and listen to soulful music. Not that
she was going to succumb to the urge. She knew the
inevitable end of wine and music. Tears of self-pity, a
nose streaming mucus and a sore head in the morning!

The house in which she occupied the first-floor
flat looked mellow in the early evening sunshine. She
loved this neighbourhood of soft Edwardian brick and
gardens filled with wisteria and love-in-a-mist and the
little pointed faces of aquilegia. The people who lived
here were mostly media people, television executives
and actors who strode the quiet streets in rumpled

corduroy or rather tatty dresses that bore exotic designer labels.

It had been Dave's idea to live here and at first she had demurred. It was too overtly chic, almost studied in its casualness, and she had feared being out of place. Now she loved it, seeing her first-floor eyrie with its heavy oak door as a sanctuary. A sanctuary that could be a heaven when Simon joined her there! And it was the best of all places for illicit meetings because her neighbours were all too taken up with their own affairs to give a damn for anything she did.

She allowed herself fifteen minutes to relax with a coffee, vowing as she did so to pack the rest of the evening with achievement so solid that it denied entry to self-pity. It was growing dusk outside and the room, filled with Victorian and Edwardian furniture, lovingly acquired over the years, began to grow pockets of semi-darkness. Liz closed her eyes, imagining the scene outside. Happy couples emerging from houses hand in hand to walk to the pub or returning, desperate to get inside and merge and cling. In the nick of time she realised where such thoughts were leading her and jumped to her feet to check her myriad house plants in case they needed water.

She was beginning to wonder if one small — one very small — drink might be permissible, when the phone rang. It was eight-thirty. Surely Simon would be home by now and unable to ring, unless . . . She leaped across the sofa to grab the receiver, already bathing and dressing in her head, defrosting chops, decanting wine, getting ready to draw him over her threshold. But it wasn't Simon on the other end of the line. 'Hello Dave,' she said, carrying the handset to an armchair. Her ex-husband's telephone calls tended to be lengthy. Might as well get comfortable.

They had been lovers for six months and then lived together for a year before they got married and love went out of the window. 'How are you?' she asked and listened to him moan about everything from Bill Clinton to the price of cheese. The day they had moved in together he had dressed in a gorilla suit to carry her over the threshold, groaning all the while at her eight and a half stones. Two years later they were hardly on speaking terms. Where had fun gone? And love? They had planned a baby for the year after they married but the baby had never materialised and now she was glad. Babies needed two parents and when babies turned into toddlers and became teenagers they needed two parents even more. Which was why she and Simon could never have more than snatched moments. Not for years and years.

She caught sight of herself in the mirror above the fireplace, her face white beneath her fringe, eyes shadowed, telltale lines from nose to chin. She was getting old and soon she would be *too* old. She tried to remember how many eggs a female was born with, millions . . . or was it thousands. She was thirty-three. How many eggs left? How much time?

She could hear Dave chuntering away. 'I'm not signing another contract — not to be arsed about by that bunch.' Fleet Street was in a state of flux again and he was feeling insecure. She made sympathetic noises but her mind was seething with anger – anger against Dave for the wasted years, against herself for thinking youth was everlasting, but most of all against Simon, who had children already and could afford to hang around.

The sheer unfairness of her thought, once acknowledged, burned out the anger. No one was to blame unless it was God or Fate or whoever or whatever wrote life's script. If she had got the exec's job at GMTV she would never have come to Daybreak. Before that, if she had failed her O-levels she would never have got a degree, never done journalism, never wound up in the media at all and never have met Simon. She laughed aloud at her train of thought. If she hadn't done her homework like a good little girl she would be happily married now, still living in Grantham probably, like the rest of her schoolmates, with two-point-four children and a house on the new estate. 'No,' she said as Dave protested at her involuntary mirth. 'No, I don't think that's funny at all. I just had a wild thought.'

'Liz . . .' Dave's voice was suddenly lower, more intimate, and Liz shuffled upright. Something was coming; better be on guard. 'I've been thinking, Liz. I don't know why . . . why now, I mean . . . well, I've never stopped thinking about you, about us . . . it's just that, this last few days . . . anyway, it's crazy us not seeing one another. After all, we're still friends.'

Liz threw back her head and blew an imaginary smoke ring. What had brought this on? Their divorce was almost final, the settlement agreed. She would take over the mortgage on this place, he would receive his share of the equity in five stages, the first due on the day the decree became final.

'So?' At the other end of the line he was expecting a response.

'So . . . yes, of course we're still friends. But I don't see the point.'

'Friends see each other, Liz. That's the point.' Liz knew she ought to argue, or at least politely disclaim, but a sudden terrible inertia had overcome her.

Simon checked the studio layout before he left for home. Yesterday there had been a jumble of colour, a too-busy backdrop to the main interview area. Satisfied that his instruction to tone it down had been carried out properly, he took a short cut across the deserted props room, settling into his jacket as he went, patting his pockets to make sure that car keys and wallet were there.

There were only emergency lights burning but he knew his way by heart, skirting the set they had used for the tribunal strand, ducking under the outstretched arm of the eight-foot gorilla they had used for every jungle-orienated item since John Logie Baird, past the pile of flats that marked a left turn for the exit and past the ten-times-life-size picture of Mandy Baker, whose short life and untimely death at the hands of her stepfather had provoked a public enquiry and national outrage that so little had been done to help her. If he

left Jane she might remarry and Rosie would be prey
to a cruel stepfather.

Every time he saw that picture of Mandy his scalp
prickled – and he saw it almost every day. Tomorrow
he would tell them to junk it – except that it served as
a reminder that television, when it got it right, was a
force for good. He had pushed the Baker case as far as he
could then – when he had been a humble producer with
time to make programmes instead of sorting squabbles
and firing people, which was all he seemed to do
nowadays. He had attended the inquest and seen the
anguish in the eyes of the PC who had given evidence
of finding the body. He had listened as the pathologist
listed the fractures, old and new, the contusions and
burn marks and bruises. And *he* had burned, as a
tale of official ineptitude and neighbourly indifference
unfolded. He had listened and burned and gone on a
crusade which might, just might, have weighted the
scales in favour of a future Mandy.

Could he do that now? Not with God in charge.
TV was becoming trivialised. It was not intrinsically
trivial – of that he was sure – but in the wrong hands
. . .! He tried to erase the tortured face of the dead
child from his mind and thought, instead of his own
children. Rosie would probably be asleep by the time
he got home but Jake would be wakeful, anxious to
chat, to talk of school or ask about work. He must
stop working fourteen-hour days and spend more time
at home.

It was OK when the children were there. It was

afterwards, when silence fell and he and Jane were alone in their mutual dislike . . . and yet he had loved her once. The memory of their lovemaking in the early days reared up in his mind as he eased his car out of the car park. He thought of Jane's body as a white column above him, the breasts, unspoilt by childbirth as taut as unripe nectarines. He remembered her moving above him and the sensation of being swept away by the new joy of it, except that the face and the breasts that preoccupied his mind did not belong to his wife. It was Liz who rode him to fulfilment now. 'Shit,' he said as the inside wheel grazed the kerb and the car juddered. He put out a hand to demist the windscreen and tried to keep his mind on the road.

If he and Jane split up, who would tell the children? And how? He knew what their reaction would be. Jake's brow would lower and his mouth would set, but he wouldn't say anything. That was always his reaction to things he couldn't fully comprehend. Resistance! He would simply refuse to acknowledge it was happening in the hope that if he held out long enough it would go away.

But Rosie would not be silent. Her mouth would pucker into an O of anguish and then she would begin to howl, her eyes growing dark and pink, her little body shrinking until she looked almost newborn. He couldn't bear his daughter's tears, had never been able to bear them. So how could he be the cause of them, inflict such utter misery upon her because he couldn't control his libido?

Suddenly he realised he had passed three sets of traffic lights. He should have left the car in the car park, where it had been for three days, but he had worried about the battery. They used Jane's car, a family saloon, at weekends, but he still loved his nippy Audi. Had he driven through the lights? He had no recollection of halting, seeing them go from red to red and amber, then to green.

He looked in the rear-view mirror. No police car, so if he'd done it he'd got away with it. He slowed his speed and returned to his thoughts.

It wasn't just lust with Liz. He wouldn't jeopardise his family for a tumble. He had never sought an affair: it had crept upon him. She was good at her job, better than he was, probably, and he had come to depend upon her. It had started with a drink, a trip to the pub suggested out of gratitude for a job well done. He had meant it to be nothing more than a quick drink, a clink of glasses to celebrate success, and then goodbye. But somewhere, halfway down the glass, he had realised he didn't want to go home.

He was on Hanger Lane now. In a moment he would turn left and the tree-lined street where he lived with Jane would be only moments away. I don't want to go home, he thought. Christ help me — I don't want to go home.

Across the hearthrug, Fred was sleeping, hands laced across belly, lips reverberating gently beneath a faint moustache of tomato sauce. He never wiped his mouth after meals. When they were young, when she'd been a bloody fool, she used to wipe it for him, demanding that he spit on the paper serviette if the stains were stubborn and refused to budge. Now, she'd given up. He didn't deserve such attention. Not since he'd denied her the new three-piece.

She had the room really nice, pale blue with a white spot above the dado, royal blue damask below. But the suite clashed! They could've had three years' free credit if he'd been reasonable but he'd just said, 'What's wrong with the old one?' over and over again until she'd wanted to belt him around the head with one of the cushions until he could see that brown and green didn't go together.

It wasn't as if he hadn't been used to nice things. He'd come from better than she had when it came to a nice home. All done on tick, but his mother was a wonder with money. Unlike Vera's own parents, who'd lived hand to mouth. She'd sat on cast-offs during her whole growing up – now she wanted a Dralon suite with fringe and ten cushions.

On her Daybreak pay she could afford paper and paint and nice teasets. Even matching curtains and duvet set. But a big purchase needed Fred behind it and Fred couldn't see what was wrong with the old suite. For a moment she contemplated stabbing him with the bread knife and buying a Parker-Knoll with his insurance, but the feeling quickly passed. She'd never seen an easy chair in Cell Block H. You didn't want to end up there!

She looked at the clock. Ten to nine and nothing on the telly for another half-hour. Monday nights were deadly unless the film on ITV was to her liking, and tonight it was more violence. *Die Hard Three* – or *Six* or *Ten*. Bruce Willis seemed to go on for ever.

For a moment she wondered what would happen if she got a lipstick from upstairs and wrote 'I am a werewolf' on Fred's forehead. He would probably go in to work tomorrow still tattooed. He never washed – not properly – and as for baths . . . I wish.

She smiled at the phrase she had picked up from the researchers. 'I wish' and 'Jee-sus' were their favourite expressions and when something went right Chris would roll his eyes to heaven and say 'Thank you, God.' She would like to win the lottery, if only for Chris's sake, except that if he came into money that Dilly would sink her hooks in quick as a flash, when anyone could see he and Amy were made for each other. And unless she was much mistaken that Dilly had been in more beds than a boarding-house flea.

Disturbed by thoughts of a nation slipping into decay she levered herself to her feet and went to put the kettle on. If they won the lottery Chris would have to fend for himself. If she won she would leave work on the spot. If they wanted notice she would pay them – in lieu.

As she carried her mug back to the fireside she thought briefly about the disturbing possibility of winning a roll-over jackpot. Seventeen million was too much for anyone. It split families. Two hundred and fifty thousand would be nice. Manageable. She would give half of it to Fred — well, not quite half, but enough to keep him happy and out of her sight. A big dollop to cancer research, something for Edie. They were sisters after all. And as for the rest, it would be spend, spend, spend.

She tried to remember how much a gigolo had cost in that item last week. A lot, but a fleabite from a quarter of a million. Not that she was up to much hanky-panky. Nowadays Fred's willy came out as often as that passion flower people went on holiday to see because it blossomed only once in a blue moon.

The thought of people booking to see Fred aroused was so delicious that she laughed aloud. For a second his lips stopped reverberating and she held her breath, but after a moment the slow breathy wobble resumed and she could relax. She sipped the tea and tried to be serious.

I'm forty-nine, she thought. Not much time left. If she had lived like Theo so that she had a colourful past, it would be different. But she had done nothing, been nowhere. Even that Dilly, at twenty-two, was more a woman of the world. It was too much to bear alone. She reached for the remote control and invited Bruce Willis to share her misery.

It was Clifford's turn to cook but he had chickened out. 'Kentucky Fried,' he said, daring them to protest as he dumped a family bucket on the table. 'Help yourselves.'

'Wait a moment,' Chris said. 'I'm not what you'd call fastidious but I do like a plate.'

'They should put you on *Hearth and Home*,' Dilly said wickedly, delving into the bucket for the breast pieces she preferred. *Hearth and Home* was the least popular item so Amy had been stuck with it for months.

Dilly pulled a face, obviously reading Chris's mind. 'I know, we're mean to Amy . . . but she asks for it. She's so nice! She exudes – she reeks – niceness. She makes us all feel unworthy and vile little creatures. We hate her and she loves us back. Christ! Anyway . . .' She wiped her nose with the grease-free back of her hand and then rubbed her inside arm against her left breast to relieve an itch. 'Do you want to go round the Grapes after?'

'We shouldn't,' Clifford said gloomily. 'We should clean up this place and get an early night. I'm still going down the Grapes, though. Can I have your fries, Dil? Ta.'

Chris shifted in his seat and reached for one of the paper napkins to use as a plate. What Dilly had said about Amy had pricked his conscience. Amy was not at all pious. She was a good sport and a mate into the bargain and he hadn't sprung to her defence. He was about to remedy this when Clifford forestalled him.

'Amy's OK. She knows her stuff and Mike Scott fancies her like mad.'

'He always goes for Asian women,' Dilly said, searching her piece of chicken carcass for one last morsel of flesh.

'I don't blame him,' Clifford said, shoving thin fries

into his mouth with banana-size fingers. 'Sultry . . .
that's what Amy is.'

'Sultry? Amy? On yer bike!' Dilly hooted and Chris
seized his chance.

'Well, I think she's attractive. Very.'

'And who are you to judge?' Dilly said indulgently. 'You know what we call you behind your
back, Chris?'

'What?' He was alarmed now. Nicknames could be
cruel. At school they had called him 'Four-eyes'.

'Thelonius,' Clifford said, wiping his mouth. 'Don't
ask me why but that's what they call you.'

'Thelonius . . .?' Chris was taken aback. What the
hell had 'Thelonius' got to do with anything.

'Thelonius Monk,' Dilly explained. 'You know, he's
a conductor or something. Something classical. Anyway,
it's the monk bit that counts. On account of you only
thinking of work!'

'He's not a conductor. He's a musician. A good one –
brilliant in fact. He plays jazz piano,' Chris said, trying
to hide his relief. Being called celibate was not what he
would have wished for but it was better than a lot of
descriptions. And at least he had defended Amy. Too late
and too little, but that too was better than nothing.

'We ought to clean this place up,' Clifford said
morosely, looking round the cluttered room but not
moving a muscle.

'It's all right.' Dilly looked mildly surprised that
anyone should object to the squalor in which they lived,
but Chris could see the thin film of dust on furniture,

the overflowing waste basket, the plant, brought in by Dilly, which had drooped and died in a corner. That was the trouble with rented accommodation: it belonged to everyone and no one, so no one felt impelled to care for it.

As he chewed on the rapidly cooling fried chicken he wondered what Amy's apartment would be like. She lived in a tree-lined street of solid red-brick houses so she was probably subsidised by wealthy parents. Or else a good manager with money, unlike Dilly, who was always skint. In any event, the place where Amy lived would be clean and orderly, like her desk. She could lay her hands on what she wanted instantly and there were usually fresh flowers on her desk — just a few — in a clear glass vase.

'Ooh, that was nice!' Dilly was licking her fingertips, one by one, before wiping her hands down her jeans. It was an awful habit and he had seen her do it before. But standing there, licking lips gleaming with grease, she looked so desirable that any trace of distaste he might have felt melted clean away.

Dilly tied up her hair and changed her shirt before they went out into the dusk. As she walked beside Chris he could smell her perfume. If Clifford had been late back from filming or played his everlasting squash anything might have happened. Why Clifford? He was big and blond and thick — but he had thighs like Schwarzenegger and didn't wear glasses.

He managed to put a hand in the small of Dilly's back as they entered the bar, and it was some small consolation when she didn't pull away. As Chris sipped his lager he wondered whether or not she might even have returned the pressure. But when they got back to the flat it was Clifford's bed she went to, not his. And all Chris had by way of consolation was the thought of clean sheets at the Imperial and a mini-bar all to himself on Thursday night.

Everything about the restaurant was discreet, except for the prices, which were outrageous. In the dim lighting Vincent smiled at the woman who sat opposite him and tried to put on a listening face. She was chattering about her new car, an automatic, and he smiled and tut-tutted in what he hoped were the right places. She was here to serve his purpose: the least he could do was be pleasant.

The had ordered boeuf en croûte as a main course and a good red wine to accompany it, but first they toyed with a salmon terrine and pretended to be close friends. The woman was small and dark with warm eyes. Jewish probably, and intelligent, so she wouldn't automatically expect dinner and bed. He felt himself relax as the second Kir Royale hit home and dared to wonder if he might even enjoy the evening.

Dave usually found the women, models, actresses, some, like this one, working in Dave's agency or one of its cohorts. A meeting in the course of business or at some public occasion would be engineered and if Vincent was interested he was presented with a mini-biog and a phone number. After that, it was up to him. The women were not wanted for sex – he could have used a high-class commercial agency for that. 'You need them for your profile, Vince. You're thirty-two . . . well twenty-nine according to your CV. It doesn't do to leave a vacuum – some sod'll fill it with dirt. We know you're straight but you have to think about rumours.'

Vincent had wanted to say 'Sod the rumours' but it wasn't fair to employ a manager and then ignore him. And some of the women were OK. He had even taken things further with a couple of them. He had nothing against women. It was relationships that scared him, or, rather, entanglements, which were what life had taught him relationships were. He thought of his mother's track record and heard his teeth chink against his glass as he clenched them. Careful! Mustn't disturb his image as Mr Unflappable.

'I saw a promo for *Daybreak*,' today. His dinner companion was smiling at him. 'You don't usually do TV . . . especially not breakfast telly.'

'I do sometimes, to promote an album.'

'I saw you on *Aspel* once and you did *Richard and Judy* last year. But the breakfast couch? With the divine Carol and the creepy Barry?'

Vincent shrugged. 'It's a means to an end. They've got a big audience. Lots of businessmen watch before they go off to the office. I need money for my Bermondsey project so I'll expose myself to the harsh light of dawn to get it. It's only two days! Some of the kids I want to help have slept out for a third of their lives.'

'OK! Don't get impassioned.' She put out a hand and touched his arm. 'Not that it doesn't become you, a hint of passion. But I wasn't criticising you. I just wondered why *Daybreak*?'

'Least zany, biggest audience. Well, relatively speaking.'

'You mean the Beeb's too po-faced and the *Big Breakfast* sends everything up and *Daybreak* is a compromise?'

'Cor-rect,' he said and raised his glass. 'Now, let's talk about you. That's a far more interesting subject. My life's already an open book. Tell me about yours.'

When she smiled her eyes gleamed. She was Jewish. They all had warm eyes. 'I thought I told you everything last time we met – when Dave introduced us. I talked my head off that night. Afterwards I felt ashamed.'

'Not at all.' Vince smiled to show he meant what he said. There had been genuine vulnerability in her voice. 'I hate those celebrity affairs. They drag. That one was better because you were there.' He smiled again but less warmly. Mustn't give the impression that he was keen. He liked her but that was all.

She told him about her family as they finished their first course and the beef was brought in. 'Do you have brothers and sisters?'

'No. I wish I did have. My mother's my only family. My father died when I was a child.'

'In Leeds? I read your cuttings this morning and they said you grew up in Leeds.'

'Yes. Roundhay Park was my stamping ground but I left early. When I was fifteen, in fact.'

'To come to London? That was brave of you. Did you come alone?' Across the table her eyes were still warm but curious also. He must be careful.

'Yes. But I knew people here – other musicians.'

'What about school – if you were only fifteen?'

'Well, almost sixteen. I'd left school.' This was what he hated, spinning tales that were half-truths and therefore could not be expected to tally with other half-truths. He made a desperate effort to rescue the conversation and move it into safer waters.

'Dave tells me you're quite a music buff. Opera, I think he said. What's your real preference?'

And then they were into the realms of Puccini and Verdi and Leeds and London could be consigned to the safety of obscurity.

Daphne was drifting into virtuous sleep when the phone rang a few inches from her ear. She struggled onto her elbow and fumbled for the receiver. 'Yes?' She was too tired and confused and far too inebriated to bother about the niceties of telephone etiquette.

'Daphne? It's Lou . . . I've been thinking. I don't want you to include Vincent in the piece. You can mention he's there . . . but a profile should be about the people who run the thing week by week.'

Daphne eased up on her pillows, wide awake now.

Last week it had been 'grab every celeb you can'. Then it had been 'not too much Vincent'. Now she was being told to leave a mega-celeb alone. Curiouser and curiouser, especially when you added it to the photographs on Lou Bryan's desk. She could still see the little hand with its blunt white-edged nails moving over the photographs, pushing the old photo out of sight. If only she had managed to get a look at that photograph. If she went in later in the week she'd definitely try.

'Well . . . if that's what you want Lou. I thought it was a golden opportunity but you're the boss.'

'Well, it doesn't matter really.' Lou was being too airy for words now. 'But I'd like this piece to be really spare. You know, informative. The anatomy of a breakfast television station. Get the backroom boys, the figures we all take for granted . . .' Lou was getting desperate and Daphne's exhaustion was returning.

'OK, Lou. I get the picture, no Vincent. Leave it to me. Now I'd like to get some sleep. I've got a six o'clock call and I was up at four this morning. I'm desperate for sleep.'

But after she had replaced the receiver and snuggled down again her mind raced furiously. Why was she being told to lay off Vincent. No, not told, *warned* off! Lou was up to something. That much was sure. Unless she simply wants to ruin my piece, Daphne thought, and she fears some real lowdown on Vincent might save it? But not even Lou would be as stupid – or as evil – as that. Or would she?

Daphne lay down and tried to slip back into sleep. Think about sheep, holidays, name objects alphabetically, recite nursery rhymes. On the second time round of 'Humpty Dumpty' she sat up and switched on the bedside lamp. If she wasn't careful she would let her paranoia over Lou cloud her judgement. There were always items brewing in a features department and photographs could lie about for years. It didn't mean there was something sinister going on. Daphne put out the light and lay down again.

She was almost drifting off to sleep when she remembered Chloe Benson. She had had five years to go to retirement when Lou Bryan had manoeuvred her out of the *Herald*. She's been saving for years to retire to Jersey and the loss of five years' salary, even with an enhanced pension, had scuppered it. Someone had tackled Lou about it and her reply had been brief. 'I'm in newspapers, not in welfare.'

She means to get rid of me, Daphne thought. But I won't let it happen. I'll make a good job of Daybreak and then I'll come up with some good ideas – real blasts – and then she'll have to grin and bear it.

But, as she turned over and tried once more to sleep, she thought of a more realistic way out of her dilemma. Follow Lou from the office and push her under a bus. That was the only certain solution.

'You're welcome to a drink,' Liz said. 'I've got Scotch and gin and wine. There might be a lager in the fridge. But I can't stay up much longer. I'm bushed.'

For once Dave was sympathetic. 'Breakfast telly's a killer,' he said. 'Ruins your social life, buggers your sex life.'

Oh no, Liz thought. We're not going down that track again. He had always blamed her job for the demise of their marriage but there had been more to it than that, so much more.

He poured himself a large Scotch and now he was flinging himself onto the sofa, lifting one leg to drape it over the arm. He's making himself at home, Liz thought, and was affronted.

'I thought we might have a meal one night this week,' he said, holding his glass up to the light and squinting at it. 'It's ages since we had a meal together. Ages since *I* had a meal, come to that. I don't know how you manage on your own . . . I find it difficult. You know, having a structure to things. I don't keep mealtimes – well, that's the job I suppose.'

Liz smiled noncommittally. 'They want to send me to Bosnia,' Dave said. 'I'm trying to get out of it. Let the young chaps go, I say. I've done my stint. I've changed, Liz. Not that I've become a homebody – but I think I'm at that stage where I want a form to things, a structure.' He had used that word twice. Structure! What he meant was he wanted someone to run his fucking life for him. The violence of her own thoughts shocked her. She had enjoyed looking after him once. What had changed?

He was putting down his glass, getting to his feet.

'Dave . . . I think you should go now!' But he wasn't ready to go.

His arms were around her, crushing her with one hand, fumbling with her robe with the other. 'Come on, Liz. We had it once. I don't know what went wrong – my fault, I suppose. But there's never been anyone but you – not for me. I love you Liz.' Her breast was exposed now, his lips on her neck and moving . . . moving.

'For God's sake, David. It's over. Can't you get that through your head?' She used his formal name to emphasise the gulf between them and now he was moving away and she was cramming her dignity back inside the cotton robe. 'Can you go now? Don't argue. Just go. It's too late. Get that through your head. It's over.'

But he was shaking his head. 'You're hurt, Liz. I don't blame you. I was an inconsiderate sod. But I've learned my lesson. I wouldn't run the risk of losing you again. I love you and I'm just enough of an egomaniac to think you still love me. Remember what it was like? Not just bed – though, by God, I've never had sex with anyone like I had with you before we got careless and let it slip away. But remember the fun, that funny little flat in Tottenham and the stockpot when you had a touch of the Delia Smith's and we both got salmonella. Please, just give it one more chance. Give me one more chance. You won't regret it.'

In a minute she would cry and he'd have her! She made her voice deliberately hostile. 'I've asked you to go. Please do it. This is not Tottenham – this is my home. I'm buying you out, remember? Now for God's sake go and let me get some sleep!'

He was shaking his head and smiling and she had to resist the impulse to hammer at him with balled fists. 'Liz.' His voice was cajoling but there was an arrogance there, an assumption that she was playing hard to get and all he had to do was persevere.

She breathed out hard and when she spoke her voice was calmer. 'Dave, I don't want to argue. I'm too tired. Let's discuss this at a more civilised time. Right now, I can hardly think straight, let alone discuss something as complicated as our relationship. We're friends – and you know I'm always there for you if you have trouble – but please, go home now.'

'OK.' He raised placatory hands. 'OK. You're tired and I'm being a pest. I'll ring you and we'll get together.' She was getting rid of him so why did he look like someone who had just scored a victory?

She let him kiss her cheek, keeping her mouth turned away, and then he was going through the door and she was closing it behind him. She could hardly shoot the bolts home because of the violent trembling in her fingers. When it was done she sank to the floor and cried with relief.

They were in bed by ten, lamps extinguished on a common 'Goodnight'. In the darkness Simon stared around, watching the familiar bedroom re-emerge as his eyes grew accustomed to the dark. Ten o'clock. His alarm set for three-forty-five. Five and three-quarter hours of night-time. The hours before *Daybreak*. If he was married to Liz he would turn to her now, put his hand on her breast, feel her reach for him, cover her mouth and kiss her savagely, sucking, needing.

'I've cancelled the milk in the morning,' Jane said into the darkness. 'Just in case you wonder . . .'

'I've usually gone by the time they deliver.' His voice was flat and unemotional. Hers had been small and vulnerable.

He reached out and sought her hand, finding it curled on her belly. It was small and slightly roughened with housework and washing and when he felt each fingertip the nails were short and sensible, the nails of a working mother. She was a good mother. Whatever else you could say about her, she loved her children.

'Do you think we could have a meal out one night?' She was pleading but not wingeing.

'I'm sure we could. Where do you want to go?'

'Anywhere. Well . . .' She was turning towards him now, confiding. 'I'd love to go to that new place . . . on James Street. Everyone says it's fab.'

'James Street it is then. Can you get a sitter?'

'Yes. And we'll let the kids have a takeaway to make up for leaving them.'

'You spoil them.'

'I love them . . .' Her breath was warm on his naked shoulder. 'Thank you for giving them to me.'

In the darkness his eyes pricked as he thought of her in the labour ward, sweating, frightened – suffering to bring forth his children. He felt a wave of pity, of shame, of guilt that turned in an instant into desire. He reached for her. 'Come here. You are a silly billy.' Beneath his hand her nipple came erect, her lips were parting. Poor little Jane, who hid behind Jane the shrew.

I am to blame for this, he thought as he entered her. And then shame and guilt were lost in the inevitable ride to fulfilment.

6

Tuesday 5.45 a.m.

Vera watched as the make-up artist spread out her tools. Dozens of lipsticks, bound in bundles with elastic bands, bottle after bottle of foundation, concealer, eyeliner, blusher. And all posh makes, Vera thought. It must cost a fortune.

At that moment Theo stuck his head through the door. On the monitor they were running the intro in studio, prior to a rehearsal. Theo looked at the dawn, the hatching eggs, the striding milkman, with a jaundiced eye. 'Morning may have broken there,' he said, 'but it's sodding well fractured here.'

'What's the matter?' Vera and the make-up girl spoke in unison. News – especially bad news – powered the engines of most of the Daybreak team.

'Carol's got a virus.' Theo put a hand to his forehead and shuddered. 'Rang poor Simon at three a.m. to say she was dying. Would we get a specialist for her?'

'What'll they do?' Vera said. 'What about Barry?'

'Oh Barry's thrilled. He's out there now, on the studio floor, throwing his arms wide and shouting, "Mine all mine". He probably expected this anyway. He rings every day to get their fortunes.' Theo paused for dramatic effect. 'Not just his own, hers as well. I saw him dial Sagittarius one day and I said, "You're a Gemini. What are you doing that for?"'

He put up a hand to cover a phlegmy cough and threw back his head. 'Do you know what he said? "I have to know what the stars have in store for her, Theo, if I'm going to keep ahead."' The dresser shook his head 'He's not the full shilling. I've said it before and I'll say it again.'

'You can manage him, though,' the make-up artist said admiringly.

Theo looked at her, a sly smile passing over his lips. 'I know where the bodies are buried.' He tapped his nose. 'That's my secret.'

'What d'you mean?' Vera was clutching her spray polish to her chest, eyes round as saucers now. This was better than you got in any of the magazines.

'Well, take his trousers,' Theo said. 'Always on about his thirty-two-inch waist. Man and boy, thirty-two inches. He's told *Hello* about it, bragged about it on *Take A Break* . . . showed his waistband to Des O'Connor. He's thirty-five and a half! I get the labels off a pal in schmutter and stitch them in before they go to the dry cleaners.

'"Just a temporary weight gain," Barry says. "I'll be back to normal in no time. No sense in giving the wrong impression, Theo."' He put out a hand to the door post. 'And to think I did *Chariots of Fire* . . .! Still, there's no justice. I've known that long enough.' He sighed heavily. 'I'd better get back in there . . . beggars can't be choosers.'

When he had gone Vera resumed a cursory dusting. 'Theo knows it all, doesn't he? They daren't cross him. I suppose. He could go to the papers.'

'They pay a fortune. Thousands.' The make-up artist was assembling her palette. 'Not that I'd ever do it — you'd have to be on your uppers to do the dirty on colleagues.'

'Yes,' Vera said. 'It's a matter of pride, isn't it?'

All the same, she thought, as she pushed the cleaning trolley along the corridor, you could do a lot with a thousand pounds. A thousand pounds . . . In her mind's eye she saw herself coming downstairs in a mink coat, carrying one of those check-cloth, leather-bound bags like the one Carol carried — the ones from Paris that cost a fortune. She would pause briefly for a last look at Fred, asleep in his chair as usual, before she went out to the waiting cab, clutching the collar of the mink.

It was a nice dream. When she and Chris won the lottery . . . She was roused from her daydream by a harassed researcher. 'Someone's been sick in the loo, Vera. I'm horribly sorry but can you fix it? I've got guests pouring in from all quarters.'

* * *

Simon was trying to convince a frightened weather girl that she was perfectly capable of sitting beside Barry and reading Carol's lines from autocue. 'I can't do it, Simon. I'm not up to it – not at a moment's notice.'. He put both hands on her arms and half-forced her down onto the settee. Her make-up was perfect, her dark hair beautifully done. She certainly looked the part.

'You *can* do it, Birgitta. You use autocue well. Leave any ad-lib to Barry. He won't expect anything from you except what's in the script. You can do it on your head. And either Liz or I will be right there, behind camera, every minute. You've got a brilliant director – he'll be with you every inch of the way. We'll all be with you.'

Birgitta smiled warily. 'Well, if you think I can do it . . .' Simon straightened up, relieved. What did it matter if she stared at the lens like a frightened rabbit as long as she kept the lines coming. The floor manager was already begging everyone to get into place for a run-through and the minutes were ticking away. Suddenly Barry appeared, beaming.

'Don't give it another thought, Simon. Leave it with me . . .' He leaned to pat the girl's trembling knee. 'You're safe with Uncle Barry.'

'No need to rely on Barry, Birgitta, darling!' Carol was standing in the doorway, her voice loud enough to be heard from one end of the studio to the other. She was dressed in a pale-blue satin tracksuit with a white chiffon scarf at the neck as she advanced on the group around the settee, a look of martyrdom on her face. When she reached them she took Simon's arm and leaned against him. 'I couldn't let you down, darling. I know how much you depend on me. Couldn't let the show go down the tubes, not when I could still walk.' The glance she directed at Barry was almost triumphant.

'We could've managed,' he said defensively. 'We had it all worked out.'

'All the difference in the world between 'managing' and a good show, Barry, darling. I couldn't take the risk. Now . . .' She turned to Simon. 'If you'll just help me to make-up, Simon . . .' Her smile flashed back to the weather girl. 'And you can go back to your nice little clouds and thunderflashes, darling. Naughty of them to put you on the spot like that. Still, no harm done.'

They moved out of the studio, Carol leaning heavily on Simon whenever she remembered. 'It's good of you to do this, Carol,' he said. 'As long as you're up to it. Is there anything I can do for you?'

Carol paused and turned to look earnestly into his face. 'Well, there is something, Simon . . . about Birgitta. I don't want her brunette.'

For a moment he was lost for words. 'But she *is* brunette, Carol.'

'We're all something, darling. But that doesn't say we have to stay that way. I don't think it helps the show to have two similar presenters. We're so alike. It's confusing.'

For a moment Simon was lost for words. There was

at least twenty-five years between Carol and Birgitta. Probably thirty. 'Well I don't know what we can do about it, Carol,' he said at last.

'You'll think of something,' she said confidently. 'When I've been so brave, coming in when I'm below par.'

'I thought you were dying when you rang me at three a.m.,' he said drily.

'I had to let you know, darling,' she said sweetly. 'The sooner the better if I hadn't been able to make it after all. It isn't fair on poor Birgitta – but when you've fixed her hair . . .' She looked at him archly. 'And you *will* fix it, Simon . . . because we both know it doesn't do to get me cross, don't we? When she looks more like herself, she may improve.'

'She *does* look like herself, you silly cow,' he said but he said it under his breath, cursing whoever had suggested Birgitta's taking Carol's place.

She had moved on to her favourite theme. 'It's for Birgitta's sake I'm doing this. I've been cursed all my adult life with my resemblance to the divine Audrey – Audrey Hepburn of course. It held me back, Simon. The parts I didn't get because I had that face, which of course was mega-famous. Still is, come to that. To my cost! So you see, I want to save Birgitta from being Carol Cusack the second as I've been the second Audrey Hepburn all these years.'

She was expecting a reply and he struggled for words. 'There's no one like you, Carol,' he said. 'I've never thought of you as anyone but a glorious . . . a unique

. . .' He was floundering now but Carol was smiling, so he had got it right after all.

He looks harassed, Daphne thought as Simon ushered her into the inner sanctum. She had heard Colin, the editor, referred to so often as God in the last twenty-four hours that she thought of him that way herself, so it was a disappointment to see a small man with a furtive frightened face seated behind a huge desk littered with bowls of seeds and nuts and sporting an impressive array of pills and medicines.

When he stood up she saw that he had a short body on very long legs, which made him of at least average height. It was only behind the desk that he appeared diminished. They exchanged platitudes and Daphne resisted the impulse to wipe away the moistness of his own cold hand, which had transferred to her own.

Around the room screens were becoming animated silently and his eyes flicked constantly to one or another. Daphne checked them off: *GMTV*, BBC *Breakfast News*, a lot of cavorting, which must be *The Big Breakfast*, and his own programme with Barry in full flow. She turned her attention back to the man behind the desk, aware that Simon was fidgeting on her right, obviously anxious to get on with more important matters.

'How are you getting on then?' God said, putting his finger tips together and resting his chin on them. He was trying to look winsome and she fought back a desire to giggle.

111

'Very well,' she said warmly. 'Everyone's being so cooperative . . .' She smiled at Simon. 'I've got all the basics now, how the team's set up, things like that. I start the individual interviews this afternoon. After that it's individual items, guests et cetera. I'm very impressed that you've nabbed Vincent!'

For once God relaxed. Smiling, he looked like a little boy and Daphne warmed to him, but even as he spoke his hand snaked out to the pill bottles. He picked one up, checked that it was Vit C and threw two or three orange tablets into his mouth in between words.

'Brilliant, isn't it? Of course, he's only doing it because of this Bermondsey thing of his! He's converting a warehouse into a hostel — well, a superior hostel. He wants to get kids off the street and into a normal lifestyle. It's sticking a finger in the dyke but he's completely sincere about it.' He pursed his lips. 'I like the guy. I went over to talk to him and his manager. I was impressed. But he's strange! It should be an interesting two days.'

'Have you always worked on breakfast TV?' Daphne asked. It was the right question and she saw the editor's eyes light up.

'Mostly . . . but not just in Britain. I worked in the States for a long time. They brought me back to set up Daybreak.' He smiled modestly. 'So it's my creation, in a way. You have to blame me for its shortcomings.'

Daphne saw Simon's eyes close momentarily, as though in pain.

'Oh, I don't see many shortcomings,' she said tactfully.

'Well . . .' God spread out deprecating hands. 'We try. And I'm a hard taskmaster, aren't I, Simon?' Simon's face had frozen into a mask of imperturbability but he didn't speak. 'We try to cover everything: home, community, fashion, cooking, human interest. And of course Barry and Carol are both experts – the best. We wouldn't employ them otherwise.'

'They're neither of them from journalistic backgrounds, I believe?' Daphne tried to sound nonchalant.

'No,' God conceded. 'Carol was a quite distinguished actress before she turned to presenting. And Barry – he's a card, isn't he? Our Barry was an Olympic hero. He'd have made a fortune nowadays.'

Simon's mask of pain was almost of death-mask proportions now and Daphne felt her lips twitch.

'Well,' she said. 'I mustn't take up too much of your time. Could you just tell me what your goal is . . . in terms of Daybreak's future, that is?'

'Easy!' God struck his desk with both palms. 'To outstrip the opposition without losing quality. Breakfast TV reaches into every home, it kickstarts the nation. So . . . standards must be high but ratings come into it, too. If there are bums on seats out there, Delia – I want them to be my bums.'

There was a small moan from the direction of the deputy editor, which quickly became a cough. 'It's Daphne,' he said apologetically, 'Daphne . . . not Delia.'

'Did I say Delia?' God smote his forehead in contrition. 'Still, the audience loves little human mistakes . . . remember Ronny Reagan and his Princess David?'

Daphne held her breath until she was out of the room and then clutched Simon's arm. 'Before you ask, I won't print a word of that. Not as a favour to you but because no one would believe it if I did.'

Chris stood behind the camera watching Carol and Barry mangle his antique-china item. He had kept it as simple as he could, delineating the differences between slipware and creamware, procelain and jasper. Now, Barry was spattering terminology over everything as though he was a Sotheby's expert and getting all of it – all of it – wrong.

Chris felt a hand slip between his arm and his side and then Dilly's voice was soft in his ear. 'Been at his textbooks, again, has he?'

'I wish,' Chris said bitterly. 'That's my brief he's murdering out there. I might as well have put it through a shredder and reassembled it.'

'You can leave the shredding to him,' Dilly said. 'Don't let it get you down, darling. None of the plebs'll be any the wiser.'

Inwardly Chris winced. Dilly was too fond of underestimating the audience. In his opinion, viewers weren't half as thick as they were supposed to be.

'Do you like that stuff?' Dilly was eyeing the items spread before the presenters.

'Ssh!' The floor manager was glaring at them, commanding silence.

'Some of it's super,' Chris mouthed. Dilly's lip curled.

'When I have a home I'm not having a thing older than nine months in it. Who wants to live in the past?'

Chris squeezed her hand with his arm and tried to remember how nice her bum looked in jeans. 'Each to his own,' he said and sighed with relief as the item came to a close and his responsibility was over for the day.

He went back to the office then, to find Amy seated at her desk. For once, she did not have a telephone to her ear and he paused by her.

'Barry's just crucified the china item,' he said.

'I saw it,' she said sympathetically. 'It looked nice. Your film was lovely – and most viewers won't detect all the glitches.'

'A five-year-old knows the difference between porcelain and earthenware, Amy. He was just waving things around and saying anything!'

'Well, it's gone – water under the bridge – and you've got Friday to look forward to, haven't you? Not to mention the night of luxury preceding it.' She was looking up at him and for a moment he wanted to reach out and kiss her cheek. It was a nice cheek, the colour of creamy coffee. And her eyes were . . . he couldn't find words to describe their dark luminosity. Besides which, she was sweet and had more brains in one finger than Dilly possessed overall.

'Ta,' he said. 'You're a mate, Amy. And you're right. I still have Friday.' If X factor wasn't there it didn't matter how pretty someone was, or how nice. Without X factor, nothing worked.

* * *

Ever since she had learned of Barry's toupee, Vera had longed to see him totally bare. Would he look like Telly Savalas or Duncan Goodhew or the guy who had played the King of Siam? Would his head be bald as an egg or speckled with alopecia? Would it rise to a point or have a curious flat place on top, like the Catholic priest's in Rosamund Street? She had snooped through half-open doorways, tried bursting in unannounced as though she thought the room unoccupied. All in vain. The secret of what lay beneath the ever so natural but slightly too luxurious hairpiece remained a secret until she grew tired of the chase and gave up. Only once had she come near and seen a shining reflection in the glass but he'd whipped his wig on too quickly for anything positive to be confirmed.

This morning all thoughts of Barry deserted her. The ferrets in the rare-pets item had turned the green room into a stable and the curse had come upon her, unannounced. She had tried the Tampax machine in the ladies' to no avail and in the end been saved by the make-up girl, who had produced a panty-pad from a cupboard.

She was supposed to check stock today and she was so far behind that she was unaware the programme was over. She pushed open Barry's door to check his cupboard, expecting him to be in studio, only to hear the sound of running water in his bathroom. She was about to turn and flee when she saw it — the hairpiece — upside down and pathetic on the table in front of the mirror.

She moved cautiously forward. In the centre of the webbed lining was a small piece of velcro – at least it looked like velcro. She put out a tentative finger – it wasn't velcro, but it was sticky to the touch. It was the toupee tape everyone used for everything from mending earrings to correcting hammer toes. So that was what held it in place!

She was still lost in wonder when the bathroom door opened and Barry appeared. At first, startled at the sight of an intruder, he looked like a large and overgrown baby, but then, as his face reddened and she saw the fringe of grey hair that tonsured his head, she realised exactly who he looked like. Friar Tuck, the Friar Tuck of the first *Robin Hood* series on the telly – the Richard Greene one they used to show in the sixties.

For a moment they stood motionless, eyes locked. At last Barry spoke, or rather gasped. 'You didn't see this,' he said and backed into the bathroom. She was turning to flee in search of someone, anyone, to tell, when he reappeared. 'Vera,' he said solemnly, advancing on her with outstretched hands. 'Vera . . .' he eyed her solemnly. 'We've always been friends, you and I, haven't we?'

She was glad to be able to lower her head in a nod and hide her twitching lips. 'Yes,' she mumbled. He had released her right hand and was reaching behind him, scrabbling for the toupee. Still holding both her left hand and her eye, he positioned the toupee on his head, moving it around until it felt right, unaware that a cow lick had fallen Hitler-like across his forehead.

'Can we keep this between us?' he pleaded. 'You know this business . . . if they can get something on you . . . there are people here who'd cut my throat . . .'

She wondered if she should tell him that everyone – *everyone* at Daybreak – knew about his hairpiece. That it was known as Dougal, after the hairy dog in *The Magic Roundabout*, and someone had once collected for it at Christmas. But she didn't have it in her to be so cruel. 'I won't say anything,' she said.

He let go her other hand and dived into his jacket. His wallet was monogrammed and well lined with notes. He pressed a fiver into her hand. 'Buy some flowers – for all you do for me. And remember' – his grin was sickly – 'mum's the word.'

She put the fiver into the pocket of her overall. 'You didn't need to do that,' she said. 'I wouldn't tell a soul. You can rely on me.'

But even as she spoke her mind was racing ahead. Wait till she told Theo, the make-up girl, Chris. She backed out of the room, smiling and nodding as she went, the five-pound note almost burning through her clothing and into her flesh.

Outside in the corridor she paused and drew breath, a foolish smile on her face. He had looked like Uncle Fester in the *Addams Family* films, Uncle Fester who had been a famous child star. What was his name? She puzzled for a moment and then began to make her way towards Theo's cubby-hole.

She was almost there when reason prevailed. Theo

was no good at keeping a secret. And when he got the wind up his tail he'd say anything to anybody. If he said something to Barry she might have to give back the five pounds. She shook her head in a show of silence and went on her way.

'Where's the journo?' Simon asked as he poured the coffee. It had been an exhausting morning and now they were rewarding themselves with a break, his office door closed. 'Can we meet tonight? he asked.

'Ta.' Liz took the cup he proffered and raised it. 'To us. Yes, do you want to come to my place?'

'Unless you'd rather go out?'

Liz shook her head. 'I'd rather be alone with you.' She had meant it as a compliment but he was looking conscience-stricken.

'It isn't fair to you, all this. Always hiding away. I never take you anywhere.'

She moved towards him. 'Shut up. I know the score. I knew it from the beginning. I'm not a seventeen-year-old, Simon. I know what I want. I'll make something simple tonight — pasta . . .' She rubbed her nose against his nose. 'And then we'll have more time for important things.'

'Like discussing the world situation,' he said solemn-ly.

She shook her head. 'Metaphysics. The world situation's beyond me.'

'I love you,' he said, reaching for her hand. 'You're sexy and funny and clever and reliable . . .'

'You're making me sound like a J-cloth,' she said, wrinkling her nose.

'What's a J-cloth?' His tone was indulgent, his eyes holding her gaze.

'Something you clean house with . . . it's all-round useful.'

'There you are, then.' He was smiling. 'That's what you are. All-round perfect.'

She was in his arms now, pressing against him, feeling him respond. Their mouths met, opened, became involved — only to separate, unfulfilled, as first one phone rang and then another. Liz put the back of her hand to her mouth and then lifted the receiver. 'Deputy editor's phone?'

'Simon here,' he barked into the other. As usual, Daybreak had proved the most demanding lover of all.

—————————————— **7** ——

Tuesday 10.00 a.m.

'Well, first,' Daphne, said, settling on the low settee, 'let me say how grateful I am for this opportunity.' They were in what was obviously a conference room of some sort, orange juice and coffee on a low table in front of them.

Carol and Barry grinned in unison. 'Our pleasure,' Barry said. Carol sighed. 'I don't know why I ever put myself in the spotlight but I did, so I accept all this.' She gestured towards Daphne's tape machine and notebook.

Daphne smiled understanding and tried to think where to begin. She would have preferred to interview them separately — and perhaps get some frank asides from each about the other — but they had been adamant that they wanted to do a joint interview.

'Tell me about your childhood,' she said to Barry. 'I

know you were a renowned athlete of course . . . but before that?'

Barry brushed an imaginary fleck from his trouser leg and crossed one elegantly shod foot over another. 'Well . . . I can't say I was born in poverty. We were comfortably off . . .' They rambled through his childhood, the discovery of his athlete prowess and his first successes. At any moment Daphne expected to hear Vangelis's *Chariots of Fire* theme strike up.

'In the end they gave in,' Barry said modestly. 'I could've had academic success but I was forced to choose. And the rest is history.' He leaned forward to collect a pile of photographs from a side table. 'These are some early pictures . . . the 1968 Olympics, that sort of thing.'

Before Daphne could take the photographs – at least a dozen, if not twenty – Carol was reaching for a similar pile. 'We thought you'd need early pics. 'That's me in panto . . . I was only seven. And then of course *Peter Pan*. I was twelve when I played Wendy. I never got to drama school – too much in demand.'

'These are marvellous,' Daphne said faintly. 'The piece is essentially about the programme but of course, you two *are* the programme.'

'I can still hear the roar of the crowd,' Barry said inconsequentially. 'You'd go out there to do your best and they'd just go mad.' His voice broke. 'It never leaves you, that sound. I can hear it sometimes when I talk to camera, the spectators willing you on.'

'The fans are so good to us,' Carol said. 'We have

our get-togethers up and down the country, of course. I love to meet them face to face. "Tell me," I say, "what do you like or dislike? We only do it for you."' Her eyes grew moist. 'And they say, "It doesn't matter about the programme content, Carol, as long as you're there."' She paused and smiled. 'And Barry of course . . . he's popular too.'

'I really feel my background brought something to the programme,' Barry said a trifle desperately. 'Like Nick Ross . . .'

'But he was a professional broadcaster,' Carol said. 'You were an amateur — which makes it all the more . . . praiseworthy.' On paper it would've seemed a compliment. Delivered deadpan it was a kidney punch.

Daphne cleared her throat. 'Now, who was here first?'

'I was . . .' Carol proffered another photograph. 'That's me on launch day. I gave up a role in *Evita* for Daybreak.'

'You hadn't been on the stage for a while,' Barry said. He was simply being truthful and wore a halo to prove it.

'I said I gave up the role, Barry. I didn't say I left it. There's a difference. Lloyd Webber was after me and so were Daybreak. You have these awful decisions to make . . . well, some of us do. You were coming to an end of your athletic career, Barry, so you were lucky.'

'Desperate,' Daphne wrote on her notebook and then scribbled it out. 'Well,' she said, taking the plunge. 'Tell me about your working relationship.'

*   *   *

'I can't believe this is happening to me!' Birgitta said. Her olive-skinned face peered out from beneath a blonde, fringed wig. She stared at herself in the make-up room mirror and then closed her eyes in desperation.

'It doesn't have to be that one,' Liz said, equal desperation in her voice. 'Try this.' Birgitta threw down the blonde wig and pulled on a strawberry-blonde one. 'There,' Liz said encouragingly.

'I look like a fairy-cake with a cherry on the top.' Tears glittered on the weather girl's lashes. 'Why is she doing this, Liz? I don't want her job. I couldn't do it even if I wanted to . . . I'm not up to it. I just want to do my own job and do it looking my best.'

'I know.' Liz sighed. 'Don't ask me to explain things because I can't. I just know that she has this bee in her bonnet. This dark-haired, wide-eyed thing . . . it's almost as though she feels she's patented the look.'

'She copied it from Audrey Hepburn!' Birgitta said. '*She* copied someone . . . *I'm* not copying *anyone*. I'm just being myself and I'm being punished for it.'

'Go blonde for a while . . . till she forgets. She's under a lot of strain . . . you know how Barry hates her.'

'Join the club,' Birgitta said.

She took off the wig and ran her fingers through her hair. 'I'll talk to my hairdresser. Some of these semi-permanents are OK. We'll sort something out. But God, I wish I *had* done domestic science. I was bloody good at it and they all said do it but I thought it was boring. If I'd only known!'

'Simon would be really grateful if you could sort something out. Just for a while. Especially while we've got this reporter poking around. She seems nice but you can never be sure . . . if she gets a whiff of discord . . . and you know how our rivals love to play up discord. They've invented enough stories — if they got a real one they'd be ecstatic.'

'Wait a moment.' The weather girl's eyes had narrowed. 'The *Herald* woman's only here till Friday. Does that mean you want something done this week?'

'If possible,' Liz said. 'Look, I'm as sick about this as you are. I think it's crazy but she's spoken to God . . .'

'Enough said.' The brunette looked into the mirror, first to tidy her fringe and then to wipe away a teardrop from either eye with a forefinger. 'It's do as I'm told or I'm out.'

'You know you'd be hard to replace,' Liz said carefully, hating what she was required to do.

'God!' Birgitta threw back her head. 'If I can just get away from here . . . I'd go anywhere, even Sky.'

'Don't do anything hasty, Birgitta. You know you're valued here.' But the other girl was glaring at her and the words died on her lips.

Sometimes, Liz thought bitterly, sometimes, I'd rather wash up in a whorehouse than work in this place.

* * *

They sat round the green room to discuss the next day's plans. 'What've we got?' Simon asked, looking down at the schedule Liz had handed him. 'Puppy farms.' He shuddered. 'Horrible idea but I suppose we're right to expose them. And darling Trevor is with us.' He rolled his eyes. 'Agony uncle is the right name for that gentleman. He'll be in my office demanding someone's blood. What's he doing?

A producer spoke up. 'Surrogate motherhood. He's got letters from both angles – the surrogate *and* the adoptive mother. We'll have them both in studio.'

'What about the dad?' Simon enquired.

'I suppose we could get him,' the producer said doubtfully. 'If you think it's necessary.'

'I think it's *very* necessary,' Simon said. 'I know you think men are redundant, Zoe, but tell me who'll fill your sperm banks when we've gone. We still have a small part to play. Get him in. I thought we did wine on Wednesdays.'

The relevant producer cleared her throat. 'We do usually . . . but he's got this new show on satellite so he asked if he could do Friday instead. I cleared it . . .'

'Yes,' Liz said. 'I said it'd be OK. He's so good to us . . .'

Simon was nodding. 'OK, OK. I only asked.'

The wine-item producer was grinning. 'You might like to know what our presenters said about it.'

'Go on,' Simon said. 'Tell me.'

'Carol said, "Tony's got his own show." Barry said, "Ooh, super."' The producer managed to make her impersonation of Barry sound really rueful. 'You know they never like anyone else to get on. So Carol said, "It'll never work. He hasn't got charisma." Barry said, "We'll have to send flowers," and she said, "Yes. Lilies!"'

There was a titter all round and then Simon drew them back to the next day's plans. 'The fashion item sounds good . . . and the Crazy Cooks strand starts tomorrow doesn't it? And you've got Hester Claire as a main guest. Not a bad menu. Not bad at all. OK, everyone. Have a good show.' He glanced at Liz and then away. 'And don't ring me with any dramas tonight. I'm having a rare night out.'

'Yes,' Liz spoke firmly. 'Any emergencies, ring me. I'll be at home all night so leave Simon alone for once.' She turned to him. 'Going anywhere nice.'

'Very nice,' he said. 'An old friend. I'm looking forward to it.'

Behind the glass the tape-op was regarding Vincent with curiosity. The singer adjusted the cans that were slung around his neck and eased his hip onto the stool. The engineer lifted his head from the sound desk and signalled that all was ready. Vincent stood up again to adjust the words of 'Ceiling in the Sky' on the stand in front of him as a disembodied voice rang out, 'We're rolling, going for a take.'

The music began to pulse – drums, keyboards, the violin high and sweet above the throbbing guitars. Outside the ring of light Vincent could see Buffy

Allen, the bass guitarist, nodding with satisfaction as
he listened to the track they had laid down earlier.
Vincent began to sing, caressing the words that told
of heartbreak and pain, cradling the lyric until it was
time to roar out despair. The engineer's face was rapt
as his hands moved over the faders.

They came to the instrumental passage and Vincent
relaxed, his eyes taking in the dark-walled, windowless
studio filled with the detritus of a recording session:
drums, percussion, amps, and in a corner the piano on
which they played around with melodies.

In front of the instruments the dog lay, her great
head resting on her front paws, hooded eyes looking
hopeful at the prospect of release from what must seem
a dark prison. In an hour – two at the most – they
would be out in the open air. The engineer lifted a
hand and aimed a pointing finger, and Vincent began
to sing again. 'Ceiling in the sky, a star for spotlight
shining way up high . . .'

He had written the words so he had no real need of
the song sheet. Behind the desk the engineer's hands,
were hovering, moving gently to and fro. It reminded
Vincent of the priest's hands at mass, laying the cloth
reverently over the host, the air shimmering above the
altar in a haze of candle smoke and incense. But that had
been a long, long time ago. He had been an altar-boy,
the hem of his surplice dragging at his first grown-up
trousers. He had been seven or eight then, so it would
have been seventy-one or -two and his father was close
to death.

As the last note of music died away his manager entered the studio. 'Nice one,' he said. 'Straight in at number one.' Vincent pulled a quizzical face but Dave ignored it. 'We have to get down to the US details, Vince. They're already yelling.'

'It's a year away,' Vincent said dismissively. He clicked his fingers and the dog stood up and stretched before padding to his side.

'They want to secure venues — we didn't give them enough time last year.'

'We still sold out.' It was not said arrogantly: it was merely defensive. He wanted to be out on the river bank with the dog, not discussing details of a tour on the other side of the world and more than a year ahead. 'This week,' he said, by way of a sop. 'Let me get this Daybreak thing out of the way and then we'll talk, I promise you.' A few moments later he was free of the gloom of the studio and on his way to freedom.

When they reached their destination the dog let out a yelp of joy and bounded ahead. Vincent saw a twig lying beside the path and picked it up. 'Juno!' The dog turned at the sound of her master's voice, the magnificent head erect, the great limbs tensed. Vincent flung the stick in a high arc and the dog leaped to catch it before it touched the ground.

There were few people about and Vincent felt a sudden sense of release. No one except the driver knew he was here. No one had recognised him. Two lovers, far ahead, arms around each other, would not have cared if they had.

He was a household name, Dave's office was lined with gold and platinum discs and in the last ten years his tax bill could have matched the National Debt — but here, on the river bank, he was just one individual out walking his dog. Nowadays, these moments of normality were more and more precious. As Vincent he was always on show, must always look the part. His simplest phrase would make headlines, so in interviews he watched his every word. John Lennon had made a throwaway remark about Jesus and been pilloried for it. Every musician since had profited from that mistake.

He saw a seat ahead and moved to sit down, stretching out his long legs in the Versace jeans. They had cost a small fortune but nothing thrilled him like those first trousers, the worsted rough against his child's skin, the wonderful mock-snakeskin belt too long for his child's waist, fastened and turned in upon itself to take up the slack. 'There now,' his father had said. 'You're a proper man now, Sammy.' He had ruffled his son's hair and smiled and Vincent had smiled back, the conspiratorial smile of man in a man's world. A week later his father was dead.

Once more, in memory, he was back in the church but this time there was no pressure of his father's bulk against him. Only his mother, fragile in black, her face bloated with weeping, her body, when he pressed against it, smelling of lily of the valley. Within two weeks the first man had appeared and it had all begun. A road to hell scented with cheap perfume. He rose to his feet and whistled up the dog. He had the awards ceremony tonight, which would have been ordeal enough, but if he didn't respond to his mother the guilt would be crippling. Better get it over with.

'And this is Theo,' Liz said. Daphne smiled and held out her hand but instead of shaking it Theo bent his head to administer a kiss.

'They told me you were a charmer,' Daphne said. 'I see what they mean.' She patted the chair beside her. 'Sit down and give me the low-down on this place.'

'Wouldn't dare, darling.' The voice was treacle laced with caustic soda. 'If I spoke . . .' He tapped his lips with a forefinger. 'It doesn't do to let it out . . .' He sat down and draped himself across an arm. 'Of course it's all small stuff here. I remember the real theatre – even telly in its early days. They *dressed* then. Nowadays they all look as though they've wandered in from the street.' He snorted his contempt. 'Can't even rise to a collar and tie, some of them.'

'What's it like here?' Daphne coaxed. 'Are they easy to work with?'

'They? Oh, you mean Pinky and Perky. I have to cast my eye over the whole production you know . . . you need an overall view.' He looked at Liz. 'God, I could kill for a drink, love. Are they breaking out something nice for our guest?' He looked up at the clock on the wall. 'The sun's over the yard-arm. It's always over the yard-arm in this place. Buds breaking, dawn breaking, fucking chickens coming out of shells.'

He leaned forward. 'Excuse the language. You were

asking about the presenters. Well, she's all right. She's been in the business a long time.' He pursed his lips. 'A very long time, but we're not allowed to talk about that. He comes from a different background of course. Some people don't hold with athletes branching out but . . . I suppose they've got to do something useful after all that leaping about. He's obedient, I'll say that for him. "You don't suit tailoring," I told him. He's more unstructured. And he listened. And . . . are you going for a bottle, darling?'

Liz had been afraid to move lest he be indiscreet but she could see he was determined to get a drink. At that moment she saw Dilly in the corridor and seized on her. 'Get a bottle of champagne from Simon's fridge . . . three glasses. Make it quick.'

She got back in time to hear Theo's *pièce de résistance*. 'I tell her, "Don't be a silly cow." As for him, "You're not on the diving board now," I say. "Do as you're told." Someone's got to rule them.'

'And if that gets printed we'll all be looking for a job.' Liz cast a despairing look at Daphne. 'Tell me you didn't hear that.'

Daphne grinned. 'I'll tone it down. How about "silly moo"? "Foolish ruminant"? I'll think of something. No, seriously, I'm not here to cause trouble. What I'm after is a few facts from you, Theo. How many outfits does Carol have? What's her dress allowance? Who picks out the day's outfit? Come on, give me chapter and verse.'

'Of course,' Theo said, rolling his cigarette between thumb and middle finger and ignoring her question.

'This lot are minnows by comparison with the old stars. Who couldn't be a household name if they're in people's living rooms five times a week? My people had mystique! People who'd never seen them worshipped them. Your Cecily Courtneidge and your Boo Laye. Postcards by the thousand, people bought. This lot give them away free. Still . . .' He sighed heavily. 'Time moves on. We're all dinosaurs now.'

Daphne scribbled in her notebook. She would have given her eye-teeth to profile Theo – the man was unique – but Lou Bryan would say 'Theo who?' and that would be the end of it. She smiled at the dresser and tried again.

'Tell me what it's like working for Carol and Barry.'

His eyes rolled. 'I don't just do them, darling. Pay attention. I have to run my eye over the whole lot of them. We like ambience on this programme. My orders come from on high. Best-dressed programme on the box . . . you don't get an accolade like that without sweat, I can tell you.'

'Are they easy to dress?'

'Swines,' he said dramatically. 'Swines. Not an ounce of taste between them . . . or if there is it's in their mouths.' He slapped his wrist. 'Naughty boy, talking out of turn. Who'd call them awkward after doing Pat Phoenix. I should coco.' He drew on his cigarette. 'No, they're lambs really. Get her Nicole Farhi or Oliver James, give him his Armani . . . you don't hear a word from them. I have a budget that would make your

eyes water. But give me custom-made . . . we called
Hardy Amies in for *Featherlight*. Cost a fortune but
the audience gasped. Gasped. It's all off the peg now.
Glamour's gone. Mortified. Putrefied! Well, anyway it's
six foot down. At least Carol and Barry have labels –
the lesser mortals are chain store half the time. Chosen
with flair, though. Chosen with flair. I wouldn't let
any of my people go on looking second-rate.'

He paused and looked at Daphne, who had ceased to
write. 'You want me to dish the dirt, don't you? Well,
I shan't. My tongue would cleave, positively cleave, if
I said a word. I could but I won't.' He paused again
and then leaned closer. 'You look for yourself. Some lies
got told in certain quarters.' He tapped his nose. 'Check
your numbers. And don't say you got it from me.'

Daphne smiled encouragingly. 'Can you be a bit more
specific?'

Theo shook his head. 'Wait for the memoirs, the
"dress and tells" I call them. You'll get it all there. I'm
going to call it *Shits I Have Dressed*. I'd like Charlton
Heston to play me in it. The man has presence. As
Larry Olivier said, the only Yank to become a great
actor. Pygmies you get nowadays. Pygmies.'

He contemplated his fag-end and then dropped it into
a nearby coffee cup. It sizzled briefly and went out.
'Out, out brief candle,' he said and stood up, brushing
ash from his tapestry waistcoat as he did so. 'Enjoyed
the chat but it won't buy the bairn a new frock, as
they say. And that drink's too long in coming. They
don't care about me.'

He's going to throw back his head, Daphne thought and was rewarded with a magnificent toss of the grey locks. She capped her pen and went in search of something less like a hologram.

Chris put his coffee down on his desk, between the piles of paper, and broke open the cellophane packet of sandwiches. Cheese and pickle in granary. He bit enthusiastically and chewed for a second before pulling forward the folder and setting about his brief for Friday. Already he had quite an amount of data on the elderly couple. It was a nice story, a genuine happy ending.

'Want a crisp?' Dilly lifted her hip onto the edge of his desk and held out a packet.

'Ta,' he said. 'Cheese and onion. Nice.' He chewed enthusiastically and then frowned. 'Is that all you're having?'

Dilly held up an admonitory finger. 'Not a word about balanced diets. I get enough of that when I ring home. What're you working on?'

'Something nice,' he said. 'A genuine love story for a change, not a Hollywood on-off affair.'

Dilly wrinkled a sceptical nose. 'I suppose you're on about that old couple. I don't think that story'll stand up – not when it comes to the crunch. Old people are too slow. You have to drag the story out of them and their heads shake and they go off at tangents. Gruesome!'

'Sometimes . . .' Amy had come up on them unseen. 'Sometimes, Dilly, you are so evil!'

'We can't all be Princess Di,' Dilly said proudly. 'I have no desire to sit by deathbeds or tend geriatrics or wipe little noses. I leave all that to the pure in heart like you, Amy. No offence, but if you had charge of this programme it would be Dullsville PLC.'

'Probably,' Amy said drily, 'but it'd have a better chance of not being blacked out by the ITC.' She turned to Chris. 'Going home this weekend?' Sometimes she and Chris travelled home together, he to York and she to Newcastle.

Chris made a rapid calculation. Clifford hadn't gone home for weeks. If he went this weekend and Dilly didn't . . . The thought of being alone with Dilly for a whole two days was intoxicating. 'I'm not sure yet,' he said. 'I'll tell you nearer Friday. But if I get through this in time I'll buy you both a beer at the Saddler's.'

'You're on,' Dilly said. 'I'm dying for a drink. That canteen swill they call coffee furs up your mouth. Talking of the canteen, have you noticed Liz and Simon when they get in there?'

She was looking at them bright-eyed, so she must be expecting something. 'What d'you mean?' Chris said.

'Well . . .' Dilly's eyes were round, her brows raised to her hairline. 'It's *Harry Met Sally*, isn't it? I mean, short of an orgasm they've everything else. Consummation over the carrot cake I call it.'

'And I call it malicious gossip,' Amy said decisively. 'Of course they're close — they work together, bird-brain. If they didn't have rapport the whole thing would break down. But if they can't even have a cup of coffee without someone talking dirty about it, God help us.'

Chris looked uneasily from one face to the other. Amy was annoyed and Dilly was both defiant and triumphant. It would end in tears.

'I wish . . .' Dilly said. 'I wish I could have a nice, pure mind like yours, Amy. Unfortunately, I'm human . . . and I'm not daft. They're at it like knives, those two, and if you can't see it, Amy, everyone else can. Can't they, Chris?'

Here it was, the moment of truth! With every fibre of his being Chris wanted to be loyal to his deputy editor and to Liz, whom he genuinely liked, but if he crossed Dilly he'd be in the dog house for days. He turned away, hating himself. 'Leave me out of it,' he said. 'I've got too much on to speculate about other people's love life. I haven't got time for one of my own, never mind anyone else's.'

Neither girl spoke but they did not need to. He felt bad enough already.

Through the darkened windows of the Mercedes Vincent could see the crowds on the pavement. They halted at traffic lights and he watched the faces of the passers-by, most of them tired, one or two frowning, here and there a look of expectancy – going to meet a lover perhaps?

'I won't be long in Twickenham,' he said. In front of him the driver's head inclined to show he'd heard. 'I'm going home then. Leave the car out. This one.

I'm taking it out myself later. It's not an early start tomorrow. Noon.' The head inclined again. Not for the first time, Vincent wondered what the driver thought of him. He was a handsome guy, broad shouldered beneath the tailored livery.

He knows more about me than most people, Vincent thought. The idea disturbed him. He cherished his privacy, hated the snapping cameras, the importuning faces that would greet him when news of his whereabouts became known. If the guy at the wheel cared to sell his itinerary he could make a fast buck, a very fast buck. He made a mental note to ensure the chauffeur received a sweetener and closed his eyes as London sped by outside. Might as well relax while he could – before he reached his mother's house and the inevitable tension set in.

But, try as he might, uncomfortable thoughts intruded. No one knew everything about him. He had to believe that. He realised his stomach muscles had tensed and breathed out, trying to let go. But even as he finished exhaling he felt the cycle begin again, the muscles tense and knot, the breath held without realising. There were people out there who did know him, knew *all* about him, knew the reality behind the glossy, blown-up pictures. And one day one of them would put two and two together and the sky would fall. He closed his eyes and didn't open them until they reached his mother's house, taking comfort from the smooth warm bulk of the dog on the seat beside him.

There were flowers in a vase on the hall table, white lilac and irises. Vincent touched them as he passed, feeling the petals dry and stiff. Artificial! In the living room the gas fire burned in spite of the summer heat. 'You've changed this room,' he said.

Beneath the bleached hair his mother's face brightened. 'Do you like it?' She changed her furniture frequently now, going through the money he gave her as though it was water. Just as well there was plenty. Even if it ended – if it all crashed about him – he would never want again. Neither would she. That was a consolation. Except that he would no longer be able to make music – unless in secret – and music meant nothing unless it was shared.

He sat down on the Dralon settee and tried to pay attention to what his mother was saying. She was alone at the moment and needed him. Soon there would be another man, another hanger-on to add to the long list since – his mind baulked at the name – since Ted. Even now, twenty years on, he couldn't remember without flinching, without hearing the voice, seductive and threatening by turns, without remembering the night he had quit the house, the rain on his face, the railway station, the faces offering succour or something worse. The lies had begun then, small lies, snowballing until now his whole life was a lie.

'I saw you on the telly this morning. Well, your picture . . . they were going on and on about you being there later on in the week. They must think a bit about you.' There was still the sound of Yorkshire in her voice, overlaid with false gentility and the London accents she had grown accustomed to since he had brought her here five years ago.

He smiled at her. 'Oh, they always blow things up. It's called hype, everything's hyped nowadays, even me. How's your cough?' he asked. Did you get your prescription renewed?'

She nodded. 'The doctor was ever so nice. Black'but a lovely manner. He says I'm underweight.' She stood up and turned side on. 'What do you think?'

She had begun to go at the abdomen but it was true she was thin. He knew she wanted a compliment, reassurance that she could still get a man. 'You look fine . . . good . . . a few extra pounds wouldn't hurt. I like you when you're a bit plumper.'

She was trying desperately to pull in her stomach, wobbling on her high heels as she did so. 'I'm still an eight. I'm glad I've kept my figure. After what I went through with you it wasn't easy but I got it back.'

Suddenly she clutched his arm. 'You do love me, Sammy, don't you? I know you've got your life to lead but I get so lonely. I need to get out more, meet people. I can't live alone. Never could. I wish I had your dad back . . . or Ted. Do you remember Ted?'

There were waves breaking in his ears, banishing thought so that it was a relief when he heard his own voice, quite calm, say, 'Yes, of course I do.'

She clutched his arms and looked into his face. 'I'm proud of you, our Sammy. I hope you know that. I loved you when you were a little lad but I never expected this. Not a household name. I still can't get used to "Vincent". You'll always be Sammy to me. And your picture everywhere — that one under glass in the bus shelter, when your last album came out, that was there for months. And every time I turn the radio on it's one of your songs. Every time. Your dad would've been proud of you . . .'

Her voice broke and he longed to open the door and run. Run anywhere. But he stayed while she blew her nose and patted his cheek. 'Your dad was the musical one, you know. I can't even carry a tune but he could come home humming something he'd heard, word perfect. Well, note perfect. You know what I mean.'

He smiled and nodded and wondered for the hundredth time what would have happened if his father had not died, slumped at the wheel of his Morris Minor, leaving a son of eight and a wife who couldn't cope alone. He reached inside his jacket for the cheque he had written earlier. It was for a thousand pounds. 'Here you are,' he said. 'Something to cheer you up.'

Tuesday 6.00 p.m.

'I can't believe we're getting out of here in daylight.'
Dilly was running down the steps as though she
feared being summoned back. She looked back at Chris
and Amy over her shoulder as if to hurry them on before
they were pursued.

They settled in a corner booth in the Saddler's Arms,
the girls drinking spritzers, Chris on lager. 'What did
you think of the show today?' Amy was looking at
Chris but it was Dilly who answered.

'I thought the guest was crap! She may have been
a big star once but she's pathetic now. I mean, what
has she done since she made *Conquest*?'

'She made that TV epic,' Chris said defensively.
'*Near and Far*. She was brill in that.' He rather liked
the faded American star with the haunted eyes above
incredible cheekbones.

Dilly shook her head. 'She's dated, darling. Face up to it. Your china item was OK. Well, it would've been except for Pinky and Perky. And I liked the fashion item . . . the VT was superb!'

'It was yours,' Chris said drily.

'I know.' Dilly was unabashed. 'That's why it was so good.'

'Do you ever get fed up?' Amy stuck an unpolished fingertip into her glass to free an ice cube. 'Well, I mean, we all get fed up but do you ever feel as though it's not what you expected? Fashion, fashion, fashion, ninety-seven ways to cook chicken and second-rate celebs for garnish . . . I didn't think it'd be like that.'

'You shouldn't have come into breakfast telly,' Dilly said practically. 'Not if you wanted to be *meaningful*.' She managed to make the last word sound foolish. 'Magazines have to cover the whole spectrum. That's what the audience wants: a little dollop of culture, a spoonful of entertainment, plenty of recipes and the latest from the high street. Specially in the early morning.'

'Throw in a mad agony uncle, a fitness freak and a weather girl and you've got Daybreak TV.' Amy had dropped into a Texas accent and flung her arms wide to accentuate her words.

'He is mad . . .' Chris was thinking of Trevor Gord, the resident agony uncle. 'He starts out with their problem and ends up giving them his own. God, he can moan.'

'I liked it when he said "You should worry!"

to that woman last week. The one with all the debt.'

'He didn't say that?' Chris said, scandalised.

'He did,' Dilly said. 'And then Barry quizzed him about his own financial affairs and he shut up. They say he's up to the eyes in debt. He put money into property while it was still selling and then the bottom fell out of the market.'

'Negative equity,' Chris said gloomily.

'He won't be down for long,' Amy said drily. 'He'll write a few more books about human misery, with his face looking soulful on the cover, and the plebs will flock to buy.'

'Books don't help.' Dilly had put an ice cube in her mouth and was sucking thoughtfully. 'You can have fun with the sexy ones – nothing like having your imagination jogged – but books can't really tell you how to live your life, can they? You have to learn that for yourself.'

The clock above the bar said six forty-five. The night is young, Chris thought and took the plunge. 'Anyone fancy a curry?' Clifford was filming in Suffolk and wouldn't be back before midnight. And Amy was a good sport. She'd clear off when she realised she was *de trop*.

But it was Dilly who cleared off, pleading an urgent need to wash her smalls, leaving him and Amy to face each other across a chequered table cloth. 'This is nice,' Amy said, leaning her elbows on the table and putting a hand either side of her face. 'Now, tell me some more about your plans. Who do you want to be – Ingmar Bergman or Cecil B. de Mille?'

'Oh, I've long since abandoned that kind of ambition. I'd just like to do something worthwhile, something that mattered.'

'Why don't you try for *This Morning*?' Amy said. '*I* have – not that I want that fact noised abroad. You know what God's like if he thinks you're being disloyal.'

Chris groaned. 'If you go to Liverpool it'll be the last straw.'

'Oh, Dilly'll console you.' Amy's lashes were fanned discreetly over her cheeks so he could not see her expression. In response her face was like a Madonna, a Botticelli – or was it a Titian? One of the old masters whose Italian Virgins had had the look of Asian women. Beautiful women.

Amy was looking up. 'I know Liverpool's not London but it's a brilliant city. I did my degree there – and *This Morning*'s a cut above this lot. Why don't you give it a try?'

'I might.' But they both knew he'd never leave Daybreak while Dilly was around. He picked up a menu. 'Come on then, this is on me.'

The five pounds she had received from Barry had almost burned a hole in Vera's pocket by the time she got home. She contemplated telling Fred of her windfall but pride prevailed and she dished up his high tea in stony silence.

After the meal they watched the TV news in a quiet that so oppressed her that in the end she murmured something about needing tea bags and made for the corner shop. She had never bought a scratch card, never really wanted to buy one. But the five pounds had come so easily – it seemed like an omen. She would buy one. Just one. Just for the hell of it and if she won she would carry her winnings back and throw them in Fred's stubborn face.

She bought a ticket from the smiling Asian behind the counter and carried it to the back of the shop to rub off the wax coating. Twenty pounds appeared then one thousand. Another twenty . . . Her heart began to beat uncomfortably fast. Three more amounts to come. If one of them was a twenty . . . She rubbed and two hundred came into view. Another thousand . . . One chance left! She rubbed cautiously and a two appeared. She bit her lip and rubbed. Another nought . . . but it was too far along. Not twenty but two hundred. For an instant she felt relief. No need to claim her winnings and draw attention to herself. No need to work out what to do with the money. No need to share it with that sod she was married to. But relief was followed almost instantly by disappointment. She marched back to the counter and put down two pound coins.

The cards were green and colourful and bore the crossed-fingers logo of the National Lottery. This time she rubbed furiously, clearing the whole card. Five thousand twice, one hundred twice, ten twice.

She rubbed again, two twenties, two tens, two ten thousands.

When she left the shop the five pounds was spent and five spent cards were in her coat pocket. She comforted herself that the money had been a gift and not hard-earned. Easy come, easy go . . . but she would never buy a scratch card again as long as she lived!

They had agreed to go to Liz's flat separately, for safety's sake, and Liz was glad of a few extra moments to prepare a welcome. She would have loved to have a bath but there wasn't time. There never was time for Simon and her.

She had managed to run a comb through her hair, open a bottle and spray herself with Chanel when Simon's ring came at the door. They clung for a moment in the hall and then she was drawing him in, tugging at his jacket, pouring his wine and settling at his feet, where he sat in her easy chair.

She flinched as his hand suddenly covered hers. 'Cheer up,' he said. 'You look like a sad little girl.'

'Not so little.' She smiled up at him. 'Do you know how old I am?'

'You're thirty-three,' he said promptly. 'I'm your boss, remember. I know your CV by heart.' His eyes dropped as he realised what she was thinking. By thirty-three most women had a child — or at least the prospect of one. As long as she stayed in a dead-end relationship with him she had neither.

Suddenly her chin tilted and when she spoke it was

with a degree of defiance. 'I could have a child,' she said. He didn't try to dissemble.

'Yes,' he said. 'You could.'

'But you hope I won't?'

He sighed then and took away his hand. 'It's not that simple, Liz. I wish it was. I wish I could give you a child and make you happy and we could all live happily ever after. But it isn't just you and I. It isn't even you and I and a baby. There are other people, other children, to be considered.'

Liz shrugged to demonstrate defeat. 'OK,' she said. 'Let's not spoil tonight. We'll think about it later. She had drawn the curtains in her bedroom when she had combed her hair. Now she looked towards the half-open door, seeing the darkened room as a sanctuary, somewhere she could crawl to in order to lick her wounds.

'Don't,' Simon said suddenly. 'Don't look like that, I can't bear it.' He pulled her up with him as he stood up, kissing her so fiercely that her lips bruised against her teeth.

They had begun to undress before putting on the light so that in the end they moved, naked and hand in hand, towards the bed, Liz leading the way through the furniture.

'We must be quick,' she said, her lips against his chest.

He groaned as her lips encountered his nipple and gripped. 'Don't think about time . . . not now.'

'I have to . . .' In the darkness she tried to make out his face. 'It's someone else's time . . . it's precious.'

'Don't say that . . . it makes it sound . . . it makes us sound . . . hole and corner.'

We *are* hole and corner, Liz thought but she did not say it aloud.

In spite of their fears about time, their guilt about partners, they took their ease, pleasuring one another, trying to make it last, avoiding the climax that must inevitably herald a parting.

We have never lain in one another's arms afterwards, Liz thought. Always she would lie in the love-warm bed, eyes closed, listening to Simon's hasty dressing, his feverish exit, torn between goodbyes to his lover and sorting out a story for the wife who was waiting. Once, when they had taken a hotel room in a strange town, they had both dressed hurriedly, sitting back to back either side of the bed to pull on socks and tights before their colleagues realised their lunch had gone on too long.

He was entering her now and she turned away her face, suddenly angry at him and then even more angry at herself for blaming him. She was as much to blame, even more, according to the politically correct. Sinful to steal anything from a sister, shameful to go to bed with your boss. They would have a dozen motives for her actions but none of them would be the simple truth.

'I love him, she thought. God help me, I love him.

And then he was thrusting and she was urging him on. Had it ever been like this with David? Her thoughts beat a staccato rhythm in time with their movements. Faster and faster so that concepts flashed through her mind, disjointed, contradictory, appalling and appealing. If she could have this — have it often — nothing else mattered. If they went on like this she would die of the pain of it. He must love her to be like this. He was using her for the one thing men wanted of a woman. Sex, sex, sex . . . In the end she feared she had screamed the word aloud as she came to climax, for he put his hand across her mouth and shushed her.

But if she had used an inappropriate word he had not heard. 'I love you,' he murmured. His body was heavy on hers, their skin sticking together so that when he moved off her they parted stickily. And then he was sliding from the bed, his pockets jingling as he pulled on trousers and tucked his shirt inside. If he went home with the smell of love on him Jane might suspect. Guess, even. That would bring matters to a head but there was danger there. He would have to decide between them and she was not at all certain what his decision would be. She felt his lips on her cheek. 'See you tomorrow. Love you.'

'See you.' She tried to sound cheerful, as though it was all right for him to leave her like this. But the words came out shakily and she held her breath, terrified he would come back to console her. That she could not bear. It was a relief when she heard the door creak open and then the closing of the outer door. She put on a CD to fill the silence and ran a bath, filling it to the brim and tipping in scented liquids with a lavish hand.

Once she had settled down and grown accustomed to

the heat, she contemplated her knees, rising pink and shining from the bath foam. She had nice knees. At least she had nice knees. She flicked foam from her forefinger and wiped tears from her eyes. It was madness to cry, even in the bath. All you got was a runny nose and swollen eyelids in the morning. Besides which, it was getting late and she had to get up at four o'clock.

She began to soap and lather, trying hard to think about tomorrow. The principal guest was Hester Claire, better known as Maisie Cowley from the soap *West Side*. She was well known to be a first-class bitch and her PR had even more side. She would have to warn Amy to fasten her seat-belt and make mega-sure that Pinky and Perky read their briefs.

In the sitting room the CD was playing. She had chosen it at random, not realising it was Vincent. The guy could write music and the smoky voice, not vocally perfect but full of expression, was just right. Suddenly she heard a new track start up. 'A Lonely Life' had been his biggest hit in 1991 but she couldn't bear to hear it now. She levered herself from the bath and ran, dripping, to switch off the CD player. She was fast but not fast enough to shut out the opening lines — 'Lonely Life . . . this is a lonely life but it's the only life, it must go on . . .'

When she climbed back into the bath she let the tears flow to mingle with the bubbles that were fading, one by one.

In the back of the cab, as it sped towards Kensington,

Daphne reviewed her day. The interviews had gone as she had expected them to go. They had put on a show and she had been able to divert them from *their* agenda very little, if at all. On the other hand she had been able to view Carol and Barry up close – Barry's paunch, the hairpiece, the loose skin beneath his chin. None of that showed on screen. Would it be fair to describe it . . . or merely say that in the flesh he was no longer the boy who had stood high on the Olympic rostrum in 1968? And then there was Carol. Carol was unbelievable! But she looked good for her age.

As the cab passed the Albert Memorial Daphne chuckled. No dewlap would dare to appear on that chin, no vein would have the impertinence to varicose those cute little legs. Perhaps she'll go on for ever, Daphne thought, and be dragged off the studio floor kicking and screaming, in the year 2010.

They were rounding the corner of Kensington Church Street and she put aside thoughts of work, fishing a compact from her handbag to touch up her make-up. In the mirror she looked tired. If the rumours were true Carol Cusack was almost as old as she was but she was still slim, her face smooth and bland, her eyes unhooded. Daphne tried widening her own eyes but the lids still dragged and she only succeeded in looking ridiculous.

She snapped shut the compact and dropped it back into her bag. For two pins she would turn the cab round and go home rather than let Brian see her looking like this. She had been thirty-six when she'd met him – 1980 and the siege at the Iranian Embassy. She had ducked suddenly when there was a loud explosion and felt an arm come round her, solid and comforting. He had been married and a sergeant in the Met then. Now he was a licensee with a dark and interesting pub in a leafy Kensington backstreet. To date he had proposed fourteen times, three times before his divorce, eleven times after. Sooner or later he would cease to make offers. The world was full of women desperate for a relationship and even at fifty-nine he was still a dish.

There were times when she had been tempted to say yes, to stick up a middle finger to Lou Bryan or her predecessor and say 'I'm off.' But something had stopped her. Ambition! The pursuit of the big story — the thing she had always dreamed of and never quite captured. And now she was reduced to doing nice factual pieces on minor institutions like Daybreak TV. But even that was better than being just a wife, an extension of someone else.

I want my own identity, she thought. Whatever it is.

She paid off the cab and ran a hand through her hair. Might as well make the best of herself. What had the ghastly Theo said today? He had been speaking about the dresser's role and she had asked him what was his most useful tool. He had lifted a finger and tapped his lips.

'This,' he said. 'The mouth. Convince them they look like a star and they'll play the part for you.'

Daphne lifted her chin, licked her lips and strode confidently through the swing doors. Brian was there, behind the counter, talking to his barmaids. His face lit up at the sight of her and he lifted the flap of the counter to draw her through, kissing her cheek as he did so. 'Hard day?' His eyes were sympathetic, the smell and the feel of him so comforting that if it had not been for the girls behind the bar she would have leaned against him and buried her face in his chest.

'The usual,' she said brightly and let herself be led into his sitting room above the bar before she went into the shelter of his arms.

Chris saw Amy as far as her street corner and stood guard until she was waving to him from the safety of her own front door. He had enjoyed the meal in spite of himself – or rather in spite of wanting desperately to be at home with Dilly. At times his mind had wandered as he imagined her moving around the flat, clad in the skimpy little robe with the hearts on it that barely covered her bum. If he had been there they might have sat on the settee together, drinking coffee, arguing amicably over which channel or no channel at all. He had become so rapt at the thought of her bare legs curled under her as she sat that Amy had had to reach over and touch him.

'You haven't gone to sleep, have you? God, I must be boring.'

He had been full of apologies then and gave her his undivided attention for at least five minutes. Now, as she disappeared inside, he turned and ran for home. It was ten to nine. With luck he'd have two hours of Dilly all to himself.

He flagged down a cab and fell onto the back seat, resisting the impulse to offer the driver a fortune to break the speed limit and cross red lights. There were things he ought to do when he got home. Friday's brief on the old couple for one, checking over tomorrow's dog brief for another, but to hell with homework. If Dilly was free and willing he would throw caution to the wind and blow the consequences.

He called 'Only me' as he entered the flat, as his father had always done when he came home. He had to call out again before there was a muffled reply from behind the bathroom door. A moment later Dilly appeared, one white towel wound turban-like around her head, a second fastened sarong-style around her naked body. Her limbs were red and steaming from the bath, her face, devoid of make-up, was suddenly vulnerable. On the way home he had told himself he wanted what every man wants: a woman to be a good fuck for an hour and then turn into a takeaway. Now, confronted with Dilly shorn of her daytime armour of denim and leather, he felt a terrible urge to protect her, to lay down his life for her if it came to it. 'Would you like a coffee?' he asked lamely and when she nodded he went to put on the kettle.

Lust returned with the kettle's whistle but it was too late. As he turned to go and take her — by force if necessary — he heard Clifford in the hall. 'God, what a day. I've been rained on, spat upon and worked with the crew from hell!' He saw Chris in the kitchen doorway. 'Is that coffee for me? Ta! I had a burger on the way back. Let's get to bed, Dil. I'll tell you about it later.'

'Thank you, God,' Chris said bitterly as Dilly allowed herself to be shepherded into the bedroom.

That is the story of my life, he thought morosely as the chat on the other side of the wall waxed and then waned into a silence punctuated only by soft groans of satisfaction.

The meal he had shared with Amy still lay heavy upon his stomach but he was suddenly seized with hunger pangs so severe that he made himself a bacon, egg and lettuce sandwich that kept him awake half the night, reverberating gently along his alimentary canal.

Tuesday 9.30 p.m.

The evening air was warm and still on Vincent's face as he stood out on the balcony. It was dusk now and the lights that stringed the river, turning it into fairyland, had just sprung to life. Opposite he could see the Embankment alive with headlights. Busy people speeding somewhere — to meetings, assignations, love trysts. He laughed aloud at his use of the old-fashioned word. Where did the mind dredge these things from? He could never remember reading the word 'tryst' — or hearing it more than once or twice — but it was lodged there, in his brain, ready to leap out at the slightest opportunity.

How much else was lodged there, seemingly forgotten? Tonight he was due at an awards ceremony. There would be a hundred clicking cameras, a thousand fans reaching out to touch, uttering appreciation, all of them thinking how lucky he was, how strong, how impregnable. None of them realising the terror beneath the façade. Inside he was still the boy, the fourteen-year-old, who had travelled so hopefully on that journey from Leeds, believing he was heading towards salvation.

He had carried a change of clothing and his post office savings book containing fourteen pounds and seven pence. Behind him he had left a note – a brief note because there was nothing much he could say.

'Dear mam,' it had said. 'Got to go to London. Sick of school and things. Don't worry. I'll be in touch. Love, Sammy.' Only two words had mattered. 'And things'. 'Things' was one of the most useful words in the language. The 'things' he had run away from had been *one* thing. Now they called it child abuse and it was discussed on TV every night, or so it seemed. Then, to him, it had been a nameless thing, a horror. 'Don't tell anyone, Sammy,' Ted had said. 'They'd take you away then and that would kill your mother.' And later, when he had rebelled, 'No one will believe you. A kid like you . . . you try telling and see how far you get.' And he had seen his mother's adoration for the new man in her life and known himself defeated.

So he had come to London like a thousand other Dick Wittingtons and been propositioned by City gents within two hours of leaving Euston. He glanced now at the gold Rolex on his wrist. Time to get ready. He stepped back and closed the windows, shutting out the

magic of the scene below. It was time for a different
kind of magic.

An hour later, immaculate in tuxedo and black tie,
he stepped from his car onto red carpet. A uniformed
commissionaire stood to attention, holding the car door.
There were crowds either side of the doorway, held
back by tasselled barriers. 'Who is he?' he heard a
woman say and then a boy's voice, 'It's Vincent . . .',
and the woman's voice again, 'Ooh, he's good-looking,
isn't he?' A hand was stretching out across the rope
barrier but he ignored it. Reach out once and you
were lost. 'Vincent! Vincent!' They were calling from
all sides now as he moved forward into the safety of the
foyer, and the screaming had begun among the younger
women. He leaned forward to hasten the moment when
he was safe inside.

He saw Esther Rantzen in the doorway Desmond
Wilcox at her side. Behind them was the tall, gaunt
figure of Sting, looking as though he wished he were in
a rain forest. Why did they all gather like this, to hear
the predictable praise, the carefully structured thank-
yous? And then someone was holding a microphone to
his lips and he was saying how glad he was to be there.

They looked in on the children before they went to bed.
Jake was asleep, face downwards, the covers rumpled
about his legs. Jane straightened them tenderly and
Simon watched her, loving the way she cared for her
children, watching the hands hover, stroke, pat. She
was a good mother.

It was Simon who smoothed Rosie's hair from her brow and tucked in her coverlet. As he did so he felt Jane's weight against his arm. 'She's lovely, isn't she?' Jane's voice was proud and Simon felt his throat constrict with emotion.

'Yes,' he said, and felt tears prick his eyes.

Once in bed Jane reached for his hand and Simon closed his eyes against the darkness, and against the guilt that flooded over him. 'I'm sorry I was such a bitch tonight!' In the darkened bedroom her voice was small, hardly audible above the ticking of the clock.

He turned on his side and put a protective arm around her. 'It was my fault. I should've been home sooner.' She had put her face into the hollow of his neck, her breath, when she spoke, warm on his skin.

'No, I ought to understand your job by now. You work so hard . . . and it's all for us.' Her hand was on his chest now, fumbling with the buttons of his pyjama jacket. Guilt and fear consumed him. What if he couldn't? And if he could, how could he live with himself? He reached up and imprisoned her hand in his own, kissing her brow to soften the gesture.

'Hush. You're not to blame for anything. And things will get better. I'm going to make changes.' Again, she was kissing him, just below the ear. She had been seventeen the first time they had kissed. She had been pretty and slender then, with a brain like a razor. Her A's had been better than his and she had given it all up for him. All that potential thrown away for a man who was betraying her. 'I love you,' she said into his hair and he felt his eyes moisten and wet his cheeks.

'I've been thinking . . .' Her voice was small and he waited. Whatever she wanted, furniture, electricals — a new house if she wanted it — she could have.

'I don't know if this is the time,' she said. In the darkness his mouth curled indulgently, thinking of the girl she had been, the good mother she had become.

'What?' he said. 'Whatever it is, you can have it.' He would think about Liz later. I love her, he thought. But I have enough love for two. And enough money to give Jane everything.

'Well . . .' she said, wriggling her hand free of his and tugging at the waistband of his pyjama trousers. 'I'd like another baby, Simon. What do you think?'

Through the wall Chris could hear the sounds of lovemaking. The sighs and movements escalating to a single cry and the contented laughter of lovers. 'Thank you, God,' he repeated aloud, putting his hands behind his head, fingers laced. It was not enough to deny him Dilly: he had to listen to someone else enjoying her. And for the second time.

He tried to reason with himself, recalling all the times Dilly had said things he had disliked. She was cynical, she was clever and empty-headed at the same time, which was no mean feat. She had decidedly short legs, which might even be bandy if she ever stood still long enough for anyone to check. She dyed her hair and sometimes ate with her fingers. And if she scratched her bum with one hand and picked her nose with the other he would still lust after her. He turned on his face with a groan and pulled the pillow over his head to block out the sounds from the next room.

He tried to think constructively, hoping to lose himself in work. But even in muffled silence it was hard to think. He would have to leave Daybreak eventually, he'd always known that. If he hadn't made it with Dilly by then at least he'd be free of her. Free of the sight of her, anyway. He had an uneasy feeling she'd still torment him, even at a distance. He gave it ten minutes before he surrendered, removed the pillow from his head and got up to make tea – and by then the room next door was silent.

Vera and Fred were in bed by ten o'clock, lying back to back at extreme edges of the bed. 'Goodnight,' Vera said as coolly as she could, to be answered with a grunt. Surly sod, she thought but without venom. She saved that for the person who had invented scratch cards. Five pounds down the sodding drain. Well, never again. That was the one consolation, that she'd learned her lesson. What she could've done with five pounds that wasn't condemned before she got it, like the rest of her money!

For a while she pondered blackmail. Barry had plenty. She could demand a tenner a week or else. She could even sell her story to a tabloid. Many a one had done that and lived to tell the tale.

She pictured herself on the cover of the *Mirror*. Or

perhaps on the *Mail on Sunday*, which was classier. She might get as much as five thousand — more if she told everything, like the way he farted all the time and talked to himself in the mirror. People would go off him and the thing everyone worried about — she'd forgotten the name but it was really just what viewers thought about presenters — would show it and he'd lose his job. No more Barry! She grinned in the darkness. She could start on Carol then. What would she do with another ten thou? And if they lost their jobs, tough!

The thought of Carol and Barry on benefit was so delicious that she turned over and slid an arm around Fred's waist. She felt a momentary flash of indignation when she realised he was already asleep. That was how much he cared about loss of married privileges! She could turn her back on him till she was blue and he wouldn't care. He'd just snore! On cue he gave a loud br-br-br and she rewarded him with a vicious dig in the ribs.

When anger subsided she went back to thoughts of ill-gotten gains. Except that she couldn't really do anyone out of a job. Not that! She'd like to see Pinky and Perky roast a little bit — knock some of the side out of them — but not ruin their lives. She shivered and snuggled closer to her husband. You didn't get any good from being a traitor. She would just have to wait for the lottery. And it needn't be the jackpot. Fred would never move a muscle if they had seventeen million. She'd like two hundred thousand. A thousand pounds for Fred . . . no, a hundred thousand, and then she could leave him with an easy mind.

She went to sleep on a glorious spending spree, the feel of silk against her skin, the scent of Chanel wafting through her dreams.

At ten-thirty Brian went downstairs to see off the last drinkers. 'I won't be long and then we can have a nightcap.' Daphne knew what he was hoping for — that she would become too tired and too involved to go home. Tonight she would have to disappoint him. She was due at Daybreak at eight a.m., not as early as yesterday and today, but bad enough.

She sipped her whisky and ginger and watched the TV as she waited, conscious of the minutes ticking away but too comfortable to care. If she was out of here by midnight, home by twelve-thirty, in bed by one, she'd get six and a half hours. She could manage on that.

It was a quarter to twelve before the sounds of laughter and shouted goodnights subsided and she heard the barmaids' taxi departing. 'Right,' Brian said when he came back into the room. 'Let's get you a refill.' He never drank downstairs and she respected him for that and for the fact that his customers accepted it. They liked him. On the odd occasion she spent time in the bar she could see that. He still had an air of authority, of solid respectability, but he was a good talker and there was a tolerance and good humour about the face. 'You look like Paul Newman,' she had told him early in their acquaintance, and he had grinned and said, 'Who's he?'

Now he filled their glasses and settled beside her on the leather settee. 'I ought to go,' she said.

He put his arm around her and pulled her closer. 'Yes,' he said. 'I'll call a cab in a little while.'

She sat for a moment, sometimes lifting her glass to squint at the amber colour of the liquid, thinking all the while of today and what she could tell him about the people she had met. But when she spoke it was not about the people at Daybreak at all.

'Are we courting?' she asked, and then was struck dumb by her own words. Courting! Where had she dredged *that* up from?

There was silence for a moment. 'Well I am,' he said at last. 'Sometimes it feels like I'm banging my head on a brick wall but I keep on. I'm not too sure about you though.' It was said seriously. Now he made a joke. 'Are you just playing with me?'

'Don't be silly.' She put out a hand to rest on his thigh. 'I'm very fond of you, you know that.' Beneath her fingers she felt him flinch.

'Fond? I can't say I care too much for 'fond'. You make me sound like an elderly uncle. Fond! Good God!'

She had annoyed him and she didn't want that. 'Come here, you silly bugger.' As they put down their drinks and moved together she took a last look at the clock. If she got out of here by half-twelve she'd be home by one . . . His lips were gentle at first and then

167

more forceful. She felt the taste of his brandy in her mouth and somehow it robbed her of the ability to calculate even time.

They made love for an hour, the slow, gentle, satisfying love of the middle-aged. I'm still alive, Daphne thought joyfully. She would be half dead in the morning but so what?

'I ought to go,' she said. His arm was across her, heavy and comforting.

'Why don't you stay?' His voice was heavy with sleep. 'We can get up as early as you like and get you a cab to your place. I'll run you across if you like.'

'No.' If she did that where would it end? 'I've got hundreds of things to do before I go to bed. Honestly. I'd like to stay . . .' Careful! Give him an inch . . .

It was too late. He was raising himself on an elbow to reach for her face and turn it gently towards him. She flinched, afraid that the lamplight shining on her would reveal too much. 'Marry me, Daphne. You can still work if you want to. I wouldn't hold you back. I don't need a wife for that.' He grinned. 'Or for this either. There are one or two who fancy me, believe it or not. But I want to live with you. I'd even sell up if you wanted it. I've got my pension and since the kids got their degrees and Jane remarried I've been able to save a bit. We'd be good together – we *are* good together.'

'I know.' She sought desperately for words to make him understand. 'It's just that I have this thing about work . . .'

'I wouldn't interfere!'

'I know . . . it's just . . . well, really . . . it's just that . . . I think I might get to like it too much. The marriage bit, I mean. It'd take the edge off me . . . can't you see that. I'd lose my edge — the incentive to chase the story. I'd rather be here with you when I should be chasing the big one.'

Except that there wouldn't be a big one. Not now. Face it, she told herself. Lou Bryan would rather lose a scoop than give it to you. You've had it, Daphne. Settle for what you can get.

But she still detached herself from the bed and struggled into her clothes. The night air caused her to shiver as they waited for the cab to arrive but Brian did not put out an arm to hold her.

He's getting fed up, she thought, but she couldn't help it. She had to go on, even though it was hopeless.

Liz had intended to be in bed by ten o'clock but by then she was curled up in a chair, feet tucked under her, a bottle of wine to hand and with a sentimental tape for background. *Songs for lovers*. She had chosen it deliberately, in the manner of one who chooses to lacerate their flesh. Sinatra's voice, smooth and warm, wrapping around her so that she could not break away. She stayed in the chair, eyes fixed on the clock, watching the precious moments of potential rest tick away, all the while remembering.

She had walked into a room at Daybreak on her first day and seen Simon standing there. He had held out his hand and said, 'Hallo. I'm Simon, new deputy ed. Who are you?' She had given him her name, all the while searching his face and liking what she saw.

But she had been cautious. TV people were actors, all of them. How often had she said, 'That was marvellous, darling – if we could just do that one little bit again', knowing as she spoke that the performance had been execrable and the presenter useless? So she had traded Simon smile for smile, for a week or more, until she could be sure that he was to be trusted.

The excitement had begun then, working together, getting things right, seeing him turn instinctively to her when he needed help, anticipating his needs, seeing his face alight when they got it right.

After that, one drink – just one drink to celebrate a job well done. She and Dave had been drifting apart then. Now the hi-fi was matching the memory: the Righteous Brothers belting out 'You've Lost That Loving Feeling.' She had lost her loving feeling for her husband and discovered a passion for her boss. The old story.

She leaned forward to fill up her glass, contemptuous now of the passage of time. What did sleep matter? She could always cope, even on four or five hours.

In the beginning she had admired the photographs on his desk. 'Lovely children . . . Your wife looks lovely . . . Is that your garden? . . . Lovely trees . . .' Lovely, lovely . . . until she had begun to see them as rivals, competitors for Simon's time, the barriers between her and happiness.

As the notes of 'Heart and Soul' trickled from the machine she got up from the chair and pressed the off button. Wine slopped from her glass and she swayed on her feet. 'Silly drunken bitch,' she said aloud. 'Silly, drunken husband-stealing bitch.'

Except that she hadn't stolen anything. Simon was safely tucked up in Jane's bed now, while she was going to an empty bed. 'I Who Have Nothing' would have been appropriate here, except that there was no music, just the eerie silence of a place where someone lived alone and was lonely.

She put the cap back on the bottle and sat down. Her head was whirling but when she leaned against the back of the chair and closed her eyes the whirling became more pronounced and she opened her eyes again. How have I come to this? she thought. She had been happy with David in the early days, seen as endearing those habits that later had made her squirm. What was it about love that blinded you to truth?

The truth about her affair with Simon was that it was going nowhere. He would never leave Jane, mercurial little Jane who was fragile and steel by turns.

Except that he loves me, Liz thought. He really loves me. But what was between them was changing. Once they had leaped upon one another as soon as the door of her flat closed. Tonight they had been almost like a married couple. Almost, but not quite.

10

Wednesday 5.00 a.m.

Liz let out a low whistle as the doors swung open and Hester Claire's entourage appeared. 'How many are there?' she murmured to Simon. His bright smile never wavered as he advanced on the incomers. Liz's first impression was that all the henchmen — there could be no other word for them — carried mobile phones, their antennae bobbing as they moved. Hester carried only a cigarette holder, which she held aloft between the first and second fingers of her right hand. *Sunset Boulevard*! Liz thought and had to school her face when she heard Simon whisper, 'Gloria Swanson.'

'Miss Claire! It's wonderful to see you here.'

Beneath the black Cleopatra fringe the kohl-rimmed eyes narrowed. 'I asked for an hour in make-up.'

'Yes,' Simon said. 'Everything's been arranged as you asked. But if there's anything at all . . .' Hester's eyes widened as she took in Simon's appearance, and decided he was fanciable.

'I'm sure everything will be fine,' Hester said. Simon thought of the two-page list that had been laid on his desk six weeks ago. It had begun with two bottles of Laurent Perrier, well chilled, and gone on through Evian water and black grapes to two dressing rooms with connecting doors.

'May I introduce the features editor, Liz Fenton. Liz will be at your disposal.' Hester's eyes never left Simon's face and Liz groaned inwardly. So she was going to be a non-person, was she? Hester was well-known for her ability to make people vanish from the scene. The cigarette holder bobbed suddenly and one of the henchmen darted forward, notebook at the ready. 'What time will I be away from here?' Hester asked.

'Well,' Simon said, 'we were hoping you'd stay with us through the programme but of course it's up to you.' He laughed nervously and Liz was surprised by his uncertainty. Hester Claire was a legend but a soap was a soap after all and she was one star among many. None of these characters would exist without their scripts so it was the writers who should be celebrated, and seldom were.

'The main interview is at seven-forty-five,' Simon was saying. 'But we did hope you'd do a tease for us near the top of the show. After the first news bulletin . . . that's about six-twenty. And then if you could be on the couch for the close of the show . . .?'

Hester sighed. 'I'm here . . . so . . .' She sighed again.

The cigarette holder bobbed towards a henchwoman. 'Have the car here at nine. I want to go to Harvey Nicks then the Ritz and Le Caprice. Tell Will to be at the Ritz for ten-thirty.' She turned her head on her neck in the manner of a puppet and smiled up at Simon. 'Well, what are we waiting for? Lead me to the slap.'

As they trailed Hester to make-up Liz counted off the retainers. There was a worried looking girl with a walkie-talkie and a permanent stoop, a hard-faced man whose eyes flicked left and right all the time, as though looking out for assassins, a man loaded down with bags and briefcase and another woman who looked like a make-up artist and carried a clutch of cosmetic cases.

'As I said' – Liz could hear an insistent note in Simon's voice, a sure sign his patience was running out – 'Liz will be on hand for you if you have any worries . . .' He didn't say 'Count me out' but he might as well have done.

Hester Claire paused in her tracks, turned her head with the curious puppet-motion and looked at Simon for a full twenty seconds. And then, as if dismissing him, her gaze flicked to Liz. 'I must have somewhere to rest before I go on. I can't share a green room with other guests.' She gave a sad smile. 'They won't leave me alone, you see. It's the price one pays.'

The make-up room, Vera's retreat at this time of the morning, was out of bounds while Hester Claire was there, so she leaned on a chair-back in Theo's wardrobe

175

room and told her tale. 'She stood in the doorway . . . just stood and looked. And then one of them − the one in the leggings − said, "Can you go, please? Miss Claire likes privacy." I nearly said, "We've had royalty in this make-up room with half the fuss" − but I didn't lower myself.'

Theo nodded sagely. 'Keep your dignity. Two pieces of advice my gaffer gave me early on. Keep your dignity and don't drink before an appearance.'

'Not at all?' Vera's eyebrows were raised.

Theo shook his head. 'Not a drop. Straight to the pores. Opens them up and you look like a washer-woman. That was what did for Fanny Craddock and half a dozen others I could mention. Their pores.'

'Never,' Vera said. She loved it when Theo got on about names, big names. 'But Fanny Craddock was a bit far back. What about this lot?' she asked.

'Ah . . .' Theo raised his shoulders and rolled his eyes. 'Say what you like about them − and personally I could write a book, a ruddy trilogy − but say what you like, they're professional. Not a drop before they go on air. Professional to their fingertips.' Yesterday he had called Barry a fucking amateur but neither of them noticed the change of heart, never mind resented it.

There was a knock at the door and Daphne Bedford appeared. Theo lurched to his feet. 'Madam,' he said and gestured to a chair.

'I'm not interrupting anything, am I?' Daphne said. 'It's just that everything − well, everybody − seems to be busy.'

'We've got visiting royalty,' Theo said. 'Haven't you heard? Queen of the Soaps? Bloody madam! Not a patch on your Pauline Fowlers or your Bet Lynches.'

'But Hester Claire's her real name, isn't it?' Daphne's brow furrowed. 'Her character's Maisie Cowley.'

'Cow by name and cow by nature,' Theo said with a toss of his head. His hand executed an upward flip. 'I'm dispensed with . . . has her own dresser. Dresser! "Who's a dresser?" I said. "Wardrobe Manager is what it says on my contract or I'm dyslexic." Still . . .' He shrugged and held out both hands, palms up. 'Stick to Matthew five, verse thirty-nine.'

'What's that?' Daphne said although she thought she knew.

Theo grinned. 'Matthew five?' He swung his hip so that his buttock was presented to his audience. 'Turn the other cheek,' he said. 'That's Matthew five.' He grinned again. 'Any chance of some coffee, Vee? This kettle's got more fur than a mink farm.'

For a moment Vera wavered, feeling that a trip to the cubbyhole where she kept her kettle might mean missing some juicy gossip. Theo smiled. 'Go on, Vee. I'll keep shtum till you get back.'

'I'm not digging,' Daphne said encouragingly. 'Theo was so good yesterday – I've got all I need.'

'You ought to speak to Vera,' Theo said. 'She knows where the bodies are buried, don't you, Vee?'

For a moment Vera contemplated telling the reporter about Barry's wig – if she did she'd be front page tomorrow – but some inner caution prevented her. Instead she rolled her eyes and tried to look mysterious, but the reporter, although smiling, didn't look interested and Vera contented herself with an enigmatic smile and exited to boil the kettle.

'And furthermore . . .' The cook's eyes were glaring and Chris blinked behind his glasses. 'Not only had I to scuttle out of make-up . . . scuttle? I was frogmarched! Frogmarched out of make-up and had to change my clothes in the loo.' He ran a hand through his blond hair. 'It gets worse.'

'You could've got changed in Theo's room,' Chris said desperately.

'Per-leese . . .' The cook's eyes glittered. 'You need a passport to get into the throne room. I'd like sight of his job specification. What is he supposed to do? I know what he does – sweet FA is what he does. What's he paid for? That's the question. Anyway . . .' The cook had made complaining his forte. 'What's the point of complaining. I'm only a cog – I'm not a big wheel like some people.'

Coming from someone with an ego the size of the Taj Mahal, that was rich, Chris thought. But there was no point in arguing with some people, and the cook was one of them.

To Chris's relief two figures had appeared in the corridor. 'Sorry, Rupert,' he said. 'I think that's Cavan O'Haggerty. I need to get him to studio.'

The ballad singer was looking around him tremulously but his manager was an old hand. 'We'll need make-up,' he said. 'Cavan likes his hair blown. We'll need a sound check. Have the group arrived?' He opened the neck of his leather jacket and turned back to his client. 'Don't go under lights till you have to, Cavan. It's the fucking Sahara in here and you know how you run in the lights.'

The singer had the eyes of a frightened rabbit. He put up a hand to his face but running under the lights was not his principal worry. 'What about the hair, though? I knew that root perm was a mistake. It'll move, Maxie. It moves and I end up looking lop-sided.' He put both hands to his curly head and clutched it in agony.

The manager was succinct. 'Shut it, Cavan. You keep the tweet coming, I'll check the hair.'

Chris had heard this interchange with mounting horror. Hester Claire and Cavan O'Haggerty, an egomaniac and a narcissist! It was too much. 'If you just come this way,' he said, 'I'm sure make-up can fix it.' He saw Amy coming towards him and rolled his eyes. She smiled, her confiding, dark-eyed smile that was so thoroughly soothing. Why couldn't he fancy Amy when she was so eminently fanciable? 'Life's a bitch,' he said inconsequentially and aloud and got a groan of agreement from the balladeer.

'I can't get used to it.' Tears coursed freely down the weather girl's face, still looking incongruous under the blonde wig Carol had imposed upon her.

'Perhaps if we changed your make-up,' Simon said. The girl did look silly, no doubt about it.

'They *have* changed it. I've even had my brows bleached, Simon. What next? My pubic hair?'

Simon shifted uncomfortably and wished he was anywhere, darkest Africa or Uranus, anywhere but here. Was this what he had sweated out a degree course for? Women's wigs? 'Look, let it go for a while and then we'll take it up with her again. She's not unreasonable . . .' Even as he spoke he felt ashamed. Carol Cusack was not only unreasonable, she was unbelievable. He pulled at his jacket as if to pull the last shreds of his credibility around him. 'I'll see what I can do. Maybe if you had a grey streak . . .'

'A streak! I'm twenty-three, Simon. You don't have grey streaks at twenty-three. Let *her* have the streak — God knows she's the right age.' She dabbed at her eyes again and then blew her nose. 'If this got out to the press, Simon. Not that I'd tell — I'm too loyal, that's my trouble. But you know what they'd make of this.'

'I hope that's not a threat.' Simon tried to keep his voice steady. There was a bloody journalist on the spot. The girl wouldn't even need to seek one out!

'No.' She had dried her eyes and tucked her handkerchief into her sleeve. 'But if I break down — or if the journo asks why I look like a circus freak with a sunflower on my head — don't blame me for that.'

When she had left his office Simon looked up at the clock. Not yet nine o'clock and he was ready to cut his throat. He pulled open a desk drawer and took out a bottle of Glenfiddich and a glass. The whisky was warm and breathtaking and unbelievably comforting and he had wanted it ever since last night when Jane had declared World War Three with that simple declaration: 'I want another baby.' He had asked for time – time to discuss, time to plan – but he knew his wife too well to think that buying time was the answer. Once Jane had something in her sights she didn't give up. So this was the moment of truth, when he had to decide what he should have decided long ago. For everyone's sake.

'Of course the whole world knows your incredible story,' Carol said. The smile she bestowed on Hester Claire was megawatt.

'Incredible,' Barry said. He leaned to touch Hester's arm and she clutched his outstretched hand and gave him a long searching smile of thanks for the gesture. She looked suddenly young and vulnerable, a fragile flower battered by life.

Opposite them Carol smiled benignly. 'But,' she said, 'just in case there's one teeny, weeny person in the whole of Britain who doesn't know you, can we go through it again.'

With an obvious effort Hester detached her gaze from Barry and transferred it to Carol. Watching on the monitor in his office, Simon groaned. He had had doubts about this interview all along but Pinky and Perky had been keen on it. They were paying for that keenness now – at least Carol was. Hester Claire was dominating the Daybreak cameras as she had dominated all nine hundred episodes of *West Side*.

'Where shall I begin?' she said wonderingly. Her hand lifted in a royal arc. 'It seems so long ago . . . my life's been a dream most of the time.' She paused and looked down at her hands – her beautiful French-manicured hands. 'And a nightmare sometimes, if I'm honest.' She raised her eyes, Joan-of-Arc-like. 'I was born in Newry. My father was a horse-dealer and my mother a concert pianist.'

'You came to London in nineteen sixty-nine,' Carol said, desperate to move on, but Barry, too, was interjecting.

'That must have been a wonderful childhood.'

'Ah . . .' Hester's eyes roved heavenwards again. 'Those Irish summers . . .' Her voice had suddenly taken on a lilting Irish brogue. 'The grass under me bare feet and the scent of the heather.'

'You were thirty-five when you came to London,' Carol said firmly. Hester turned on her a look of gentle forgiveness.

'*Twenty*-five, Carol. I remember seeing you in *Thunderfly* and thinking how well you played the mother.'

Carol slapped her script playfully. 'Twenty-five. Of course. I'll box our researcher's ears. Yes, I had to play twenty years on in *Thunderfly* and I was still green as an actress then.'

'Hester ten; home team one,' Simon said aloud and refilled his glass. He was raising it to his lips when one of the internal phones buzzed. 'Simon here.'

'There's a bloody massacre going on out there!' The editor was almost crying at the other end of the line.

'Yes,' Simon said cheerfully. 'It is a bit like the Christians and the lions.'

'There's nothing Christian about those two.' The editor's words were punctuated by the vigorous crunching of pills. 'Who set this up? I know who'll pay the fucking price for it! I know who'll be thrown to the lions! I dreamed of those two last night . . . I was in a cage and they were poking me through the bars. Get in here, Simon. I'm not facing this on my own!'

Liz tried to keep her mind on the scene in front of her but all she could think of was the look of abject misery on Simon's face when he had arrived this morning. Twice she had asked him what was wrong but he had fobbed her off. She had hoped they could get together at the show's end but now it was obvious that there would have to be a post-mortem and it could go on for hours.

She closed her eyes and tried to remember last night. He had kissed her closed eyelids and then let his lips travel slowly to her mouth, her neck, the valley between her breasts. Her eyes snapped open again. In another minute she would groan with pleasure and the whole studio would look at her — a scene from *When Harry met Sally*.

Out there in the arena Barry was holding forth. 'No

one has held the nation's heart like you, Hester.' He smiled cheerfully at Carol as if to invite her agreement. She smiled and did not speak but the white area around her mouth deepened. Instead she stared into her camera and put the tip of her tongue to the edge of her teeth. We all know who's the nation's sweetheart, the gesture said and Liz's heart sank. There would be hell to pay after this. Carol did not like competition and Barry was making the most of it.

She turned as she felt breath on her neck. 'It's only me.' The man behind her had dark glasses covering his eyes. It was Trevor, Daybreak's resident agony-uncle. Liz disliked his over-the-top manner on screen and his naked ambition off.

'I thought you'd gone,' she whispered.

Again he was breathing on her neck and she had to resist, the desire to squirm away. 'I wanted to tie up the phone-in details for tomorrow. I'm getting seven minutes, Liz. Seven minutes! You can't say hello-goodbye in seven minutes.'

'Things are complicated tomorrow, Trevor. We've got Vincent coming in.'

'Oh, I know you've got Vincent. All I've heard today is Vincent, Vincent, Vincent. I really question this whole business of celebrities. Who puts bums on living-room seats day after day after day? Your regulars, that's who. Not Vincent – he'll come and go. I'll be here next week. Someone should remember that.'

He sounded bitter but Liz felt no sympathy. He had made a fortune out of videos and books on sex and relationships and still the wrangling over his fees took months each time his contract was reviewed.

'It's a big scoop for us, Trevor. You know how elusive – reclusive – Vincent is. And he's a world figure.' The floor-manager was casting angry looks in their direction, wanting total quiet. Liz turned back to the studio floor. Carol's right leg was swinging backwards and forwards, a bad sign.

'I'm not sure I agree with you, Hester,' she was saying.

Damn Trevor, Liz thought. 'Now I've lost the thread.' But Barry still had firm hold and was twisting it for all he was worth.

'I agree with you, Hester. That's the new way of thinking – a fresh approach!'

'Fasten your seat belt,' Trevor whispered in her ear and this time he was right.

'My God,' Dilly said. 'She scrambled Carol. Scer-rambulled! Someone'll pay for this.'

'Barry made it worse,' Chris said mournfully. He held up both hands in a doggy-begging gesture. 'Like a great big St Bernard, he was. Hester this, Hester that. He could've shown a bit of solidarity.'

'I don't blame him,' Dilly said, swinging into line beside them in the corridor. 'He knows Carol does better than him in audience appreciation. He's trying to level things up.'

'I don't believe those figures.' Amy was thoughtful. 'I think they doctor them for Pinky and Perky – and they can't let us have the true figures because you know nothing's secret here.'

'They *are* popular,' Chris said. 'They're a national institution.'

'So's prison and the income tax,' Dilly said. 'They're institutions but they're not popular.'

They were at the door of make-up now and Chris peeled away from the other two. 'I've got to collect the Irish guy. See you later.'

In the make-up room Cavan O'Haggerty was anxiously regarding his mirror-image. Above his well-bronzed face his curly hair had been blow-waved to an auburn halo. He glanced at the make-up girl. 'Perhaps a bit more spray?' She sprayed a cloud of lacquer over his hair. He preened. 'A bit more?' She sprayed again. He put up a finger to his temple. 'On there?' Another squirt. Oxygen was becoming in short supply as he turned to his manager. 'What do you think, Maxie? Will it hold?'

The manager's world-weary face contorted. 'Cavan, a fucking bulldozer wouldn't move that hair.'

Daphne had been aware of the mounting tension as the interview continued. She had left a tape in her video so she could review the programme tonight, but as the exchanges went on she took fright that she might not have programmed it properly and resorted to taking notes. She saw Carol turn her back as soon as they said farewell to Hester Claire, leaving Barry to escort the star past the cameras, bowing and scraping as he went. The next item was a taped piece on jewellery, so she capped her pen and put notebook and pen into her bag. She wanted to catch the editor if she could. He had avoided her so far, except for that brief welcome. Perhaps she could corner him now.

The door of his room was ajar and she could hear voices. She put an eye to the crack and saw that it was Simon, the deputy editor, who was in there. A phone rang and she saw the editor snatch it up. He listened for a moment and then slammed it down. 'She's gone ballistic, Simon. She's coming up here while they're running VT. I can't face it. Enough's enough.' He produced a wide briefcase from under the desk and began to throw papers into it. 'I'm off and I'm not saying if I'll be back.'

'Steady on, Colin.' Simon didn't sound too certain and Daphne felt her lips twitch. Carol Cusack was all of five feet but she had two men running scared. 'You're making too much of it.'

Colin emptied a scoop of capsules into his hand and popped them into his mouth. He began talking before the Evian water had washed them down, so that his words came out in a splutter.

'I can't take any more. If it's not her it's him. Me first! No, me! There's a disease in this team, Simon. A virus!'

'There's nothing wrong here,' Simon said calmly. 'Two egos got out of control out there, that's all.'

'Exactly! Colin was moving round the desk to reach his coat. 'Two egos out of control and neither of them is mine. Why? Because I haven't got an ego left. It's been squashed between two monsters . . .'

There was the sound of clicking heels on the corridor and Carol Cusack swept past Daphne. The editor's right hand froze on the neck of his coat, the briefcase fell to the floor. 'Carol!' he cried, suddenly holding out both hands. 'That was magic. Let me get you a drink. You were superb.'

The Irish singer had mangled 'Anyone Who Had a Heart'. Now Barry was giving the menu for the following day. 'And we'll have Vincent – yes, the real Vincent – live in the studio.'

Vincent pressed the remote control and watched Barry fade to a dot in the centre of the screen. The *real* Vincent! He smiled wryly. Will the real Vincent stand up? They might interview him for ever and not come within a mile of the truth. He picked up the phone and ordered his car round.

Already he was regretting his promise to appear on *Daybreak*, but it was too late now. Still, he had become so practised at lying over the years that he scarcely knew the truth himself. And Carol and Barry were not Jeremy Paxman. He would concentrate on the project and its future. Rescuing runaways from the streets. A drop-in for drop-outs. He could keep the subject going for ever if he had to.

But he would be wary about accepting other appearances, however good the cause. He had felt strange these last few days, as though the tide of his life, steady for the last year or so, had suddenly begun to run swift again, swift and deep for he had no real idea of what was happening, only that he could sense a change.

He let himself out onto the landing and summoned the lift. He was due at the recording studio at ten but they could take the river route. He loved the river, had always loved it, had clung to it at times when its moving waters had seemed to invite him to end it all.

The car was waiting at the side door. He paused on the pavement for a moment, lifting his face to the morning sky and drawing in the fresh air. He was about to get into the car when the flashes came, and the rapid clicking of a shutter as a high-speed camera snapped away. He tried to school his face, knowing how you could be caught open-mouthed, looking like a gargoyle, but it was too late. The cameraman uttered a cheery 'Ta' and scurried away.

'Sorry about that,' the chauffeur said as he held the door for Vincent.

'Who was he?' Vincent asked. 'I don't know him.'

'He's from the *Herald*,' the driver said. 'I don't know his name but he's a *Herald* man. And a bit of a rascal by all accounts.'

They moved smoothly through the traffic, the sea of cars around them weaving and interweaving. It was a miracle that there were not more crashes. They halted at traffic lights and he glanced at the pavement. There was a girl cowering in a doorway. Something about her — the thin, yard-long legs, the plastic-leather bomber jacket, the tuft of fair hair above a pinched face —

reminded him of Julie. She had been his first real friend in London, sharing her precious ciggies with him, warning him never, ever to get addicted to crack like her, using her age advantage to act like an older sister.

'I smoked weed at first, Sammy, but I never touched heroin. Bad scene. With crack you've got to have it — that's why you don't go near it, mate. But I need it — it's better than men.' She had been locked in a relentless crack/crime lifestyle but she had been kind to him. 'I'll come off it one day,' she had told him confidently. 'It's not easy to come off it and I'm not ready to come off it yet. I need that twenty-quid rock, Sammy. Got to have it. But I will come off it. I want my kid back off the foster home. That's why I take crack — 'cos I'm lonely. When I come off it and I get the kid I won't need it.'

He had known there was a vicious circle in there somewhere and she was caught in it, but she had put her arm around him and that was all that mattered.

She had told him he was right to run away. He had told her of the nightly intrusions into his bedroom, the sickening threats, the fear, and she had called his step-father a sod and promised to cut off his balls. 'But you were right to scarper, Sammy. Otherwise they'd've put you in care and that's no good. I was in care until I was sixteen. I was always in a room on me own, locked up. That's why prison has no effect on me now. I've been in Styal, Drake Hall, Risley . . . you name it. It's great in prison . . . except you put on loads of weight.'

Three weeks later Julie was found dead in an alley near London Bridge station. He heard about it from another girl. 'Seven knife wounds,' she had said succinctly and Sammy had gone away to throw up the burger he had bought with a hand-out. That night, more afraid than ever, he had gone into a hostel.

The lights changed and the car leaped forward, leaving the girl in the doorway behind.

11

Wednesday 9.20 a.m.

'What a disaster!' The producer was pouring coffee as she spoke, tipping up the pot to catch the last dregs.

'It was good telly,' Dilly said gleefully. 'Robocop versus the Terminator.'

'Who won?' Chris asked although he knew the answer to his question.

'Well, not the home team.' Amy's brow was furrowed. 'Whose idea was it to ask Hester? I mean, she's notorious. All actresses are megalomaniacs.'

'Carol's an actress,' Dilly said. 'She tells you that every time she opens her mouth. According to her, presenting *Daybreak* is a well-paid kind of resting . . .'

'. . . from which she will emerge to enchant the audience at the National,' the producer finished. 'It was the editor who booked Hester. He met her at the RTA and thought himself a very clever Dick to get her.'

'He better watch his dick when Carol gets up from studio.' Dilly obviously thought the whole thing a huge joke. She was perched on the edge of a table, hugging one knee. The others were thinking about the fall-out from one of Carol's tantrums and the trickle-down if God took the horrors.

'Carol liked the dog item . . .' Dilly was grinning. 'So did I, especially when it peed on Barry's shoe. That long steady stream . . . and the look of disbelief on his face! God . . . it was beautiful.'

They were all joining in the laughter when the editor's secretary appeared. She smiled at them but the curl of her lip said 'Skiving again?'

'I'm sorry to interrupt,' she said, 'but I've got someone outside who wants to see Hester Claire. It's obviously a fan — she's got a huge bouquet and a card a yard wide.'

'Hester's gone,' Chris said. 'Whisked off in a Daimler as soon as the end credits rolled.'

'I'll see her off if you like.' Dilly was standing up, smoothing down her skirt, smiling sweetly at the secretary.

'Thank you. You're such a help, Dilly.' But as the woman exited Dilly plopped back into her chair.

'Aren't you going? Amy said.

Dilly shook her head. 'Let the boring old fart wait. They'll stand around for hours when they're obsessed. I'll go in a minute.' But it was Amy who exited quietly to see to the fan, leaving Chris feeling distinctly ill at ease.

'You should've done that,' he said.

Dilly pointed. 'I would've done. I was going . . . give me a break!' And then she smiled and Chris felt his resolve melt.

'I know,' he said. 'I know.'

Daphne had sought refuge in the wardrobe room, where Theo brought her a coffee strong enough to float a spoon. Perhaps this explained his rich brown voice, although the fug of cigarette smoke that wreathed the room was probably more responsible. She drank it gratefully while he gave her his opinion of the morning's show. 'Carol'll bounce back of course. That's why she's stayed at the top for so long. Resilience. Besides, as I told her, she's Carol Cusack. Hester Claire's a myth – the product of someone else's script. I've seen them come and I've seen them go. Take their script away and they're nothing!'

'Well,' Daphne said. 'I suppose I should get going when I've had this. I'm talking to the researchers after lunch.' Theo was opening his mouth to give her his opinion on the entire team when the phone rang. He picked it from the wall and held it to his ear for a moment before holding it out to Daphne.

'It's for you-hoo,' he said, pointing his finger in lottery style. As she took it she wondered if Theo was ever off duty. What was he like when it was all over and he went home to wherever he laid his

head? A moment later all thoughts of Theo left her as
she heard the eager note in Lou Bryan's voice.

'Daphne – at last. They've looked all over for you
. . . where are you hiding away? Never mind, there
isn't time. Listen, I want you to come over here as
soon as you can.'

'Now?' Daphne said.

'No – not until you've got what we need. Can anyone
hear you? Don't speak – just say yes or no. I need the
exact times – exact – that Vincent is entering and
leaving the studios tomorrow. Going in would be better,
fewer people around. We don't want to tip off the rest.
Get the times and the entrances . . . is he coming in by
some back door, that sort of thing. And, Daphne, above
all, don't let anyone know we're interested.'

'How do I find out without showing interest?'
Daphne said, turning her face away from Theo's
curious gaze.

'I don't know . . . you'll think of something. Ask
about security – make it general, but get the facts and
then get in here. And Daphne' – there was an ominous
pause – 'get it right.'

'And I will not – will *not* . . .' The cook's pink jowls
quivered. 'I will not be upstaged by a Rottweiler.'

'What do you mean?' Liz tried to sound calm but it
wasn't easy.

'I mean that when I've slaved over an item I expect it
to be treated with respect, Liz. They were still laughing
about the wretched dog when the cameras came to me –

you could hear it all round the studio. And it went on. Right through my crème brûlée.'

'It was tension,' Liz said. 'Well, the release of tension. It was a very fraught morning. When the dog peed everyone cracked.'

She tried very hard to concentrate on what the man was saying but it wasn't easy. Constantly, Simon's image floated before her, Simon looking small and grey and anxious . . . and he had looked like that *before* the fracas on the studio floor, when he entered the building in fact, so that she felt as though he had been somehow diminished since he had left her bed the night before.

Had he spoken to Jane? Was that it? She tried to remember what he had said as he left her flat. Had there been some hint that he was about to bring it all to a head? Had he told Jane the truth? And if so, what was the result?

She had eased the irate cook out of her office and was reaching for the internal phone to call Simon when an outside line rang. 'Liz Fenton's phone.' It was David on the other end of the line. 'Hello,' she said cautiously. Two calls in two days. What was up?

'I wondered . . . well, if you're at a loose end tonight I thought we might grab a meal somewhere . . .'

'Sorry . . .' She spoke automatically in a gesture of self-protection, and then waffled because she didn't have an excuse ready. She was always at a loose end at nights now and they both knew it. Except that David didn't know about Simon, so perhaps he assumed she had a better social life than she in fact had.

'I'd love to . . . well, it would be nice . . . but . . .'
Inspiration struck suddenly. 'I don't know whether you
saw the show . . . well, Hester Claire was guesting
and she and Carol got across one another. Anyway,
the upshot is we're all going out tonight to discuss
what went wrong. Carol's furious, as you can imagine.
She's not used to being upstaged.' It was a relief when
he accepted her excuses and she could put down
the phone.

But as she got down to work a feeling of guilt
pervaded her. All he had wanted was a meal, a talk
for old times, sake. That was no big deal. And they
had been together a long time. If she had never met
Simon she might have gone on thinking David and
she belonged together. For a moment she was swept
with nostalgia, remembering his face, young and eager,
anxious to be a good husband. But only for a moment –
in the end it had been grim for both of them. It was a
temptation to look back with rose-coloured spectacles,
but it wouldn't do!

Simon tried to keep his mind on his editor's stream of
consciousness but his own thoughts intruded. Another
baby? Jane's face had been so eager . . . and yet
shy, like the first time she had told him she was
pregnant and for a brief instant he had thought it
the end of the world. He had been twenty-one, a year
off graduation. Jane was nineteen and both of them
belonged to conventional families. Useless to suggest
any other way out than up the aisle. In that moment

he had seen his dreams of a bright future evaporating before his eyes.

And yet it had all worked out. They had been happy. *Very* happy, sometimes. And he didn't regret the kids – anything but. All the same . . . The editor was talking about tomorrow now – about Vincent – and Simon struggled to respond, but it was difficult. Did he love Jane? Had he loved her once and lost it somewhere along the line? Whatever the truth, Jane was jeopardising the future he had planned with Liz. He had intended to wait until Jake changed schools and was settled. Rosie would be seven then, comfortably into primary school, so that his leaving would cause the minimum upheaval. Then he had intended making proper provision for Jane and the children and going to Liz. To start a new life.

If he gave in to Jane's need of another child – a child that would add years to the waiting – Liz would never forgive him. If he didn't, he would have to give Jane a damned good reason why not. They had money and space and Jane had time on her hands. If he just said no she would smell a rat. Unless he pleaded the responsibility factor. He could tell her he wanted to go freelance. That would work. Everyone they knew was setting up on their own – independent production was the new growth industry. She would buy that and accept that money might be short for a while. He was tying up loose ends in his mind when he realised Colin was staring at him.

'Sorry,' he said. 'I drifted off for a second. I was thinking about tomorrow.'

'That's what we were talking about . . .' Colin made an irritable grab for some tofu and Simon was saved by Liz knocking and entering.

'I'm not interrupting . . .?'

The editor waved a preremptory hand. 'Come in, Liz. We're talking about the arrangements for Vincent — it's your concern anyway. Are you sure you've got everything taped?'

'He's coming in by the goods entrance at five-forty,' Liz said. 'He doesn't need long in make-up with that tan. They can do him on the floor if they have to — he's at the top of the show.'

She was interrupted by the phone ringing. Colin looked at it with anxiety. 'You don't think it's Carol again, do you?' The battle with Carol had left its mark.

'She's gone,' Simon said. He looked at his watch. 'She can't be home yet and I doubt she's ringing from the car. She wears her sleep mask in the car.' He leaned across and picked up the receiver. 'Editor's phone?'

At once Liz knew it was Jane on the other end of the line. She could recognise the hunted look, the way Simon's face took on the aspect of guilt, the way he avoided meeting her gaze.

'Yes,' he was saying. 'I suppose we could.' And then, as if he realised he was being lukewarm, 'Yes, that sounds great. OK. I'll try for seven o'clock.' He smiled sheepishly as he put down the phone.

'It was Jane,' he said. 'She's booked a sitter for tonight . . . apparently we're going out.' Across the desk his eyes were beseeching. They seemed to say, 'Understand. I don't want this. It's not of my doing. Forgive me, Liz.'

She understood the message but she was in no mood for forgiving. 'How nice,' she said. 'Now, can we get back to Vincent?' And she hoped as she spoke that neither of the men would detect the pain that must surely show in her voice.

The DAT had just arrived from the studio for Vincent's opinion. He settled in a chair, Juno heavy across his feet, and listened. Opposite him, Dave, his manager lay back in his chair, eyes closed. The music was good, melodic and with a strong beat, but as Vincent listened a different vision intruded: a man in a navy donkey jacket smiling cheerfully as he withdrew his camera and turned on his heel. What had the man said? 'Thank you' or 'That'll do nicely'? It had been something like that.

Vincent stared unseeing at the dark walls, the grey leather upholstery, the vivid cushions. He tried to concentrate on the music but the image was stubborn. Perhaps the man had merely been an amateur collector. God knows, there were thousands of them, snapping away like paparazzi, treasuring their imperfect pictures. But the movements had been too slick, too assured. It had been over in a second and then the man had scarpered. Amateurs hung around, desperate for a word, savouring each moment with what they thought was a star.

'Vince!' He realised the manager was rebuking him and straightened up in his chair.

'It's good, isn't it? Not quite how I envisaged it but . . . good.' Another track was beginning and they both settled back, Dave to listen intently, Vincent to remember.

There had been a banner hanging on the wall of the church. As a small child the fancy lettering had fascinated him, and then the Latin words, '*Capiosa ab deum redemptio*', which meant, so his mother explained, that God had enough forgiveness for everyone. Later on, when he had felt himself defiled – a sinner – he had wondered if it was true. Did God have enough forgiveness? Would he be forgiven? He had murmured the Act of Humility over and over, hoping it would assuage his pain. And then the prayer for others, for children could not be sinners according to Father Crone. 'O Jesus, have pity on poor sinners, and save them from hell.' But he had been in hell already so there had seemed to be no point.

Now, he turned his attention back to the music. 'Good,' he said, nodding sagely, 'good,' hoping Dave would think the new tracks had had his undivided attention.

He had prayed so hard for the burden to be lifted. 'O Jesus, wash away my sins with your Precious Blood. In the moment of temptation may I always say: "My Jesus, mercy! Mary, help!"' But his sin had not come out of temptation: it had been forced upon him. Perhaps that was why the pleas had not worked, so that in the end he had had no choice but to run away.

Chris was coming out of the canteen when Amy caught him. 'I was wondering,' she said. 'You know I'm doing this thing on genealogy next week . . . I wondered if you'd give me a few tips. Oh, I know you're not an expert but you seemed more clued up than me when we had forward planning. And I thought' – she drew in her breath – 'I thought I might buy you a pizza and we could discuss it. If you're not doing anything, that is.'

It was an invitation to more than discussion and they both knew it.

'I'd love to, Amy.' Chris was flailing around for excuses and each of them knew that too. 'Maybe later in the week. It's just that tonight . . .'

'I know,' Amy said soothingly, anxious now only to extricate herself from an embarrassing situation. 'Forget I mentioned it.'

'Later in the week,' Chris said, half sorry that he had reacted so swiftly. Except that Clifford was away again and with a bit of luck Dilly might be home alone.

Vera had overheard the conversation in the corridor and was disappointed in her protégé.

'He's a fool,' she told Theo as they shared a pot of tea and a packet of cheese-and-coleslaw sandwiches she had fetched from the canteen. Theo had put his cigarette in the saucer of his coffee cup, from which it sent up plaintive smoke signals. Vera turned her head away and coughed meaningfully, but he took no notice.

'They're all turned on by a tight little arse,' he said gloomily. 'I suppose it's nature but it does get in the way.'

'Amy's better looking.' Vera was indignant. 'As for that Dilly — and that's a silly name to start with — she's a . . . I know the word I want . . . it's "cone" or something . . .'

'What's it mean?' Theo said.

'It means she always copies off someone else. This week she's Liz Hurley, next week that one off the lottery, the one that chews her words.'

'Anthea Turner,' Theo supplied.

'That's her. Like I said, one minute one thing, next day another. She's never herself, that's what I mean.'

'"Clone",' Theo said, wiping his mouth with a silk handkerchief and taking up his cigarette.

'"Clone",' Vera said gratefully. 'I'd've gone mad trying to think of it if you hadn't. Anyway, she's a clone and she's not particular, either, about who she sleeps with.'

'Like Hester Claire,' Theo said. 'She's been in more hotel rooms than a Gideon bible, that one.'

'Get away.' Vera moved closer, eyes bright.

'That's how she got the part in *West Side*,' he said. 'It's common knowledge in the trade.'

'She's good though. You can't deny that.'

'She's good now,' Theo said. 'You should've seen her when she started: funny, gawky little thing, all tits and kneecaps.'

'Did you know her then?'

'I've known them all, Vee. If I'd taken my chances I'd've been on top now. But first it was mother and then I had a mortgage. If I'd been a free agent I wouldn't be sitting here now, I can tell you.'

'No.' Vera began to gather up the remnants of their feast. 'We'd none of us be here if we had a choice.'

Theo fished in his pocket and produced a crumpled fiver. 'Get some of those scratch cards, Vee. Make us a fortune.'

But Vera was shaking her head vigorously. 'I'm not buying any more of them, Theo. It's rubbing money away. The first week you couldn't move but someone'd won. When do you hear it now? I'll put you in our syndicate for the lottery if you like. If Chris says it's OK, which he will. But I wouldn't encourage an enemy to buy a scratch card, let alone a friend.'

Theo shrugged. 'OK. I only suggested it. If it'd been your precious Chris you'd've said yes. You've got a soft spot for that lad.'

'I don't deny it,' Vera said defiantly. No point in denying it. Chris was the son she'd like to have had, a genuinely nice young man and clever into the bargain. 'There's nothing wrong with Chris except that he lives with that Dilly. She'd cause trouble in Eden.'

'They're all the same, researchers,' Theo said gloomily. 'Live together, eat together ... you see them

205

come in fresh, bright as buttons. They look on the bulletin board for a flat to share, move in with another researcher and five minutes later you can't tell them apart.'

'Well, it was a black day for Chris when he moved in with her,' Vera said. 'Why couldn't he've moved in with Amy? She'd be good for him.'

'Amy doesn't share.' Theo said. 'Wealthy parents. She's got her own place.'

'There you are then,' Vera said. 'If he had the sense to choose Amy he'd fall in for a bit of money. But you can't tell kids!'

'Not this lot, you can't,' Theo said. 'Cloth-eared little bastards, most of them.'

Liz had made up her mind to avoid Simon for the rest of the day if she could. He had seemed so weak on the phone, his words telling a different story from the expression on his face. It was always the same, always would be the same. 'You knew it,' she told herself over and over as she skimmed through letters, altering a comma here, a dot there, and adding her signature. She had always hated casual infidelities and despised women who consented to them. How could you do that to another woman? And here she was, screwing Jane . . . or rather, screwing Jane's husband, which was worse. Except that there was nothing casual about her feelings for Simon.

She was planning a night of sympathetic self-indulgence when he entered her office.

'Don't be like that,' he said miserably as she tried to turn him to stone with a glance.

'Like what?' She had meant to sound together and slightly amused but hadn't succeeded. She sounded like someone who was about to cry. She could feel the tears building up, threatening to shame her.

'I couldn't help it, darling. Not there, with him listening.'

'You could have said no. You could have said there was a meeting. You didn't want to say no to her, Simon. Why don't you admit it?'

'It's not easy.' He was moving to pinion her arms, force her to look into his face. If he did that she'd be lost! She twisted free and moved to put the desk between them.

'Just answer me one question, Simon. Are you going out with her tonight? And I'll be greedy – I'll ask for another answer. Will you take her home after your nice meal – or whatever she's got planned – and take her to bed? Will you fuck her, Simon, like you fucked me last night. Or perhaps she's better. Perhaps I presume to even include myself . . .'

He moved swiftly to grab her and shake her. 'Stop it, Liz. Stop it. You don't mean that. You make it – us – sound shit-awful. I love you. You know that. But I can't just shake off my wife as though she was something I'd stepped in on the street.'

'Get out, Simon,' she said wearily, all fight gone out of her. 'We'll talk about this later. Just go, please.'

When he had gone she went back to her letters,

but it was an effort. All she could think of was Jane, getting ready for a joyful night out while she was going home alone.

That was how it was every time they met, at her place, or for a snatched drink. She closed her eyes, thinking of the scene she had played in a hundred times.

'I ought to go,' Simon would say, looking at his watch. Around them the pub would hum softly, workers going home, young lovers ready to make a night of it, guilty couples like them snatching a few stolen moments together.

'Yes,' Liz would say. 'You shouldn't be late again tonight.' As she sipped her wine she would think how it would be when he got home. There would be lights in the windows, warmth, the smell of food cooking, a dog bounding to be petted, children competing for attention . . . and Jane, another adult to speak with even if that conversation was arid, perhaps hostile.

He lives, she would think sadly. And I exist. When she got home the flat would be warm, thanks to a time switch, but there would be no welcoming lights, no sound, no dog's tongue to lick a welcome, no human voice to say 'You're home!' And the fact that she had chosen it was no consolation at all. If I go home tonight I'll go mad, she thought. Wearily she reached for an outside line. 'David, if your offer still stands, I'm free.'

It was lunchtime when Daphne arrived at the *Herald*

offices and most of the desks in the newsroom were empty. In Lou Bryan's office three people were gathered, but at the sight of Daphne Lou gestured to the other two to leave. 'Did you get it?'

'I've got approximate times,' Daphne said but she made no move to produce them. 'I'm dying to know why you want this.'

'I'm doing a piece on him this weekend,' Lou said impatiently 'I know exactly what I want . . .'

'We're awash with pics of Vincent,' Daphne said. 'Why another? And why taken on the hoof? They're never any good?'

'What we've got won't do,' Lou said. Her eyes had dropped and Daphne knew she was wondering how little she needed to give away to secure Daphne's cooperation. 'I want a picture of him looking startled, Daphne. Off guard. And it must be up to date – as though it was taken just after we sprang our story. We tried this morning but they're not good enough.'

'What story?' Daphne said, lowering her bag to the floor and sinking into a chair. 'It's obviously something big so why doesn't someone tell me?'

'You don't need to know, Daphne. It's nothing to do with the Daybreak piece. God, I'd've thought you had your hands full without wanting to get involved . . .'

'I *am* involved,' Daphne interrupted. 'If I'm getting info for you I'm involved so . . . do I get to know or don't I?'

12

Wednesday 7.00 p.m.

'Meat's a bit tough,' Fred said, poking his teeth with his tongue and, when that failed, using a finger to explore.

Vera had put the meat in the slow cooker the night before, chopping onions and carrots when she was drooping with tiredness. It had simmered all day and still he complained. Ungrateful sod! But all she said was, 'There's a pudding.' It was only shop-bought treacle sponge with in-built custard that tasted like nothing and everything but it took three minutes in the microwave and he was too greedy to know the difference.

'What?' He was still eating the steak and kidney, tough or not, as he spoke.

'Treacle sponge,' Vera said. When she won the lottery she would never cook again. As she served

the pudding she thought of what she would do with
the money. Leave Fred! That would be number one!
Then she might go abroad. She had read an article
on cruising once. It said you had to allow sixty pounds
for tips to cabin staff. Sixty pounds! If there were ten
cabins that would be six hundred quid in tips and not
a penny to the tax man. She was in the wrong job,
that was a fact. In seven years at Daybreak all she'd
had was a bottle of perfume, two lots of after-dinner
mints and the five pounds from Barry, which was less
of a tip than a bribe. Hush money!

She turned her mind back to cruises – in particular
the cruise on which she would meet a rich widower
who looked like Des O'Connor and was after her body
rather than her money.

She was still thinking of him when she climbed into
bed and it was a bit of a letdown when it was Fred's
hand rather than the Des O'Connor look-alike's that
stole round her waist and fiddled with the buttons
of her nightgown. For a moment she wavered, torn
between making love with Des in abstract and sex for
real with Fred. In the nick of time she remembered his
ungratefulness over the meat. 'Not now, Fred,' she said
and turned to where Des was waiting for her on the boat
deck, his white tuxedo stark against the navy-blue and
starlit sky.

But the dream – it wasn't a daydream because it
was night-time and she was in bed – the dream lasted
only a moment or two before reality intervened. She
would never go on a cruise and, even if she did, no

one who looked like Des O'connor would give her a second glance.

She felt a tear slide from her eye and trickle down onto the pillow. She put a furtive finger to her cheek and wiped it away, knowing that tears left unwiped made you sore. Where had life gone? Or where had it gone wrong? She had dreamed of Fred once, not in a white tuxedo, admittedly, but handsome and virile, which was what every man should be – and wasn't, according to Theo.

She thought of the days when he used to wait for her, sitting astride his motorbike, a young god. He had sold the bike when they set up but he still grew wistful when someone roared past on a Harley Davidson. If they'd had children . . . but that wasn't an automatic recipe for happiness. She could think of dozens who'd had families and split up. At least she and Fred were still together. She turned over and put out a tentative hand but by that time Fred was fast asleep.

Daphne had travelled by cab from the *Herald* offices to her flat, but even as she tried to set about a mountain of household tasks she knew it was no good. If she didn't have someone to talk to her head would explode. As she loaded the washing machine she thought of what Lou Bryan had told her and, the more she thought of it, the less she liked it.

Lou had spread the dossier out before her on the desk. 'I got into it by chance. We needed pictures for a series on homelessness and the picture desk sent me a pile of stuff. I was looking through it with Dennis when he pointed out that one of them – one of the men on the photo – was the guy who went to jail for procuring kids . . . rent boys. You remember – Harry Quinn. He got seven years. We decided not to use it because we didn't want to cloud the issue and we'd used it before, so I put it aside and it didn't get sent back to the picture library with the others. I found it after Dennis had gone, and you know the way something ticks away at the back of your mind? I knew there was something in it, I just didn't know what.'

She had produced the picture then and flourished it. 'And then I twigged. That face – that one there . . .' She stabbed with a forefinger. 'The boy on the right . . . is Vincent. Oh, Vincent ten or more years ago, but Vincent all right. You know how distinctive his features are. So I put Mike onto it. That's what he's been doing the last few weeks. And he's done a brilliant job. Brilliant!'

'So Vincent was homeless,' Daphne had said. 'So what? He's never denied he had it rough when he came to London.'

'He never said he was a rent boy,' Lou said triumphantly. 'That's one little fact he somehow forgot to mention!'

At first Daphne had refused to believe it – not Vincent, upright, talented, famous Vincent who had been seen out with the world's most beautiful women – but it was all there. Dates, facts, figures – and the damning photograph.

Now, as the washer ceased to fill and began to churn, Daphne straightened up and wiped her hands as if to rid them of unpleasant facts. I don't like this, she thought, and was glad that her details of Vincent's arrival tomorrow had been fairly vague. The less she had to do with his downfall the better.

In the sitting room she dialled Brian's number. 'I'm coming over. Is that OK?'

On the way to Brian's pub she thought of how Saturday's paper would look. It's cover would be splashed with horrific headlines – 'sensation', 'scandal', 'bombshell'. Headlines designed to wrap fish and chips or be consigned to dustbins – but not before they had devastated a life. Vincent's life.

He would never make music again, or, if he did, no one would buy it so no one would hear it. She had a sudden picture of him, alone, degraded, picking out a tune with a single finger in an empty room. And was he rich enough to lose his livelihood and still survive? Probably, but that wasn't the point. When you had a talent you wanted to use it. Her talent was words. What would she do if someone prevented her from exercising it?

She could always write a novel. She'd always wanted to do that. She could marry Brian and produce a blockbuster under another name. So perhaps Vincent could survive, too. But in spite of this crumb of comfort it was a relief to pour the whole story out to Brian, someone who would die before he would betray a confidence. She told him everything, keeping her eyes half shut so as not to miss a single detail.

When she looked up Brian was shaking his head from side to side. 'It's a mucky trade you're in, Daphne. You know that.'

'I know.' She tried both to sound and to feel philosophical but it wasn't easy. 'And I know what Lou would say: if we don't use it, someone else will. But it turns my stomach, Brain. She's sat on this for weeks. They've stalked him, for God's sake. And now I'm playing a part in bringing down the guillotine.' She drained her glass and held it out for a refill. 'What do you think this will do to him?'

Brian shrugged. 'I don't know a lot about the bloke. I'm a Sinatra man, remember. Some of them would revel in it – but if he's another type . . . I suppose it could finish him. Still . . .' He filled her glass and returned it. 'There's nowt – as they say in Macclesfield – you can do about it.'

'What's Macclesfield got to do with it?'

'Not a thing. You've got me talking rubbish so let's be sensible. There is one thing you can do. Marry me and leave the whole can of worms behind you.'

'Be sensible.' She sipped her gin and tonic and then put down the glass. 'Can it be true? I mean I've seen him, Brian. He's an attractive man. Successful, sensitive . . . talented. It seems a far cry from . . . well, you know.'

'Being for sale?' He was putting it bluntly deliberately and they both knew it. 'I was on vice for years. I joined the Met thinking there'd be ladies of the night on every street corner and pimps in Cadillacs. Well, there's plenty of them. What I wasn't prepared for was the trade in lads. 'Fresh meat' they called them . . . but only for a while. They had a quick sell-by date – after that they were dregs.'

'It's horrific,' Daphne said. 'Why doesn't someone stop it?'

'How? Catch them coming off the trains or the buses or the long-distance lorries? Half of them are running from abuse at home. Sometimes I used to think the whole world was putrid. Festering, even. Not that your average homosexual is after kids. They're the most doting uncles in the world, your average gay. And ninety per cent of child abuse is carried out by heterosexuals. But the trade in little boys is scary. It scared me. You'd get one come down to London and just vanish. According to a Sally Army guy I knew – a guy I've got respect for – they're taken to a country house and kept until the fuss dies down. If no one misses them they're used for a snuff movie.'

'You mean they're killed?' The glass had halted halfway to Daphne's lips.

'According to my bloke. You've seen the cases that get to court. They broke up a ring a few months ago. It was in all the papers. Yours, I shouldn't wonder. But your average rent boy survives. If he's gay so be it. If he's not he drags himself up by his boot straps . . .'

'. . . and becomes a rock star?' Daphne's eyes were round.

'Could be. I don't know. But the fact that he

was caught up in the meat trade tells you little or nothing about friend Vincent – except that he was lucky. Very lucky!'

The restaurant was small and dim and intimate. 'Remember the last time we were here?' David said as they waited for their first course.

'Yes.' In spite of her doubts about being here, Liz smiled. 'It was the night you proposed.' They had known each other six weeks and she had been so in love she had wished away each perfect course so that they could go to bed.

He reached out now and covered her hand with his own. 'This is nice. Like old times.' But as they ate and drank she was remembering more than those first days and nights of passion. It had gone wrong so quickly. Not that either of them had been unfaithful – at least not as far as she knew. It was his selfishness, his total lack of consideration for anyone or anything other than himself, that had caused her to hate him in the end. Or that was what she had told herself then. Perhaps all that had happened was that they had fallen out of love.

'I've missed you, Lilla,' he said as the first course was cleared. The use of his pet name for her was scary and she felt like saying, 'Hey, not so quick!' Not ever, really. She would never go back to David, whatever happened between her and Simon.

The waiter came to pour wine and then another to serve. David always got that kind of attention, probably because he was a good tipper. No, not a good tipper, an extravagant one. He had gone on giving out tips like an emir even when she was worried to death about money.

'Tell me what you've been doing,' she said when they were alone again. 'And, more important, what your plans are.' She kept her voice steady and as cool as courtesy allowed, in an attempt to show him that whatever had been between them was over, and now they were acquaintances, no more. And yet, had he been any more selfish than Simon? Or taken her more for granted? She lifted her glass and drained it, trying not to answer her own questions.

'You know what I've been doing,' he said. 'At least I hope you do. I hope you read every word I write, or what's the use of a byline?'

She smiled. 'All right, so I know what you've written. Some good stuff, incidentally, but don't let it go to your head.' He was a good journalist, incisive, sometimes witty, always clearheaded. If only he'd been able to communicate like that in his private life.

'This is nice,' he said again and would have reached for her hand again if she hadn't made a great show of lifting her glass and playing with her cutlery, remembering suddenly that somewhere, in some other restaurant, Simon might be reaching for Jane's hand, reminding her of old times, completely forgetting everything except that he was with his wife.

The meal, in their favourite trattoria, had been large

and rich. Now, well fortified with red wine and coffee and liqueurs, they sat opposite one another, almost silent. Jane's hand was supporting her head, her blonde hair falling to cover it, her face flushed with wine and contentment. 'You look about fourteen,' Simon said. He had intended to keep tonight unsentimental but the mood of the evening was becoming more mellow by the minute.

'Hah!' Jane threw back her head to laugh, but for once it was mirth without rancour. If only it could always be like this. 'It's the booze,' she said, her words slightly slurred. 'You're seeing me through a lovely haze of alcohol, darling. I'm old and my bottom's gone — sagged to my knees. I looked at myself in the shower room yesterday and I thought, Everything's going!'

So that was it, Simon thought. The cosmetic clock was ticking and she wanted to prove she was still young and fertile. 'You're twenty-eight, Jane,' he said gently. '*Twenty*-eight. Nothing has sagged — well, not from where I'm sitting. You look like an adorable sixth-former.' He was laying it on too thick. Too late, he realised he was flirting with her — as he had done so long ago. 'I think we'll have another Armagnac,' he said and lifted a hand to the wine waiter.

'I'm not as nice as I was then.' She looked rueful as she spoke and Simon shook his head to contradict her words. 'It's true,' she said. 'Sometimes I hear myself speak, shout, scream, and I can hardly believe it's me. Because I do love you, you know, all of you.'

'I know.' This time his voice was gentle and he didn't regret it.

'Do you love me?'

It was a straight question but he tried to dodge it, remembering Liz, who was sitting alone in her flat now, crying for all he knew. 'Don't be silly, Jane.'

'Yes, but do you?'

'Of course I do.'

'Do what?' She was going to keep going till she got what she wanted.

'I love you.'

'Oh darling.' Her face was melting, as it always did when he was fair to her, when he behaved as a husband should.

'I love you very much,' he said. 'You and the children are my life.' It was true. And untrue. And life was shit and he couldn't stand much more of it.

Chris had cherished high hopes of the evening. If something happened to detain Clifford, if all went well . . . anything could happen. He ran it through in his mind a thousand times, rehearsing the perfect seduction, becoming so involved that the cab driver had to say, 'All right, guv?' when he failed to alight at his door.

Once inside he showered and used an underarm deodorant and the last of his Paco Rabanne. For good measure he sprayed his mouth with Amplex and then breathed into his hand and sniffed. It seemed OK but he sprayed again to be on the safe side.

He was trying on and discarding the third shirt when Dilly let herself into the hall.

'It's me.' She had a Waitrose carrier bag in one hand and a bottle of Chardonnay in the other.

'Special occasion?' he asked, merely for something to say, so it was devastating when she replied, in uncharacteristically embarrassed fashion, with eyes downcast, 'Well . . . not really . . . just . . . well . . . Cliff and I . . . oh, you know it's not that we're an item . . . but it's ten weeks . . .'

'Ten weeks of what?'

'Us, cretin. Cliff and me.' She had coloured up so that her eyes looked bright in a fevered face.

'Oh,' Chris said, suddenly feeling foolish. 'Just as well I'm off out then. Wouldn't want to be a gooseberry.'

The look of relief on her face would have been laughable if it hadn't been tragic. He let himself out into the summer evening, wondering where he could find the nearest equivalent of Beachy Head, from which to throw himself.

Wednesday 9.30 p.m.

V incent was in his favourite place, his eyrie above
the river. And tonight no gala occasion to attend,
no last-minute recording session to put the final touches
to his work. He smiled, remembering the long haul to
this moment, the luxury of being alone.

In the beginning the pressure to succeed had been
immense. 'If we haven't had a big hit by the third
single, we're out,' Peter, the lead singer with Frame,
had said and they had known he was right. The other
boys had left university to form Frame. If it didn't work
they had something to return to. He had nothing. So he
had gritted his teeth through the grotty club circuit,
thrown together with three young men he hardly knew
and might not have chosen as friends.

When they had achieved a modicum of success and
had a manager, his instructions had been explicit. 'You

don't exist alone. Twenty-four hours a day you are Frame. I don't want to see pics of you anywhere on your own, no getting drunk, no girlfriends, no scandal.' And Vincent, who was Sammy, had listened and shivered.

But he had also listened and learned. About looking good, about honing his body and choosing his clothes, about the need to smile all the time. And he had learned about music. His first song went out as a Frame creation, but 'Lonely Life' changed everything. Suddenly he was 'gifted'. The manager treated him with respect. The others both respected and resented him as one hit followed another. When the split came it was a relief. Now he could please himself what he did and he chose not to smile.

Again, he sipped his tomato juice, savouring the tang of the Worcester sauce, holding the chilled glass against his face for a second, trying all the while to make up his mind. Should he go out tonight with that unbelievably early call ahead of him?

He could ring that nice Louise woman. He liked her but not enough for it to matter. There was Kim Garroway. If she was in she'd jump at an invitation, however short the notice. He liked Kim . . . quite liked her. She was a model but she had a brain, and if he had to be seen in public with a woman from time to time she was less boring than most. But she *was* a model, and that had implications. For a fleeting second he wondered what it would be like to have a real relationship, to have a woman who wouldn't take three hours to get ready and go off to check her make-up every fifteen seconds. He particularly hated their hands, their unreal hands that could only flutter for fear of breaking a nail. Kim was a little more real than most but that still meant drawbacks.

He decided to take a shower while he made up his mind. He let the water cascade over his closed eyes. It didn't pay to analyse things too much, that he knew only too well. Forget people and think of music. There was a tune running through his mind, or rather a fragment of a tune. It had first occurred to him on the drive home — F sharp, F, A, B flat, A flat, G, D sharp, A flat, He had picked out the notes on the piano later. As he lathered his hair and soaped his long legs he hummed to himself.

If he felt like it tomorrow he'd play around with it — it might make something. It had certainly helped him to make up his mind. He would do the sensible thing and go to bed, even though the car was waiting in the underground car park, positioned for an easy drive out.

He liked to drive himself, feel the power of the huge engine beneath him, but it was possible only at night and then it could be awkward if he was caught at traffic lights. It would be difficult on Thursday and Friday — getting in and out of the Daybreak studios. His presence had been well advertised. There were bound to be crowds. He would just have to leave it to the studio and his driver. Perhaps there'd be a side door. They usually arranged things for him, and thank God they did. He hated the feeling of hands plucking at him.

He hated getting up early, loathed the searching morning light, the dry mouth and the aching head that often accompanied it. But when he was in bed, lights out, the radio burbling gently in his ear, he knew that sleep would be a long time coming. He hated the night, too, had hated it since he was seven.

There had been three men before Ted. Each of them had come bearing gifts, ready to play football, pat his head or give him rides in the car. Until they were in. Until the gilt wore off the gingerbread.

The rows would begin then – his mother and the current man going at it hammer and tongs. And then the man would be gone – in the night usually – and if he asked where he was his mother would shake her head and say, 'None of your business.' But it had been his business because it had been his life too.

Ted had brought gifts at first, but with Ted the gifts had gone on. And the kindness, the warmth, the hugs. He had especially liked the hugs until he began to realise they were not like the hugs his father had given him. Not like them at all.

He had not known how to tell anyone – especially not his mother! There had been no Childline, no TV documentaries. Had he heard the words 'sexual abuse'? He doubted it. In the end he had packed his rucksack and run away and in his first two hours wandering the streets of London he had been propositioned three times. Out of the frying pan into the fire! It would have been funny really, except that it was tragic – the cold and the hunger and the terrible, overweening fear.

And then he had met Harry. In a hostel, the one place he had felt safe in since he came to London. The man had been so clever at first. Not a rush of affection, not even a rush of attention. Just a casual word, a pat on the shoulder, a pound coin once or twice. 'Have a butty on me.' He had been so grateful to Harry, grateful for kindness that asked nothing in return.

'You can't stay here Sammy,' Harry had said the night of the fight, laying down the clipboard he carried like a badge of office. There had been two newcomers at the hostel. They had taken beds either side of Sammy's and then proceeded to fight. At the time it had seemed very real; with hindsight he could see it had been fixed. Harry had stepped in with the offer of refuge at his place and Sammy had seized on it. He had been chicken, in the jargon of the streets. Fresh meat – what every punter was looking for.

For a week he had lived in the Highbury flat, revelling in unlimited hot water, good food and, above all, peace and cleanliness. Harry had even given him gifts – an Argyll sweater in soft wool and an acoustic guitar so he could make music. And then Harry had brought home the punter. 'You owe me this,' he had said bluntly. 'This once . . . you owe me a favour.' And Sammy the boy had thought of the dark and the cold outside and given way.

After that, it hadn't seemed to matter. This was what he was meant for, it was all that was on offer. A bitter fatalism had numbed him for a few weeks, long enough for him to cease to cry, long enough to realise what happend to chickens when they lost their youth.

They had found a boy dead of smack in the arches and someone had said, 'He was one of Harry's once.' Vincent had looked down at the ashen face, strangely pure and chiselled in death, and seen his own face a year or so on. Even the street was better than that.

It was the guitar that saved him in the end, a nice touch of irony in that it was a gift from his predator. He had waited until Harry's back was turned and left with the rucksack he had brought from Leeds and the guitar, and within two weeks he had moved in with two of the boys who eventually formed Frame with him, paying his share of the rent by busking in the tube.

It had been easier to tell them he had just arrived in London and he had stuck to the story for years. And then his mother had moved to London in pursuit of one of her men. He had never lost touch with her, more for her sake than his, but he had not told her why he had run away from home. And she had never asked him, which meant she knew.

Now, he turned on his side in the darkness and tried to compose his mind. Tomorrow he must do his best for the project. That was what mattered. The past was dead and buried. If he could provide for others a refuge from the Harry Quinns of this world something would be gained.

'I ought to go,' Daphne said but she didn't move. Instead

she held out her glass and Brian gave her another inch of Scotch and a dash of dry ginger.

'What are you going to do, then?' Brian asked. He was lying back in his chair, his jacket discarded, his tie loosened and his top shirt button undone.

Sitting opposite him, legs curled under her, Daphne pursed her lips. 'I don't know. Nothing, I suppose. What can I do? It's too late, anyway. And even if he tried for an injunction, you can't stop the truth coming out. If he was one of that guy's stable – and I trust Mike, he doesn't invent things – if Vincent was this Sammy kid it'll come out.'

'OK.' Brian shrugged. 'If it's inevitable why agonise over it? Forget it!'

'You know I can't.' There was an angry note in her voice and she made a little moue of apology. 'It's not your fault, I know. It's just that hearing about him over the last couple of days, his plans for this refuge he's building, I feel mean.'

'You're not writing the story,' Brian said. It sounded as though he was making excuses for her but she could sense his disapproval of the whole affair. He had been tough when he was in the Met, but he had been fair. He thought the Vincent business unsavoury and in her heart she agreed with him.

Looking at him, the great, satisfying bulk of him in the chair opposite, she felt a surge of satisfaction that he still fancied her after all these years. He was a good-looking man. Anyone would fancy him. Did I break up his marriage? she wondered. Their relationship had been platonic until after Brenda had left him and she had gone off with a retired sergeant, so perhaps Daphne had played no part in it.

They had become lovers as soon as he'd put in for his divorce and he had proposed the day his decree was made absolute. He had proposed then and gone on proposing and she had gone on saying no almost automatically.

But I wanted him tonight, she thought. I needed him.

If the time came when he wasn't there, could she manage without him? Probably, but life wouldn't be half as pleasant.

Reluctantly she got to her feet. 'I must go. It's late.' He put down his glass and stood up too and she moved into the circle of his arms.

'Get a night's sleep,' he said. 'You never know, it might all have gone away by morning.'

But as her cab wended its way homewards she knew it wouldn't go away.

I don't like what's happening, she thought. I don't like the way I feel. I just don't know what to do about it.

Chris had stayed in the coffee bar as long as he dared and then retreated to the pub to drown his sorrows. For a while he watched the doors, half hoping to see them swing open and reveal Cliff and Dilly. But as he downed his third vodka and tonic he acknowledged that they were doubtless in bed by now, at it like knives.

230

The thought depressed him so much that he ordered another drink and sat regarding it mournfully. It wasn't just Dilly, although the thought of her and Clifford together was churning his gut. It was work as well — the happy anticipation of each item he worked on and then the dawning realisation that it wasn't working out as he had hoped. Even when he didn't get a bollocking for cocking things up, he felt distisfaction. *Self*-dissatisfaction, which was the worst of all.

He sipped his drink, even though he didn't really want it now, and tried to think positively. There was Friday to look forward to, after all. A nice, wholesome item. He had a sudden picture of Dilly at the mention of the words 'wholesome' and 'nice'. She would screw up her face as though he had said something vile. 'Wholesome' was out as far as Dilly was concerned. 'Hot' and 'wicked' were in, 'sharp' was OK . . . but not 'wholesome' — and his English teacher had always said 'nice' was meaningless.

For a moment he contemplated buying a bottle of vodka and drinking it on the way home. But it wouldn't help, and in the morning he'd be bitterly regretful. He emptied his glass and carried it back to the bar on his way out, earning a 'Ta' and a smile from the barmaid. It was an encouraging smile, reminiscent of the smiles Amy gave him, and as he trudged home he wondered why he couldn't be like other men and settle for what he could get. Cliff had Dilly, but if he didn't he would undoubtedly shag anything that had a pulse!

There was an empty coke can in the gutter and Chris

kicked it moodily for a hundred yards or so, seeing it as Clifford's head. Cliffy was thick. No two ways about it. But he must have something to keep Dilly eating out of his hand.

Chris thought of her, as she had been earlier that evening, clutching the carrier bag of groceries. She was willing to cook for a bastard who never pulled his weight with washing up or hoovering and left dirty socks and underpants strewn everywhere.

Perhaps he'd have blotted his copybook over supper. His type was bound to slip up somewhere, and Dilly, for all her daftness, was no fool. She has a better degree than a lot of researchers so she must have a brain. 'But no judgement,' he said mournfully with no one to hear him but a cat crouched on a wall. The flat was in total darkness when he got home, confirming his worst fears.

The moment they were naked in the bed together Liz regretted it but by then it was too late. She was not ruthless enough to cry 'Hold' at the last moment. Dave entered her and she turned her face away, hoping that the amount they had drunk would not render him incapable so that it went on and on for ever and ever.

His face was pressing against her face, his lips scrabbling for her mouth but that she would not surrender. She had been lying inert, hoping for it to be over, but now, desperate for release, she entered into it, touching, tugging, moving her body in a frenzy of encouragement, trying not to cry out against a predicament that was of her own making. When at last he shuddered and gasped she reared up and *faked* her orgasm.

Why had she done it? She had loved him once, no doubt about that. She found she was half smiling in the darkness, remembering those first, sweet, novel moments of intimacy. But it was over. She had put the past away and moved on. She loved Simon now, belonged to Simon, was saving – or should have saved – herself for that. Instead she had made love – feigned or otherwise, she had done it – with another man.

She was glad when enough time had passed for her to ease herself out of the bed and reach for a robe.

'I'll fix you a drink before you go,' she said. 'I can't say stay because I've got to get some sleep. You know my wake-up time.' For a moment he did not stir and she held her breath until at last he began to move and she knew she would soon be alone. That made it possible for her to smile as they drank and nod her head when he said, 'See you?'

'Give me a ring,' she called, knowing it was the worst thing she could say.

She turned the shower's flow to cold and put both nightdress and robe into the laundry box before she stepped under the icy water. Served her right! When at last she reached up to turn off the water she leaned her forehead against the tiled wall and cried with shame and frustration and self-pity.

Back in her bedroom, towel-wrapped, she stripped her bed and put on clean linen. 'How could you?' she

asked herself over and over again. It was not just the
act of sex, although loveless sex was bad enough. It was
what Dave would make of it, seeing it as an invitation
to begin the whole ball game again.

I must be mad, she thought.

But, as long as the present situation went on, she was
vulnerable. She must make Simon see that they were
wasting time. When at last she ran a comb through
her damp hair and climbed into bed it was to sleep the
sleep of someone who has made up her mind.

Simon had to help Jane out of the car, her legs buckling
on her high heels, her head lolling foolishly as she
giggled her way into the house. Simon paid off the sitter
with one hand, supporting Jane with the other. 'We've
had a bit of a celebration,' he said by way of excuse. The
sitter smiled the world-weary smile of one who has seen
it all and went in search of her car keys.

Upstairs he sat his wife on the bed and began to
remove her jewellery. She kept shaking her head from
side to side as he tried to unhook her drop earrings.
'Guess what,' she said, when at last he succeeded. She
was gazing up at him and trying to look seductive but
already her eyes were closing.

'What?' he said.

She leaned her head against his chest and her words,
when they came out, were mumbled but not so mumbled
that he could not hear. 'I'll be pregnant by the morning.'
She gave a little sigh and then she slept and he felt tears
coursing down his cheeks as he lowered her against the

pillows. What was he doing to her that she felt like this, seeing pregnancy as the only thing to solve her problems?

'I'm sorry,' he said, his lips against her hair, and then he was stripping her, doing it tenderly, holding her upright with one hand while he slipped the flowered nightshirt over her head and down to cover the thin white limbs.

I love her, he thought. I just don't want to fuck her.

He tried to remember when he had gone off his wife. Had it been when he met Liz? Or was it before that, when he had watched her in labour and almost screamed with horror himself at what he was putting her through? He could never forget she was the mother of his children. It would always be there, binding him to her but putting a curtain between them because it made her somehow holy and beyond the act of sex. A man never thought of sex as the road to procreation. It was women who thought like that. Most men wanted love and freedom in equal measure.

He had never acknowledged this feeling before and it shocked him. When he had folded Jane tenderly into the sheets he sat on the edge of the bed, elbows on knees, head supported in his cupped hands, and tried to still a brain teeming with alcohol and uncomfortable thoughts.

He had let things slide, his marriage and his relationship with Liz. God, he had been a shit all round, fair to no one. But how was he to resolve it? Where should he go? He was filled with a sudden longing to get away, to put as much distance as he could between himself and every form of emotional entanglement. But he couldn't do that. He would have to work it out somehow.

In the dark Vera snaked out a hand and switched on the bedside radio. It was Frank Sinatra, so that was lucky. But the song he was singing was a sad one, the lament of a man alone in a bar in the wee small hours,

That's the story of my life, Vera thought 'and switched channels. All she got was a droning voice going on about water supply in some country she'd never heard of and which, as far as Vera could make out, got what water it had for nothing, which was more than she and Fred did. What they had to pay in water rates was a scandal, considering all the water company had to do was pray for rain.

Frustrated, she turned over and slipped her hand between Fred's arm and his side. She liked the comforting bulk of him in bed and at least when he was asleep he wasn't complaining. She lay for a moment considering whether she should let the matter of the three-piece go and stop letting it rankle. If only he'd bring her a little present sometimes. Not something useful. He often brought in useful things but inside her there was a frivolous, glamorous creature who wanted — needed — a single rose or a frilly garter or one of those cut-glass scent bottles with glass stoppers that you up-ended and dabbed on your neck.

Glamour. She rolled the word around in her head.

Rita Hayworth. She had been glamorous. Princess Di was glamorous, and Anthea Turner. Who wouldn't look glamorous on what she was making out of the lottery.

Thinking of the lottery was a mistake because it reminded her of the lost five pounds. Furious, she withdrew her hand from her husband's side and gave him a dig for his pains, turning on her side so that her back was to him.

Think about something else, she urged herself and turned her thoughts to tomorrow. They were having that pop singer on, Vincent. Now *he* was glamorous, the image of Cary Grant, who had been glamour personified.

She punched her pillow and concentrated on Vincent. In the darkness the digital clock glowed twelve-fifteen. Vincent was probably in a nightclub with someone gorgeous now. Catherine Zeta Jones or Naomi Campbell. They would gaze into each other's eyes and he would reach out and take a single rose from the display in the centre of the table and she would take it from him and touch it to her lips. When sleep came at last Vera was smiling a truly contented smile.

At twelve-thirty Vincent abandoned sleep, crossing to the window to pull a cord that sent the heavy curtains gliding back to reveal London, a fairyland of lights below. There was still traffic on the bridges, the lights of cars winking as they travelled across Waterloo Bridge to be lost in the maze of lights in the South Bank.

He turned to his right, seeking Blackfriars Bridge and the great *Express* building. There had been an alley near there, near the underpass, where he had existed for a week once, living like a vole in the darkness.

In the dark, the cobbles gleaming wetly, the eyes of a passing rat shining like emeralds, he had prayed the familiar mantras of his childhood and half expected the holy angel to materialise. But there had been no angel. Only Harry Quinn. And after Harry there had been no peaceful sleep for a long time, not until 'Lonely Life' had made him rich and his third AIDS test had shown him to be HIV-negative. He turned wearily and went back to bed, leaving the lights strung along the river like a handful of diamonds thrown down by the gods.

14

Thursday 5.30 a.m.

Simon was down at the service door long before Vincent's expected arrival. It was cold in the windowless corridor and he shivered and thrust his hands into his pockets. Outside day was breaking. Inside, in the dingy concrete bowels of the TV station, it was deepest night and winter night at that.

At 5.40 he pressed the bar to open the door and stepped out. Just in time. A limousine was nosing carefully into the back street and gliding to a halt in front of him.

Where he came from Simon did not know, but, as the doors of the car opened and Vincent and his entourage emerged, a man appeared from nowhere. Before Simon could step forward he took a running step towards the car and then, with the star half in and half out of the door, the newcomer crouched and raised the camera he was carrying.

Simon saw the singer's mouth open — whether in protest or question he did not know — there was the sound of the camera shutter and then, as Vincent straightened, the camera clicked again.

'Wait!' Someone was shouting but the photographer was legging it up the backstreet and a car, a green Golf, was backing towards him. A moment later he was inside and the car was gathering speed and rounding the corner into the mass of traffic on the main road.

'What the hell was that?' The man who had shouted was shaking his head in a puzzled fashion but there was something in his expression that suggested he had more than half an idea of what was behind the stolen photo.

As if he had read Simon's thoughts he turned. 'Sorry . . . I was just knocked out of kilter. I'm Dave Behan, Vincent's manager.'

'Simon Stringer, deputy editor. Shall we get inside?'

'Good idea.' It was Vincent who spoke. Up close he was thinner than Simon had envisaged. His face was perhaps not as handsome as the blow-ups but there was a grave — almost stern — quality there that Simon had not expected.

They walked the bleak corridors, Simon and the singer hesitating in doorways, each trying to usher the other ahead. Only the manager strode confidently forward, hands thrust into jacket pockets.

'We're very grateful to you for coming in,' Simon said as they neared the green room.

'Not at all.' Vincent smiled suddenly and Simon

warmed to him, seeing the vulnerability there. 'Not at all,' the singer said again. 'I'm the one who should be grateful. You're giving me a wonderful opportunity to talk about the project — at least, I hope you are. Acres of time?'

'Not quite acres, I'm afraid.' Simon pushed open the green room door and gestured to a chair. 'But we hope you'll be pleased with the way it turns out. I'll leave the details to Liz, our features editor. She'll take you through it step by step. In the meantime . . .' He was moving towards the buffet when Dave interrupted.

'Black for him. Milk and two sugars for me, please.'

Simon poured the coffee, wondering as he did so where the hell were the researchers who should be here, greeting guests. 'As I said' — he handed over the cups — 'Liz will explain the format of the show. Basically, the live items are interspersed with the VT — that stands for videotape, but I suppose you know that. Basically, it's films we've made to illustrate an item or strands. Strands are films which run over six or eight weeks, occasionally twelve. They're the stock items — you know, celebs' homes, famous gardens. Today's is street markets. How to make best use of them, which is famous for what . . . you know the kind of thing. But it's the interviews that come out top in audience appreciation. We're expecting our viewing figures to go up with you here.'

Vincent smiled wryly but the manager's face brightened. 'I should hope so. When will you know?'

'We'll have the overnights tomorrow. Official figures later. But there'll be an upswing, no doubt about it. Now, if you'll excuse me, I'll find Liz. Make yourselves comfortable. Someone will be with you before long.

Chris had greeted his guests, a couple who were there to discuss their prizewinning garden, and conveyed them to the green room when he saw Dilly coming out of the loo. She had been strangely silent when he had seen her before he left the flat and Clifford had not appeared at all. Now, she looked glum and there were faint mascara stains around her eyes. Surely she couldn't have been crying. Not Dilly! A wave of protectiveness rose up in him, but when he spoke his voice sounded gruff to his ears.

'What's up with you?'

'What do you mean?' So he'd been right. Her voice was strangely subdued. As if she detected his suspicion she spoke again.

'They told me I was doing Vincent but all they really wanted was the brief – the donkey-work. Simon met him at the door and Liz's taking him around. It makes you sick.'

There was more to her despondency than being deprived of Vincent. Disappointments like that were everyday stuff to researchers. 'What else?' he said. 'I know you. It's more than getting an unfair deal.'

'I'm finished with Cliff, if that's what you mean.'

'Oh, yeah!' He tried to sound disbelieving but

however hard he tried he couldn't help sounding gleeful. 'Any reason?'

'Because he's a sod. A selfish swine.' She had fallen into step beside him and he had to struggle to resist putting his arm around her.

'How come you've just found this out?'

'So *you* think he's a swine?'

'I didn't say that,' Chris said defensively. They'd be friends again tomorrow and she'd tell Cliff everything. 'I just asked what'd changed your mind. He was God's gift yesterday.'

They had reached the studio door and were about to go their separate ways. Dilly's face was turned up to him and her despondent mouth was inches from his own. What would happen if he kissed her now? Hard!

'He fell asleep!' she said. 'After all that build-up . . . I burned my finger — look — and after all that effort the sod said "I'm tired", and turned over. Not even a thank-you.'

'It'd've been different if it was me,' Chris said fervently but he said it under his breath.

He has nice eyes, Liz thought, as she conducted Vincent to make-up. He smiled and nodded as she chatted away, trying to put him at ease, but she could see that he was a man grimly determined to do what needed to be done and then get the hell out of it.

He wouldn't be here if it wasn't for his precious charity, she thought and warmed to him because of it.

When he was seated in the high, swing chair, a make-up cape around his shoulders, she gave him a script to look at. 'Anything special?' the make-up artist asked.

Vincent shook his head. 'Anything to take the shine off.'

'Another brownie point,' Liz thought, thinking of the pipsqueaks in his industry who came in with their list of shading, highlighting, mascara and eyeliner — complete with exact makes and shade numbers. And that was just the men!

Vincent was studying the run-through. 'So you want me at five past six . . .?'

'The top of the show, actually. There'll be a wide shot showing you on the settee with Carol and Barry and then we'll go to news and come back to your first spot at 6.05.'

'And the film?'

'We have VT of the Bermondsey project and vox pop from young homeless. That goes out at seven-forty-five. That's our peak viewing — we thought you'd like it there to get maximum impact — and then, if it's OK with you, we'd like you at the end of the show. Just easy chat before the outro.'

He was nodding and as she relaxed Liz thought longingly of the end of the show, when at last she might have the chance of a few moments alone with Simon. The shame and self-disgust of the previous evening had formed a heavy knot in the centre of her chest. Should she tell Simon she had had sex with

David? Had he the right to know? He never told her when it happened with Jane — and of course it did. Every night, probably. She realised her knuckles had whitened where they gripped the back of the make-up chair. 'Well,' she said, 'I'm leaving you in good hands. Just shout when you're ready.' He was lying back in the chair now, a pink nylon cape covering his shoulders. But when she looked at his face she saw that the eyes fixed on her face were kindly, as though he knew what she was going through.

Daphne arrived in the studio as the film on the Bermondsey project was going out. She stood to watch it on a monitor, seeing the strained young faces of the cardboard-box dwellers, hearing Vincent tell of his dream, for a dream it obviously was — or rather a crusade, for she saw the haven that was rising out of the shell of the old warehouse. Would it survive if Vincent went down? Would Vincent survive Lou Bryan's exposé?

When the Bermondsey item was over the agony uncle took his place on the sofa. He wore a white poloneck sweater and a gold and enamel crucifix hung on a chain around his neck. His earnest and cherubic face was Dickensian, topped as it was by a halo of yellow curls. If Theo hadn't already given Daphne the lowdown she might have thought him an OK guy. Until he opened his mouth!

It was a mean little mouth, she realised. Hiding tiny white teeth that made her think of Red Riding Hood.

A caller was complaining about her husband. 'I should tell him to' — he nodded his head sharply to denote an obscenity — 'off, if I was you.' He waved aloft the letter from the obviously unhappy wife. 'I get scores of these. All of you pouring your heart out — get off your backsides, I say, and leave the effing so and so's.' He beamed right and left at the two presenters. 'You only have one life — isn't that so? — don't waste it on some oik who treats you like rubbish. Get out, darling — that's my advice. Get out and get yourself a good time.'

Not a word about loneliness or lack of money or who got the kids or the dog or the grandfather clock. Just 'Get out and live'. If only it was that easy. She looked around her. Gerry Malone, the photographer, should be here at any moment. She'd like at least one pic of the programme in session.

On the other side of the studio she could see Liz, the features editor. She was frowning, as though she echoed Daphne's sentiments.

I'd like to know what's going on between her and Simon, Daphne thought. But I've got troubles enough.

She had two more days to watch Vincent at close quarters and then one day till the trap was sprung! Lou was expecting the Vincent exposure to beef up the flagging Saturday sales so at least he was going to be sacrificed in a good cause!

The agony uncle had finished his spot and the studio sprang to life as adverts filled the monitor screens scattered around the studio. Next to Daphne a member of the studio crew was blowing a reddened nose. 'Got a cold?' Daphne asked sympathetically. The man was about to reply when the agony uncle swept past. He looked at the man's watery eyes and shuddered. 'Don't come near me with that — I can't stand infections.'

What a charlatan, Daphne thought as she watched him go. And then she thought of the way she had smiled at Vincent earlier. Was she any better?

It was ten past eight. Only fifty minutes to go and everything he was responsible for would be over and done without mishap. Chris relaxed against a pillar and then decided to go in search of something to eat. There might be a sarny left in the green room. If not, he could nip to the canteen. Ever since Dilly had sprung her surprise he had been famished. And excited! It churned inside him like a hurricane. She and Cliff were no longer an item. Please God it would last.

The green room was empty except for the solitary figure of Vincent. It was strange to see the megastar alone. Presumably his entourage were up in the gallery, watching them put out the show. Chris smiled at the singer. 'Are you OK? Can I get you anything . . . coffee tea . . .?' They had spoken briefly over the phone before he made the Bermondsey film but the singer was a hard guy to get to know.

'I'd like a coke — diet, if possible.' Vincent had risen from his seat and Chris was surprised to find that he was taller than the singer. On screen, and in photos, Vincent gave the impression of height and strength. The reality was somewhat frailer but much more approachable.

'There's a machine in the corridor,' Chris said, hand going to his pocket.

Vincent was grimacing. 'I know. The sad fact is I don't have any change. Any money on me, come to that. We . . . I . . . well, it's door to door in the car nowadays. I've got plastic . . .' He grinned. 'But you can't put that in a drinks machine.'

Chris smiled back and pulled out a coin. 'I've got some change.' Their eyes met in mutual amusement and liking. 'I rather care for being in a position to fork out for a megastar.'

'I'm grateful, man. I'm grateful.'

The coke was obtained and handed over and Chris poured himself a coffee and perched on the opposite sofa. 'It must be difficult – being recognized all the time. Still, I suppose it's what you worked for . . .'

Vincent was smiling. 'At first,' he said. 'It's OK at first. Even elating. And then you begin to realise you're in a cage. The first time it struck me was in Safeway. I'd bummed around for a year or two and learned to shop on the cheap – you know, things on their sell-by dates, bashed cans . . . I went in one day – just leaped in with a trolley and made for the bargains. I was having a ball until I heard the whispering. "Look at him! Fancy that! All his money!" I crawled out of there – I put the goods back and I beat it. A door had clanged and I hadn't realised it.'

Chris was leaning forward, waiting to hear more,

when Dilly appeared, clipboard in hand, looking flustered. 'Here you are,' she said to Vincent. 'I thought I'd lost you. Is there anything I can get you?' Her eyes flashed at Chris and he got the message: this is my chance . . . beat it.

'Well,' he said, 'if you're OK I'll be off. It was nice talking to you.' Dilly's lashes were fluttering, one hip jutting above perfectly curved legs.

'Thanks Chris,' she said and he knew he was dismissed.

Vera had made good use of her break in the canteen, keeping her fellow cleaners rapt with her tales of Vincent at close quarters. What she had not been able to observe she invented, making up whole chunks of imaginary conversation between herself and the megastar. In the end, when she was running out of fantasy, she stood up. 'Well, I best get back. You never know what you're missing in that place.' Her position as studio cleaner gave her a certain cachet but today's pre-eminence was heady stuff.

'See if you can get us an autograph, Vee,' someone said. 'Or a signed picture. Ooh, I think he's lovely. Mean and moody. He's better than that Sting!'

She carried a bacon-and-egg butty back to Theo's den and was rewarded with a pat on the arm. 'Ta, Vee. I need this. Carol's drained me this morning. Drained me. All on account of yesterday, of course. On and on she's gone. If they could wire her gob to a generator they could close down Dounreay.' He bit into his butty and closed his eyes in ecstasy. 'Ooh, lovely. You can say what you like about cholesterol but you can't beat a bit of fat!'

For a moment she was tempted to tell him about Barry and the five-pound note but caution prevailed. If the worse came to the worst, she could blackmail Barry and sail away from Fred on the *QE2*.

'You have a life with those two, don't you?' she said sympathetically.

Theo's eyes rolled. 'Don't tell me. But that's been my lot, Vee. Uphill! It doesn't do to look back but you can't help it, sometimes. When I think of what I could've done . . . Jesus!'

He leaned forward suddenly, eyes glittering. 'Friend Barry was upset the other day. Wouldn't say why but I've got my suspicions. He said someone came into his room while he was peeing. He said they were going through the drawers . . .'

Vera felt her face flush and her scalp prickle. 'Go on,' she said. He was talking about her, she knew it!

'What I think,' Theo said dramatically, 'is that they caught him up to something. Without his rug, probably. And he didn't like it. He's breathing fire − he'll have them sacked, just watch it. It may take time but he'll do it. That swine never forgets.'

As she collected her cleaning implements from the cupboard Vera felt waves of panic come and go. If she lost her job − and who would take her word against Barry's? − what would she do? How would they manage?

But as she began to sweep and dust two things consoled her: the thought of what she could sell to the papers if Barry forced her hand and the rock-solid knowledge that Fred would see her through. Whatever else he might be, he wasn't one to let you down when the crunch came.

Simon settled back in his chair and looked from one monitor to another. Comparing sets, *GMTV* was coming out on top. He made a note to speak to the designer. In the *Daybreak* studio the fitness guru was leaping about, all limbs and leotard. 'And one and two . . .' she exhorted. Simon smiled to himself, picturing viewers limbering up in front of their TV sets. A likely story!

He sipped his coffee and tried to watch with an analytical eye but it was difficult not to think about the mess his life was in. He had sought and sought for a solution that could be fair to everyone. Could Jane survive if he left her? He could provide for her, he could be there for her whenever she needed him but would that be enough? And if he stayed with Jane would Liz accept a secondary role for ever . . . or for the foreseeable future? If he went, what about the kids? If he stayed, what about Liz's right to a child?

In the beginning he had been horrified at the intensity of his feelings for Liz. He had never even contemplated being unfaithful to Jane, accepting that the pattern of his life had been settled for him in that one brief moment of foolishness when Jake had been

conceived. Besides, he had loved her. He did love her.
There were a thousand things that bound them together
– she was part of his growing up, for God's sake.

But he had not bargained on the way she would
change with pregnancy. Almost from the beginning she
had been like someone possessed, talking babies, reading
about babies, planning not just for herself but for him.
They had gone almost from the church to antenatal
classes and she had assumed – taken it for granted –
that he would be there at the birth, taking part in it
as though he too was delivering a child.

He had tried to draw back, to explain his reservations, but she would have none of it. This was
going to be the greatest experience of his life. He
had wanted to ask how the hell she knew, but
faced with such monumental maternal certainty he
had fallen silent. And afterwards, things had never
been the same.

And then Liz had come into his life. Independent,
self-possessed Liz, who was everything a man could
wish for. Until now. For he could sense their relationship changing. Irrespective of the stresses imposed upon
it by secrecy, something was happening, some kind of
internal combustion. Would he fall out of love with
Liz? But he loved Jane still. If anything happened to
her he would be devastated.

Who do I love? he thought, the women's faces and
bodies becoming intertwined in his mind. Was it Jane,
whose lips caressed his neck? Liz whose limbs so
completely fitted to his own? Sickened at his own

inability to marshal his thoughts, he seized the remote control and turned up the *Daybreak* sound.

Carol was talking to Barry now, smiling at him with a saccharin sweetness. 'You don't need a fitness regime, darling – you're amazing . . . for your age.' Simon groaned and shut down the sound, knowing that Barry would be bending his ear within minutes of the closing credits.

The blonde and silly researcher was riding shotgun on Vincent but Daphne was not to be deterred. She held out a hand as she entered the green room. 'Daphne Bedford. I'm with the *Herald*.'

He shook her hand and nodded but his eyes were wary. She hastened to put him at ease. 'I'm doing a profile of the show. I've been here all week. It's five days in the life of breakfast TV – you know the sort of thing. I'll be mentioning you're the star guest and if you gave me a quote I'd like it but I'm not going to grill you.'

His smile of relief was heartfelt and she felt her own heart sink. In front of her was a charming and certainly vulnerable young man. She was presenting herself as a friend, someone who posed no threat to him. On Saturday he would know her for the liar she surely was – he would know enough about the press to know she must have been aware of the exposé as she smiled into his eyes and shook his hand.

She poured herself a coffee and sat down. 'Your

Bermondsey project sounds fascinating. Tell me about it.'

He pursed his lips and blew. 'Where do I begin? Well, when I came to London from the provinces' – he hesitated for a second – 'I was lucky. I found somewhere fairly quickly. But I can remember feeling scared.' I wrote a song about it, 'Ceiling in the sky''.' He grinned. 'It sounds romantic, the sky for a cover . . .'

'But not when it rains,' Daphne finished for him.

'Exactly. So once I had a bit of clout – and some cash – I thought, why not create a hostel? Hence Bermondsey.'

'Not everyone would've been so generous.' Daphne's gaze held his and his eyes didn't waver.

'It's not purely me. A lot of guys've chipped in. I'm not another Geldof. For God's sake don't say that.'

'Why not a St Vincent? It sounds better than St Bob.'

'There's already a perfectly good saint called Vincent – besides, I'm more of a sinner than a saint.'

Daphne thought of Lou's instruction not to make too much of Vincent and then decided to throw caution to the wind.

'Tell me a bit about your background. You were born in Manchester?'

'Leeds. I was born to good Catholic parents in Leeds. That's how I know my saints.'

'Was it a musical family?'

'Not really. We went to church a lot – I remember the music there . . .' He fell silent and Daphne tried another trick.

'Do you have brothers and sisters?'

'No. I'm an only child. My father died when I was quite young, so there were no more children.'

'And your mother?'

'Oh, she's still around. She lives in London actually. She moved down here — it seemed to make sense. But she likes to keep out of the limelight.'

Daphne laughed but she could see that he was becoming uneasy now and she was glad she could turn to the blonde researcher and say, 'Do you know where my photographer is? He was taking random shots last time I saw him but I'd like a pic of Vincent.'

_____ *15* __

T he young researcher with the short skirt had
   guided him back to a place behind the cameras.
'Not long now,' she said encouragingly and Vincent felt
a weight lifting from him. One more brief appearance
— 'no more questions, just a few goodbyes as the credits
roll,' they'd said — and he was free, the first, and
arguably the worst, day over. And the *Herald* journalist
had been human — nice, even. So that was good.

On the monitor he could see the signs of the
Zodiac sailing by, one by one, each with a message. Aquarius, Pisces . . . He waited for his own
sign, Gemini, to appear. All a load of codswallop,
of course, but comforting when it was good tidings.
'The sun in your sign should make you feel that
life is fun-loving and pleasurable but still you feel
as though a shadow hangs over you. Your worries

will soon be over and a new and brighter period begin.'

In spite of himself he felt cheered — and then arms were urging him forward, into the arena. Someone was fastening a microphone to his lapel and hiding the cable beneath his jacket and Carol Cusack was smiling encouragement and patting his knee. He took a deep breath and prepared to smile his way into the credits.

Liz watched him, noticing the tenseness beneath the smile that the viewer would not see. And yet he was proving to be a joy to interview. Not even Pinky and Perky would be able to spoil it. Things were going well today — for once. Carol and Barry were cooing at each other, none of the items had overrun and there had been a satisfying number of calls to the duty desk to say 'Well done!'

She was there to collect Vincent at the end and carry him back to God's office for the champagne that was reserved for VIPs. While she waited she tried not to let her mounting anger overcome her.

Damn Simon! He's using me, she thought and knew as she thought it that it was untrue. She had had users in her life but Simon was not one of them. We are part of a tragedy, she thought. None of us to blame, all of us caught in a whirlpool of love and deceit.

She closed her eyes, experiencing an almost physical sense of being sucked down, beneath the surface of life, to a place of non-status and lonely weekends and even lonelier bank holidays. Last Christmas they had just become lovers and she had endured the holiday in a fever of anticipation of their next meeting, so that it had almost passed in a flash. This year — if they lasted till Christmas — would be different. This year, Christmas would be hell on earth.

The studio sprang to life as the programme ended. The crew were seizing furniture and props, cameramen retreating, cables leaping and writhing about their feet. She moved to Vincent's side. 'Nearly over. Just the outro and then the editor's hoping you'll join him for a drink.'

For a moment she thought the singer would refuse but at last he nodded. 'Fine,' he said. 'My manager's in the box. Can somebody retrieve him?'

'Yes.' Liz put a hand on his elbow. 'Watch the cables. I thought the interview went well. Were you happy?'

Vincent nodded. 'Yes. It was fine from my point of view. I got the chance to say what needed to be said. Were you happy with it?'

'Very!' They had to keep their voices low so Liz smiled radiantly to emphasise her pleasure. She saw Vincent's eyes flash momentarily, as men's eyes always did when they recognised a woman as a sexual being, but then the reaction was gone and he was serious again.

'I'd be grateful to hear about any feedback about the project.'

'Of course. We'll help all we can. And if I can help personally, let me know. I'd quite like to get involved in a cause.' Even to her own ears — or perhaps especially to her own ears — her voice sounded wistful.

'You can come and run it for us,' Vincent said.

'Hah!' She raised her eyes in appreciation of the joke.

'I'm quite serious. We'll need administrators. If you're ever interested give me a buzz. You seem to have your hands on the reins here.'

'Don't you believe it.' Liz shook a rueful head. 'Today we've been lucky.' They were out of the studio now and moving towards the editor's office.

'Well you know how to reach me — or Dave. He's not as keen on the project as I am but he'd make sure we got together to see if there was any possibility . . .' He fished for a card 'Here's the number of my private line.'

He means it, Liz thought and was relieved when the door to God's room loomed up.

They had all disappeared into Colin Frost's office and Vera seized her chance to tidy up. She could do with getting off promptly today, not that there was much to go home for. She thought of the advert she had seen in Sunday's paper. 'Is your man lying down on the job?' It had gone on to extol the virtue of a herbal potion but it would take more than ginseng and cinnamon to liven up Fred. On top of which she had the worry about Barry and his threats to Theo. He wouldn't dare get her the sack. She'd expose him if he did.

She decanted the cold coffee remnants into the empty jug and threw the waxed paper cups into the litter bin. There was one egg mayonnaise sandwich left and she nibbled the soft bits and threw the crusts after the paper cups. When the table was cleared she sprayed it with cleaner and wiped it until it was shiny before she turned her attention to the settees that lined the room.

She was plumping up the scatter cushions when she saw the pound coin. She picked it up and hesitated. The editor's secretary kept lost property but would she want to be bothered with a pound coin? Vera tried to think who had been sitting there. Several people had passed through the green room but she could only remember Vincent sitting in that particular spot. Vincent was rich – a millionaire . . . She looked at the coin for a moment and then she dropped it into her overall pocket.

'So.' Daphne smiled. 'How d'you think it went?' The young man's eyes blinked behind his spectacles.

'OK,' he said. 'Good, in fact.'

'Yes,' Daphne said. 'Better than yesterday's, I thought. I liked Vincent – and his project. Who did the film?'

Chris was blinking again but this time proudly. 'I did the Bermondsey bits. It was . . . well, OK, I suppose.'

'It was bloody good,' Daphne said. 'I liked the way you wove in the kids' faces . . .'

'The cutaways,' he said. 'Yes, I thought that would work.'

'You really got the impression of them being lifted up from the streets – onwards and up.'

'It'll be a good thing if it comes off.' Chris was serious now, his coffee cup forgotten in his hands.

'Do you think he can bring it off?'

He nodded vigorously. 'If anyone can, he can. I mean, he's bigger than Geldof and look what *he* did.'

'Let's hope nothing stops it, then.'

Daphne felt her cheeks flush. You fucking hypocrite, she thought. By Saturday lunchtime it might all have come tumbling down like a house of cards. It was a relief when the deputy editor appeared and invited her to a glass of champagne.

'I thought the show was good today,' she said as they moved along the corridor.

'Yes. Having Vincent is a big coup. He's quite extra-ordinary in that he's a household name, but we don't really know a lot about him. Not in depth. Hopefully today and tomorrow will help with that a little.'

Daphne nodded but she was thinking of Saturday. Vincent would certainly be known in depth once the *Herald* hit the streets.

At that moment Gerry Malone appeared round a corner, his neck strewn with cameras, his spectacles pushed up onto his head so that he resembled an earnest birdwatcher.

'Did you get everything, Gerry?'

'I think so.' He consulted the list she had given him. 'I need to get Theo. Theo, Wardrobe it says here. Where do I find him?'

'Well done, Chris!' He turned at the sound of Amy's voice but it was not the Amy of the sober suits or neat T-shirts that stood there. It was an exotic creature in a shimmering sari, her abundant dark hair tamed into a bun low on the nape of her neck, earrings dangling and bracelets chinking on her slender wrists.

'What's with you?' he said.

'All right.' She held up a hand, palm outwards. 'No need to sound so shocked. It's for Rachel's item on ethnic fashion. This is my Sunday-go-to-meeting sari.'

'You look stunning,' he said.

'Thank you.' That was what he liked about Amy. No mucking about!

'Anyway,' she said. 'I just wanted you to know your Vincent film was fab.'

'Thanks,' he said, suddenly unsure of how to proceed with this strange woman who was no longer just a pal but looked like a sex-symbol. It was a relief when Liz bore down on them with celebratory glasses of champagne, the reward for an especially good programme. But after Liz had moved on he was left with the same embarrassment. 'Well,' he said, raising his glass, 'here's to you. You really do look great.'

Amy clinked glasses but pursed her lips. 'What you're saying, Chris, is that I normally look a dog.'

'No . . . no, I don't mean . . . I mean, no, you always look . . . nice . . .'

'Nice! Chris, you are digging yourself into a hole.' He felt his scalp prickle, a sure sign that he was going to blush. God, this was awful.

'All right,' Amy said kindly, extending a jingling wrist to pat his arm. 'All right, you've been punished enough. Thank you very much for your compliment.

263

It's appreciated. Now, drink up and then I can go and revert to my normal, boring self.'

But she had rehabilitated him enough to respond in kind.

'You are never boring — and not normal either. No one here's normal. Cheers!'

The editor's office was roomy but now it could hardly hold everyone who had thronged there. Carol and Barry had raced for Colin's chair so that they could dominate the assembly and Carol had won, graciously allowing Barry to perch on the edge of the desk beside her.

Liz and Colin's secretary, had supplied champagne all round and now everyone was laughing and chattering with the animation of people who had delivered a satisfactory performance and were pleased with themselves.

Simon stood, sipping his champagne, trying not to catch Liz's eye, trying not to think about anything except that the day had gone well. He was watching Vincent's manager, deep in conversation with God — unlike his client, who was staring out of the window — when one of the phones on the desk rang.

'It's for you.' God was handing him the phone and Simon moved as far away as he could from the hubbub before he put the receiver to his ear.

At the other end of the line Jane sounded positively cheerful and full of compliments. 'Yes, it was a great show, wasn't it?' He listened as she babbled on about nothing in particular. He looked up and saw that Liz was watching him and he felt a faint sweat break out over his scalp. 'Darling, was there something special. It's just a bit difficult at the moment . . .'

He raised his eyes again to meet Liz's eyes and saw her lips form a mocking 'Darling?' He turned away, hunching his shoulder. For God's sake get on with it, he silently urged, but Jane was in full flow.

'I just wanted to say I love you and I'm sorry I didn't wake up before you left. I was out like a light. Are you OK?'

'Yes, yes I'm fine.'

'No hangover?'

'No, not so you'd notice.' Behind him the office seemed suddenly silent. Were they listening? For God's sake hurry up, he urged his wife silently. It seemed an age that he hung there, pinioned between his mistress and his wife, unable to break free of either.

16

'Well done, everyone.' Liz had seen off the last of the guests and returned to the office. She looked around her colleagues, all glowing because none of them had had a strip torn off them and God was pleased!

She was about to return to her own office when Chris approached her. 'I need some cash, Liz.' She raised her brows in mock horror and he hurried to explain. 'I'm nannying that old couple — tomorrow's human interest item. They're booked into the Imperial. So am I — Sarah OK'd it. I'll need tips and taxis and things.'

'See me when we've got rid of everyone. And don't forget your receipts!' She was walking back to the office when Simon came towards her. She felt a terrible mixture of anger and pity when she saw his expression. Sheepish and hopeful. Or shifty and devious? The words tumbled round in her brain as they halted, by unspoken consent, at the photocopier.

She pretended to be busy with paper. He stood with his back half turned to her. Like characters in B-movies, she thought bitterly.

'Liz . . . about Jane's call . . .'

'Don't tell me about Jane's call!' The viciousness in her own voice took her by surprise. 'I don't care about Jane's call — it's not my fucking business.'

'I'm only —'

'Shut up. I've told you — it's not my business. What *is* my business is what you're doing to my life . . . no, what *I'm* doing to my life! I'm as much to blame as you. I want out of this situation, Simon. One way or another, I want out. I can wait if you can give me some idea of what I'm waiting for — but I can't go on like this, wondering if there's anything there for me at the end of it all.'

'It's not that easy, Liz.'

'Well, it'll just have to be because I can't stand it, Simon. I want an answer and I want it now — this week. Which means tomorrow because, as we both know, weekends are out of the question!'

'Darling . . .' It was the wrong word and they both knew it as they turned on their heels to go their separate ways.

'Told you it would be OK,' Dave said. They were pausing at traffic lights and the manager stared out through the smoked glass, scrutinising the pedestrians

268

who could not scrutinise him. They were confident words but Vincent could sense a tension in Dave, an avoidance of eye contact, a nervous fidgeting of fingers. If it had not been for the bulk of the driver in front of them he would have asked a question, but this was not the moment.

He waited until they were safe in the penthouse, the lift returned to the ground, the doors shut, the dog over her first frantic leapings and ready to settle at her master's feet.

'What's up?' Vincent asked. They knew each other well enough not to dissemble.

'I don't know. And that's gen. I have no concrete reason to feel twitchy – but I do. That geezer – the photographer . . . And I got a call from Len Sleightholme today – a fishing expedition. You know what he's like if he thinks someone else is onto something. Still – what the shit – you get tomorrow over, we agree the final pressing with Omega and we can have a month somewhere warm and as far away as possible.'

'Why would Sleightholme call?' Len Sleightholme was the doyen of the entertainment columnists. Usually he had the story first. 'Did you ask him?'

'Of course,' Dave said. 'He didn't know anything. Nothing concrete. He just said the grass was rustling. You know the way the buzz goes round.'

'Could it be all the promos we've put out on the project?'

'No. It's more than that. You didn't say anything to that journo from the *Herald*, did you?'

'The usual. She asked about Bermondsey.'

'And that's all?'

'Yeah. She was OK.' Vincent frowned, trying to remember. It *had* been OK, hadn't it?

'Let's forget it.' Dave raised beringed hands. 'It's me. I'm getting paranoid. Now. One or two things to sign and then I'm off.'

'So I'll be there at Euston . . . I'm tall and thin and I wear glasses . . . hey, I'll carry a red folder. You'll see me at the barrier.'

Chris was smiling as he put down the phone. There had been genuine excitement at the other end of the line. He was still smiling beatifically, rocking back on his chair, when Amy approached his desk, changed now into her usual garb. She regarded his beaming face.

'You've won the lottery?'

Chris shook his head. 'Guess again.'

'You've been given a director's course?'

'Nope.' He swung his chair back to the floor. 'I have just encountered true love. Real, twenty-two-carat love . . .' She was looking mystified. 'The old couple we're using tomorrow. You know, World War Two romance. And I'm booked in to the Imperial tonight, to look after them, and for once – for once, my Amy – we will have a *nice* item. No sleaze, no hype, no yuck – just real people. I can hardly wait!'

Daphne had made her goodbyes and was ready to

leave the studio when Liz came up to her. 'Is every-thing OK?'

The features editor looked tired and somehow older than she had seemed at the beginning of the week and Daphne tried to reassure her. 'It's going well, Liz. Everyone's been helpful and I've enjoyed myself. It's going to make a good piece.'

Liz had put up a hand to her head. She rubbed wearily and then looked at Daphne again. 'Would you like a drink before you go? There's still some champagne – or coffee.'

'Have you any plans for lunch?' Daphne said. 'I don't mean to be rude but you look shattered.'

'I haven't time . . .' Liz began and then stuck out her chin. 'Yes, I have. Will the canteen do? I can have something sent to my office.'

They ate excellent sandwiches and drank mineral water, making small talk all the while, and then Daphne fished in her bag. 'Are you ready for coffee?' She produced a small silver flask. 'This is my favourite whiskey – Bushmills. A slug in coffee does wonders.'

They drank the warm and now redolent brew for a moment and then Liz said, 'That's better.'

'Things a bit tough at the moment?' Daphne said sympathetically.

'Bloody. Oh, not just this place, though God knows it can be a killer. I'm . . . I'm in the process of divorcing my husband. You know how it is. Anyway . . . what did you think of Vincent?'

'I thought he was lovely,' Daphne said, accepting the

change of subject. 'Not a bit starry, totally unarrogant – and he looks as though he washes.'

'He was more intelligent than I expected.' Liz smiled. 'He offered me a job. Well, sort of – not something I think I could do – but it was nice to be asked. Well . . . *half* asked.'

'It's always nice to be offered a job,' Daphne said fervently. 'Especially in my line of work. You're more likely to get the order of the boot! Tell me more.'

But Liz was half smiling into her glass and it was a minute before she answered. 'He was probably just flannelling. You know, 'What a marvellous job you do et cetera et cetera' – but he said they'd need people to run this Bermondsey thing and I could apply. Really, they need a social worker.'

'God forbid,' Daphne said. 'But you're not thinking of leaving Daybreak, are you?'

'Constantly! That's off the record, by the way. Telly is not the glamorous job it appears, you know. Frustration's the name of the game most of the time. And – I suppose because of my divorce and things – I feel frustrated anyway.'

Things? Daphne, thought, but forbore to comment. Instead she asked, 'Well, as you say, it's always nice to be offered a job, whether out of politeness or not.'

'How long have you been at the *Herald*?'

'For ever,' Daphne said. 'Or it feels like for ever. I've got a new features editor. That's the rub at the moment. We don't see eye to eye.'

'Would you like another coffee?' Liz asked sympathetically.

'Yes.' Daphne fished in her bag and shook the flask. 'Just enough for two tinctures. We deserve them.'

'You can say that again,' said Liz and eased from her seat.

It was raining when he reached the South Bank and, when he arrived at his apartment, Vincent crossed straight to the window, eager to see the river in the rain.

But as he looked out at cars crawling now along the embankment he was thinking of the woman with the tired eyes. Liz Fenton. She had seemed genuinely interested in Bermondsey, although her eyes had flicked constantly around the room, keeping tabs on everything. That was what had made him think of her as an administrator, that feeling that she was holding rein on everything. But why would someone leave a satisfactory job in the media for the uphill struggle that Bermondsey would inevitably be?

He stood for a moment, revelling in the feeling that he had his home to himself. Soon he would take out Juno and run with her in the rain but now, for a moment, he wanted to enjoy this feeling of being in his eyrie, high above the streets.

As a child he had always felt exultation when he was somehow safe, preferably somewhere where no one knew of his presence and he was unobserved.

But you were never unobserved. The eye of God was on you all the time, all-knowing, all-judging.

His father had once told him rain was God's tears for the world. Now he looked at the tears trickling down the huge windows and found himself repeating yet another mantra of childhood. '*Agnus Dei, qui tollis peccata mundi* . . .' Lamb of God, you take away the sins of the world.

It was strange the way the religious elements of his childhood kept floating up. He hadn't been to church proper since he came to London. Nowadays Langans was his church, the columns of the tabloids his confessional, so journalists would like to believe.

And he wasn't a frightened little boy any more, needing to cling to the banner that promised forgiveness. He was a man of power. Three years ago this room would have been awash with hangers-on. It had driven him crazy until he realised the solution was within his own grasp. They had been banished to a discreet office in Baker Street, from where they ran his business empire, and Dave was his only line of communication to the outside world. What he wanted, he could have, as long as he could pay for it. Surely that was forgiveness enough.

There was a steady drizzle as Vera got off the bus and she had to pause on the corner and wipe her forehead before she could go on. She tucked her coat around her and hurried towards the corner shop. She needed bread and milk and a quarter of the salami Fred liked in his sarnies.

The friendly sounds of the shop closed around her as she entered: the hum of large freezers and cheerful banter between the Asian shopkeeper and his Cockney customers. He was teasing one woman about her thirst for a scratch-card win. 'Don't call the helpline, Mary. I'm your helpline. I sell the tickets. I want to be there for the big wins.' He grinned around. 'Very lucky shop, this. I got the lucky tickets, make me an offer.'

'I'll give you five pence for one,' someone said, and they all laughed as the shop owner sliced ox tongue onto greasproof paper.

'That's all they're worth,' Vera said. 'I've had my fingers burned, I can tell you.' The thought of the lost five pounds still rankled as she tried to squeeze moisture from her wet hair.

'Well, I'm not giving up.' A stout woman clasped plump, beringed fingers over her purse and stuck out her chin as she spoke. 'Someone's got to win, might as well be me. One day!'

'It's for you-hoo,' the shopkeeper yodelled, pointing the meat fork he was holding at his customers. It was a random gesture but he had actually pointed at Vera and she felt her scalp prickle. That's how it would be for someone, the finger of fate reaching out of the heavens and pointing to one lucky so-and-so. Did it mean anything, that gesture? Was fate telling her something? She had only enough money for the milk and bread and her bus fare tomorrow.

She was shuffling forward to claim her turn when she remembered the pound coin she had found. Lying there on the leather cushions. Better than a pointed finger. It was still there, in the pocket of the overall she wore beneath her coat.

As he opened the till to add up her other purchases she scrabbled feverishly. 'Might as well have one of those cards,' she said. 'This might be my night.'

Thursday 6.00 p.m.

Vera had served up Fred's tea and tried to put on a semblance of eating herself. Now, freed from the dining table, she sat in her chair and pretended to be watching Oprah Winfrey. But all she could see, eyes open or closed, was the numbers swimming into view when she had scratched the card.

She had been too proud to scratch it in the shop with so many people there, so she had carried it home. She had laid her things down in the hall and put the card on the kitchen table. There was a knife lying there, moist and crumby with cheese where Fred had cut himself a piece of Wensleydale. She had picked it up, holding it halfway down, feeling the blade dig into her fingers, and rubbed. Twenty pounds. Two hundred pounds. Five thousand pounds. Five thousand pounds. Twenty pounds. And then, as she was getting ready to bin it, another number. Five thousand pounds, clear at first and then, as she half realised, receding until it was out of focus and she had to lift the ticket almost to touch her eyeball before she could grasp the truth.

I have won five thousand pounds. I have won five thousand pounds. She had wanted to shout it out loud but some instinct kept her mute. When she dished up his meal he said, 'Anything fresh?' and for a single trembling second she almost told him, but what came out was, 'No, nothing much. That Vincent was on the programme.' And after that it was too late for confession.

Now they sat in silence, the TV set burbling away in the corner of the room. Five thousand pounds! The most she had ever had in her life was a hundred and twenty. Five thousand was – she did rapid calculations in her head – nearly forty times that.

At seven o'clock Vera retreated upstairs and lay down on her bed. She didn't feel as she would have expected to feel after a windfall. She felt awful, so awful that she had resorted to Alka Seltzer. But the feeling in her stomach was more than wind. It was a compound of excitement and apprehension, or pure, unadulterated joy and terror.

She was rich. But, instead of thinking of the hundreds of things she now had access to that had been out of reach before, she was filled with a terrible desire to save money, even begrudging the money it had cost to ring the Lottery Helpline.

Perhaps it would turn her funny. She'd heard of that

before: old women found dead in indescribable hovels who turned out to be worth a fortune. If she invested, her money would grow. But investment was not the issue at the moment. The burning question was what to do about Fred.

If he knew she'd come into money he'd never part with a penny again. She knew him. On the other hand, could she keep her win a secret for ever? She'd need a bank account now – Chris would help her with that and never tell a soul. But she had married Fred with a vow to share. If she stayed married to him how could she keep her good fortune to herself?

So it wasn't just a question of to tell or not to tell. It was a question of whether or not to stay. She turned on her side and closed her eyes, hoping for a little respite in sleep, but she was still awake when Fred pushed open the bedroom door. 'Are you OK, Vera pet?' There was the chink of a spoon in a saucer. 'I thought you might like a cup of tea.'

The first thing Daphne did when she hit the house was run a bath, tipping in bath oil as though she was frying tonight, dipping in a finger to whisk up over-hot water and then, as pain seized her, snatching it out again. She left the taps running and went to check her answering machine. 'Ring me, Daphne.' Lou's voice was curt. Daphne went back to the bathroom, turned off the taps and settled in a chair before she rang the *Herald* offices. This could turn out to be a long phone call.

'Lou . . . it's Daphne. You wanted me?'

'Daphne! Yes. How did it go today?' Lou was trying to be polite, which put Daphne on guard.

'It went well, Lou. I got some good stuff. The piece is shaping up nicely.'

'Was Vincent there? Well, of course he was there. I watched him. I mean, did you see him?'

'Yes. We had a nice chat.' Two could play at being subtle, Daphne thought, wriggling into a more comfortable position.

'But you didn't say anything?' Now Lou was openly anxious.

'Of course not.' She allowed her irritation to show in her voice. 'What do you take me for, Lou? I have been at this game for quite a long time.' As the words left her lips she regretted them. Lou would take that as a retirement notice!

But Lou was sounding mollified at the other end of the line. 'I know. I only asked because this is such a coup. If anything went wrong I'd kill myself.'

'I wish,' Daphne thought. Aloud she said, 'I just got on with my piece . . . and Gerry got some good pics. Well, he said he was pleased and you know how choosy he is.'

'Good,' Lou said but she sounded totally uninterested in the Daybreak piece, having got what she came for: reassurance that she was on course for a triumph over the Vincent piece.

They made their goodbyes and Daphne put down the phone and went in search of the bath she now felt surely in need of.

It was impossible to sit down until she had run in some cold and then the water level was dangerously high, so that it slopped just below her mouth and threatened to overflow if she moved about. She had brought the ghetto-blaster into the bathroom, running it from an outside plug, and put on a Vincent tape. 'Lonely life . . . this is a lonely life . . .' That had been his big hit in 1990 . . . or was it 1991? Three years ago or four, it seemed like yesterday. Brian had bought her the album because she kept humming it under her breath.

Vincent had been little known then, except to the cognoscenti. Now he was famous, a megastar, and a megastar with a mission. She thought of him today, obviously ill at ease and desperately anxious to escape but sticking it out because the cause was a worthy one.

'Oh shit,' she said aloud. 'Oh shit!' But swearing didn't help. Nothing helped to erase the memory of his face, the shy smile, the way he had kept a low profile when anyone else of his status would have made waves. She lay back in the scented water and tried to think up ruses to stop the exposé going ahead. It was useless. Short of murdering Lou Bryan there was not a bloody thing she could do about it. She heaved herself out of the water and went in search of a drink.

'Only me.' Chris pocketed his key and shut the door of the flat. He had an hour and a half to shower, pack an overnight bag and get over to Euston, but there was time for a coffee. He was filling the kettle and wondering just who else was in the flat, when Dilly appeared in the kitchen doorway.

'I thought you were back at the treadmill,' he said. 'Want a coffee?'

She shook her head and hitched a hip onto the pine table. 'Nope. Ta. I've just got in. Cliffy won't be back till midnight. He left a message on the answering machine. I'm sick of him always being off somewhere while I'm tied to the grindstone. It's just as well we're finished.'

'You can do strands next year,' Chris comforted. 'Cliff'll've gone by then and you'll have a good chance. I wouldn't put in for it — not my scene. Amy wants to go to documentaries and none of the rest are up to it.' He stirred his coffee and sipped. 'Ooh, I needed that.'

Dilly was smiling at him, swinging a bare leg backwards and forwards as she perched on the table. 'You are a sweetie, Chris. I know I give you a hard time sometimes but you're always trying to cheer me up.' She raised both her arms. 'Come here and get a hug.'

For a moment Chris stood still, unable to believe his ears and also unable to move. Of course she was kidding . . . well, not kidding, just being friendly. His brain screamed caution but his treacherous body was betraying him. He put down the mug and moved forward until her two thin scented arms were round his neck, her lips brushing his cheek, his temple, the corner of his eye. He kept his eyes down, seeing the curve of her shoulder, the faint gold hairs on her arms, the tiny hole in the lobe of her ear where once an earring had hung.

'Hey!' She had drawn back her head and was looking up at him. 'Put your arms around me, dope – unless you don't want to, that is?'

Beneath his hands her cotton sweater was riding up, moving until his fingers encountered the bare flesh of her torso, the rib cage barely beneath the surface. He expected an outcry but none came, not even when he turned his head so that his mouth encountered her mouth, two sets of lips touching, opening, fusing.

He moved his fingers then, up over the thin ribs to the place where her breast swelled. There was a singing in his ears now and although he desperately needed air he could not contemplate removing his mouth from hers. His fingers probed gently until they met her nipple, tiny and hard and erect.

I'm dreaming, he thought, but it didn't matter. Dream or reality, this was what he had been born for.

Liz would have stayed at her desk, immersing herself in work to shut out everything else, but the prospect of coming face to face with Simon was intimidating. There had been a sea-change in their relationship and she knew it. Before, they had always sought each other out after a spat. This time she was avoiding Simon and the very fact that he had not sought her out showed that he felt the same.

So she resolutely put aside matters crying out to be finalised, locked her desk and quit her office. She could have summoned up a cab and charged it to the company but she felt a need to walk in the open air, and even the rain did not deter her.

She walked from the studio towards the City, not caring whether she was going in the right direction, oblivious of the rain upon her face, even when it ran in rivulets between her collar and her neck. People blundered past her, hurrying to get into the dry. A woman, face hidden behind an umbrella, bumped into her and cursed her for not getting out of the way but Liz simply plodded on. In a way, it felt good to be cold and wet and degraded. She kept on walking until the water penetrated her summer shoes and the unpleasant squelching sensation forced her aboard a passing bus.

She had to stand at first and then a window seat came vacant and she squeezed gratefully past the knees of a smiling black woman who was getting out soon and didn't want to move.

She leaned her face against the glass and thought of the night ahead. Would Simon ring and if he did would she speak to him? Should she let the phone ring or put on the answerphone? But the question that kept intruding, however hard she tried to suppress it, was whether Simon would respond to her ultimatum and what her own reaction to his answer would be.

She was regretting her action now. It didn't do to issue ultimatums, not in any sector of life, but especially not in love. Or work. And in effect she had issued a double ultimatum, for if she and Simon were to split she couldn't continue to work at Daybreak; that much was certain.

*   *   *

Simon stayed in his office until Amy, his favourite among the researchers, came in to ask his opinion on an item she was handling. 'Everyone gone?' he asked as casually as he could.

The Asian girl's smile was wry. 'Of course not. We're all out there, heads down. We have this terrible slavedriver of a deputy editor . . .'

'All right,' he said. 'I only asked.' And then he said, nonchalantly, 'Is Liz in her office?'

'No. Liz's gone home for once. About half an hour ago. I saw her waiting for the lift.'

'Ah,' he said, keeping his eyes glued to the documents Amy had given him. 'Never mind, I'll see her tomorrow.' Fifteen minutes later he was out of his office and making his way to the outer doors. He had a sudden longing to get home, to take stock, to sit at the family table and remind himself of his situation.

There were cries of delight as he opened the door and extracted his key from the lock. 'Daddy!' Rosie was hurling herself into his arms and Jane appeared in the kitchen doorway.

'Darling . . . what a lovely surprise. I'm afraid your meal isn't ready. You're never home this early.' And then she was in the fold of his arm, nibbling his ear and whispering. 'Sorry I got pissed last night, darling. Were you OK? But wasn't it good?'

He hoisted his daughter still higher and looked down into his wife's face. 'I missed you all so I left everything on my desk and came home.' He smiled as he spoke, but his own hypocrisy was gnawing at him. How easily he might be standing in Liz's hall now, saying, 'I missed you so I rang home and made an excuse.'

Rosie was shrieking, 'Daddy, daddy', to get his attention but some strange chemistry was changing the words as they fell from her childish mouth so that the sound that rang in his ears was 'Liar, liar!'

'Euston,' Chris said and subsided onto the back seat. As the taxi moved away from the kerb he closed his eyes and put his head back against the leather of the cab's upholstery. He wanted — he *needed* — to still his thoughts, make sense of it, remember every detail. Had it happened? It had happened, his spent body was evidence of that. But how? And why?

It's what I wanted, he told himself. He tried to remember it . . . it had been good. Of course it had been good! Fantastic, even. Fucking fantastic! But the pun did not amuse. It's what I wanted, he told himself again. Or it's what I thought I wanted. I scored! With Dilly! Dilly, for God's sake.

Just for once the runes had fallen right — so why did he feel so goddamn flat?

They had stayed where they were for a few seconds, kissing, exploring — and then she had begun to urge him towards the bedroom. He had never been in her room before. Not properly in. Usually he was pounding on her closed door or half in the doorway carrying on a conversation as she searched for something she had lost and needed desperately. Now he was drawn into its cluttered and scented depth and she was reaching crossed arms to pull her sweater up and over her head.

Her breasts had come into view then, round and full. He had wanted to bring his mouth down on them, crush them in his fingers, and even as he thought it she reached out and took his head between her hands and pulled it down to fulfil his wish.

At first his only fear had been that he would come too soon and disgrace himself. He had felt it happening – or threatening to happen – before he could sling off his own clothes. Must be a good lover. Foreplay. Foreplay! Every article he had ever read was coursing through his brain but none of the information was sticking. What did he do now? There had been sex before, with a dozen or more partners, but never a consummation like this, the climax of months of wanting. She was laughing at his frenzied attempts to hold back so that he might pleasure her, guiding him into her until their bodies were beating a frenzied tattoo and it was over. 'Was it good?' Dilly had said, panting, and he had said, 'Yes. Brilliant.' But all the time a funny little phrase was running through his mind: 'Travelling is better than arriving.'

When the kids had gone to bed they sat down to their meal, either side of the table. 'This is so nice,' Jane said. 'Can you do it more often?' Simon smiled but his chicken stuck in his throat. This would be his life for the rest of his days. He looked at his wife's face, softened now because she was happy but capable of contorting with rage if he forced her to it. And he had forced her, putting all the weight of marriage and parenthood onto her, seeing providing as his only role. As long as he brought home the money, nothing else mattered. Or so he had thought. Now he knew better.

Could he stay with Jane? Looking across at her as she sliced the dessert and handed him a plate he knew that he loved her, but it was not the love he had wanted, the love that burned within you and made you feel alive.

'It was a lovely meal, Jane,' he said. 'I'll just nip up and check the kids and then I'll make the coffee. You put your feet up.'

'It's OK,' she said. 'You're the one who's had a hard day.' She looked happy as she spoke and he knew she meant it. On other days she had said just the opposite. 'You sit at a desk all day and issue orders and I'm here with two kids, run off my feet. Try it — you try it — you wouldn't last a day.'

What had effected the change? He knew but didn't want to admit it. She was inspired at the thought of another pregnancy. She liked being pregnant, was always radiant and fulfilled, never grumbling about clothes or the fact that she couldn't sleep on her face as she liked to do. Never minded being sick for three months and ungainly for six. He had married a woman who was born to be a mother, which was the female function if you thought about it. Jane was fulfilling her natural role. He was the one who was out of step, who wanted to deny the purpose of life, which was to reproduce.

What the hell am I going to do? he thought as he moved apple pie round and round his mouth.

It was not until he stood, looking down on his sleeping children, that he knew, beyond doubt, what he must do. He must stay and complete the task he had started in one mad moment in the back of a Ford Cortina.

18

Friday 4.30 a.m.

In the night Chris had dreamed of cats, black cats, ginger cats, a white cat big as a house with green glass eyes. It was a relief when his alarm call came and he could sit up in the wide hotel bed and feel the sweat cool on his naked body. He sat, eyes shut, thinking of the moment when he must face the office. Would they know? Was it written in his face? Would Clifford crease him for poaching?

He tried to savour the memory. In parts it had been as good as, even better than, he had dreamed it would be. So why, unless he concentrated, did he keep thinking of Amy and what she would say when she knew? And she *would* know. Nothing in that office could be secret for long. Would he ever have a relationship like that of the elderly couple in the room next door? Their every glance had radiated total trust and undying love. Was Dilly capable of fidelity? He wanted to think so but reason said not. Her routine had been well oiled, as expert as his had been inept.

In the end he threw back the splendid bed linen and took a cold shower. His breakfast came at 4.45 – the full works as it was on the company.

He relished the crisp bacon, the well-packed sausages, the mushrooms, tomato, hash browns and finally the fried egg, which he put whole into his mouth so as not to lose one atom of the runny stuff. He was cramming toast into his mouth as he took a last look round the room before going next door to collect his charges.

He could hear them behind the door, whispering hastily to each other. At last Sid opened the door a crack. 'Oh, it's you, Chris.' He opened the door wider and motioned him inside.

'You haven't eaten your breakfast?' He had ordered full English breakfasts for them when he had ordered his own.

Mary turned wide eyes on him. 'It's the middle of the night, pet. I couldn't touch a bite. The tea was nice, though, and Sid had one of those puff pastry things.'

'Croissants,' Chris said. 'Well, we'll get you something at the studio. Tell me when you feel like it. Now, are you ready?'

He shepherded them into the lift, carrying their bags himself. The hotel corridors were quiet and deserted at this unearthly hour. As the lift doors closed he looked at his charges reflected in the mirrored walls, seeing their hands snake out until they touched and held. That was love, taking comfort from each other. However his relationship with Dilly turned out, last night had been a good screw, no more. He knew that now. As he handed the lovers into the waiting car he felt such a wave of affection for them that it threatened to choke him.

Simon had closed his eyes, trying to catch a few tranquil moments before the car reached the studios. Then his phone rang. It was God, sounding alert but speaking softly so as not to wake whoever was sharing his bed. 'Simon, I've got reservations about the running order. Too tight. We need about six minutes out by my reckoning.'

'Six minutes?' Simon tried not to let his irritation show. The editor had had the script since two o'clock yesterday. Why make changes now, when everyone was locked into it? 'Difficult to shave that much,' he said, trying not to sound confrontational.

'You can't.' The answer came back pat so the sod had already decided what was out. This wasn't going to be a discussion: it was going to be an execution. 'Drop the old couple – I had doubts about that from the start. It's five and a half. Take thirty seconds off the intro – it waffles on a bit, anyway.'

For a moment Simon was tempted to rebel, but a sudden weariness had overtaken him. He was fighting for his ruddy life – his emotional life anyway – and had neither the energy nor the inclination to fend for anyone else. 'OK,' he said. 'If that's how you want it.

We couldn't tamper with the Vincent slots — they're cast-iron. See you later.'

Once upon a time he would have stood his ground, argued that decency demanded the old couple got at least a showing after their long journey. He winced as he thought of their families, waiting at home, videos probably preset. Jesus Christ! Well, at least they could give them a phone to make calls — and a whopping present. Liz would see to that. Liz! He shouldn't have let thoughts of Liz intrude. Last night Jane had whispered, 'You will always love me, Simon, won't you?' and he had answered, 'Always.'

'I wish I were dead,' he said under his breath and turned his face to the window to look out at passing London through unseeing eyes.

The notes were there in Vincent's head when he woke. F sharp, F, A, B flat, A flat, G, D sharp, A flat. He picked them out on his keyboard as he towelled hair wet from the shower. He felt a sense of relief now that it was Friday. One more ordeal at Daybreak and duty was discharged. And it wasn't really fair to call it an ordeal. Yesterday had been easy enough. They'd all been helpful, especially Liz Fenton. He might take her to dinner sometime, except that she was probably heavily involved elsewhere.

He crossed to the window and pulled back the drapes. Above the river the morning sky was clear blue, the dome of St Paul's appearing to have a rosy halo. He felt a sudden surge of excitement, of anticipation. Perhaps there were good times ahead.

As he padded on bare feet towards his dressing room he was smiling. Once he finished in the studio and the album was in production he could take off. Sun and sand and acres of deserted beach. He deserved it. He wouldn't go till Bermondsey was on course but even that was going well. And perhaps he had a passable song gestating inside him. He began to hum once more.

'I'm sorry, Chris. We'll have to pull your item.' Simon had called the researcher into his office to detach him from the old couple, to whom he seemed to be bonded, judging from the way he was hovering over them.

'I don't understand.' Behind his glasses, the young man's eyes were startled. 'You don't mean . . .'

'Colin says we're too tight. He wants six minutes out. Yours is the only thing we can drop today. Everything else is a fixture for one reason or another. I'm sorry. Make it up to them. Take them to lunch – anywhere you like . . .'

'They've come two hundred and fifty miles.' Chris's voice was almost a squeak. 'They're . . . they're over the moon about being on the show. Their families are watching, Simon. You can't do this!'

He looked close to tears and Simon felt a surge of sympathy. But if he said he agreed and didn't want to do it himself, the argument would go on and on. 'I'm sorry,' he said shortly. 'I don't give the orders, I take them. Like you do! Now go and get rid of them, as diplomatically as you can. This is not a benevolent institution, Chris. This is television.'

Daphne leaned her head against the cab's upholstery and thought about tomorrow. No need to set the alarm, no haggard face in the bathroom mirror — well, not before noon anyway. Tonight she might go over to the pub, stay over even. She felt like a bender.

And Brian was so good to her. As they moved towards the Daybreak studios she listed his virtues. He was steady. He was faithful . . . it was his wife who had left him. He was good in bed, He was considerate. He was sexy. She cast a guilty look at the driver, sure his eyes would be on the rear-view mirror wondering why the hell she was smiling vacantly, but mercifully his eyes were fixed on the traffic.

He was moderately well-off if you counted his police pension, and he loved her. That above all. I am loved, she thought and was uncomfortably aware that if he ever got fed up and went elsewhere she would be unloved.

Shit, she thought, determined to have a well-laced coffee as soon as she hit the studios. But even as those same studios appeared through the windscreen she knew that no amount of alcohol would help tonight. Whatever she did, wherever she was, there would be only one topic on her mind: Vincent, and the fate that would overtake him when the *Herald* hit the streets.

She made straight for the green room and poured herself a coffee, augmenting it from her pocket flask because, sooner or later this morning, she would come face to face with Vincent and she didn't know how she would bear it.

'Look at that . . . and that . . . and that!' Birgitta, the weather girl was hurling letters onto Liz's desk. 'And this one says I look like Paula Yates — I can't bear it!'

Liz shuffled the letters, seeing a phrase here and there . . . 'most unbecoming' . . . 'look a right mess'. And one, written in green ink, which began, 'Welcome earthling'. She cleared her throat to disguise an uncomfortable chuckle and looked up at Birgitta. 'There's always resistance to change. You know that. Viewers want you to stay the way you were but that doesn't mean you should. Change is good for you.'

The girl leaned forward to put her hands on the desktop and stare into Liz's face from a distance of six inches. 'This isn't change, Liz. It's total bloody destruction. If this was any other industry, I could sue. But because it *is* this industry that bitch can do what she likes with me. I'm expendable. My hair's expendable. What will she want to change next. My knees resemble hers? Chop them off! My nose? That could go! But not my tits. My tits are different to hers because she hasn't got any! Unless the cow's facing backwards and those two little . . . protruberances are her shoulder blades! Oh God, I could go mad.' Beneath the platinum wig her face stared out, defiantly brunette.

'You'll have to put up with it for now,' Liz said wearily. 'Give Simon time — he'll sort something out.'

But as she uttered the words she pondered. *She* had given Simon time — eight months of her life, to be precise. And what had he sorted out?

This was crunch time, she told herself firmly as she went in search of coffee. She had issued an ultimatum! But as she returned, carefully balancing cup and saucer, she couldn't help remembering how many times in the past six months she had backed down when deadlines had not been met.

Vera paused in her tidying of Barry's dressing room and listened as the two presenters, above her on the monitor, catalogued the highlights of the show ahead. 'And of course we have Vincent with us . . .'

A shot of Vincent, smiling uncomfortably, appeared on the monitor and Vera raised a hand to blow him a kiss. She had five thousand pounds thanks to Vincent and his pound coin. Or she would have when she had done the necessary. She had phoned the helpline, preferring that to marching into the shop and letting the world know her business. They had asked her about publicity and she had said not a word. Not that five thousand was special. The tone of the helpline had told her that. Chickenfeed! But to her . . . she still felt weak at the thought of it. Five thousand one-pound coins would stretch for miles. And all she had to do was take the ticket to a Camelot regional office to be validated and for a security check — and then she got the cash.

Where would she keep it? Not in a bank. She'd

never had a bank account except the Giro and that was in Fred's name. She could hide it in the house, but where was safe from burglars — and from Fred? He was always rummaging around for something he'd lost or thought he'd had once. He never threw anything out. Or brought anything in, the mean sod. Everything's down to me, she thought bitterly. He was nice with that cup of tea last night but that was just a flash in the pan.

Well, things were different now. She was a woman of substance, just like a Barbara Taylor whatsit heroine! She looked around at walls lined with photographs of Barry at various stages of his career. No need to blackmail him now. He could go on thinking his wig was his little secret. Perhaps, when she left, she could scrawl 'Bare as a badger's bum' across his mirror in make-up. Just to remind him she knew.

She was enjoying this lovely daydream when Theo poked his head round the door. 'Any chance of a brew, Vee? I've got a nice little titbit about our Carol.'

'What?' She was instantly alert.

'I'll tell you when we have our cuppa.'

'Now!' The possession of five thousand pounds was making her bold. Theo blinked and obeyed.

'Well, apparently she went to lunch with Victor Kerslake last week.' He paused for astonishment but Vera's brow only puckered. 'Who's he?'

'The boss! The Big White Chief. He *is* Daybreak.'

'Oh,' Vera said, unimpressed. 'So what happened?' If it was only lunch that was nothing.'

'They went to lunch. She had her Jean Muir on — the grey number, plain as a dye . . . stunning. Well, she has the figure for a Jean Muir, flat as a board.'

'I know,' Vera said. 'Go on.'

'All right.' Theo was peeved. 'I'm doing my best. Well, they came back to his office and he says, "We're going to discuss contracts. Don't disturb us." I've heard it called some things but "contracts" is a new one.'

'What d'you mean?' Vera was curious now. She had never heard of innuendo but she knew what rolling eyeballs meant. Sex!

'They were in there an hour and when they came out . . .' Theo paused for maximum effect. 'When they came out, all business talk and "Mr Kerslake" and "Miss Cusack" . . .' He paused again until Vera's fierce expression forced him into a denouement. 'The Jean Muir was inside out. Label out the back, seams outside. Well, you know Jean Muir seams . . . works of art . . . but still . . .'

'You mean . . . she'd had her frock off?'

'I mean they'd been *at* it, darling — rumpy-pumpy. In the nuddy! I should be careful at her age, if I was her. Still, they say it keeps you young! Now, where's that tea?'

But Vera had money and money was power. 'Sorry,' she said sweetly. 'I've got to do their rooms while they're on.'

Carol was smiling benignly from the monitor as Vera cleaned her dressing room.

The fast cat, Vera thought, remembering the inside-out dress. She sank into the padded chair and looked at herself in the mirror with its ring of bright lights. Could she manage a sex life like Carol's? She leaned closer and grinned at herself in the mirror, thinking that the chance would be a fine thing. Fred would never be a sex fiend. He'd been keen enough before they married but the urge seemed to leave him at the altar.

In the beginning she'd tried all the tricks – saucy underwear, perfume, making the first move. And most of the time all he'd said was, 'Leave off, Vee.' Every time she picked up a magazine they were on about multiple orgasm. A single one would be nice!

Still, she had five thousand pounds now. Enough for a gigolo like Richard Gere. She would start with the tea dances. Everyone said you could pick up there. And if she was careful with the cash she could afford a cruise. She lolled back in Carol Cusack's chair and made plans.

Vincent had mastered the art of the Daybreak phone now. He dialled nine and then the site number. As the number rang out he watched the little cleaner – the one who looked like Hilda Ogden – as she ran a cloth over the hospitality trolley and removed the used cups and saucers. She had a faraway look in her eye. Probably thinking about her kids or her grandchildren. She must be fifty at least.

As the receiver was lifted at the other end of the line the cleaner looked up and caught him watching her. She smiled suddenly, dazzlingly, her face transformed. He tried to grin back, wondering just what had provoked such enthusiasm, and then a voice spoke at the other end of the line and he turned his attention to his beloved project.

The call was detailed and took a long time. Halfway through, he transferred the receiver to his other hand and half turned in his chair. The journalist from the *Herald* was watching him now and she too smiled at the sight of him, but her smiling was not as joyful as the little cleaner's. In fact, if he had not known better, he'd have thought it was the smile of someone in the grip of acute embarrassment.

Daphne let her smile slip as Vincent returned to his conversation. He was talking about the Bermondsey project, stressing that a certain kind of skirting board must be used for the bedrooms. Deep skirting board, not what he called 'piddling little two-inch stuff'. God, he was immersing himself in his hostel. If something went wrong . . .?

She thought of his songs. The lyrics were always sensitive. And sad. Above all they were sad, the words of someone who knew the meaning of pain. And if he didn't know already he certainly would know tomorrow. Discomforted, she got to her feet and went in search of a loo.

'I've tried to placate her, Simon,' Liz said. 'It won't work. She looks stupid and she knows it. Birgitta's no fool. We wouldn't employ her if she was.' She had come to his office on business, the business of a weather girl who looked like Little Weed.

'What do you expect me to do?' He was throwing back the ball. As usual, it would be up to her to decide and that wasn't fair.

'I expect you to earn your salary, Simon. I expect you to make a professional decision, instead of leaving things in the hope they'll sort themselves out. You're good at that! Very good, but this time it won't work.'

She had meant to wound him and she had succeeded. She saw that from the way his jaw had clenched. She saw it in his eyes, the eyes of a man on the rack. Now for the *coup de grâce*. 'I mean it, Simon. Birgitta won't wait much longer, and neither will I.'

'It's not as easy as that.'

'I know.' Suddenly she felt guilty. After all, she was free to make decisions. He was fettered, with bands of iron. He couldn't just walk out as she could, and if he did those iron fetters would become elastic, constantly pulling him back.

Even if I get him, she thought, I will never have him completely. I can get him out of his children's home, I can't get them out of his heart.

She put out a hand and touched his arm. 'We can't talk now. But you've got to do something about Birgitta. She's getting ready to snap.'

After half an hour on the studio floor Daphne sought sanctuary in the wardrobe room. 'Have you had enough of the madhouse?' Theo asked sympathetically and fetched them each a coffee.

'I think it's getting up early all this week.' Daphne said when he returned. Wouldn't do to confide her misery in Theo. He was the last person in the world with whom to share a secret. Not that it would be a secret after tomorrow.

'I thought you might've got pissed off with our friends,' Theo said. 'God knows they get on my wick. Insincere? That's not the word. They'll say anything to anyone as long as it gets them well in.'

In spite of her inner turmoil, Daphne felt her lips twitch. This was pot calling kettle with a vengeance. 'Who do you mean?' she asked.

'All of them!' Theo flung back his white mane and flicked ash from his cigarette. 'I mean, if they start out as human beings, they catch the smit. Come in sincere, go out shits. Well, it's the same in your game. I bet you . . .' suddenly he hesitated, wondering how to extricate himself.

'You bet I was a nice girl?' Daphne suggested.

'You still are!' Theo said gallantly but Daphne could not let go.

'No, I'm not,' she said. 'You're right. It makes shits of us all, the media. Oh, we don't all wield the knife but we're in there, snouts in the trough. My salary's paid out of other people's misery, Theo. And the worst thing is, I know it.'

'Oh Gawd!' Theo said. 'I can see I've touched a nerve here. Should've kept me gob shut. We couldn't do without the media, darling. I mean, we need to know.'

'Of course we do – of course we need to know, Theo. But there's something else that creeps in along with the information and that's spite! What's the quickest way to become Queen of Fleet Street? Be a bitch! How to become a television icon? Raise your tits and your skirt and host a sex show!'

'That's not spite,' Theo said. 'That's being outrageous. Don't tell me about that, darling. I've had to watch it strangle talent.' Suddenly his eyes rolled heavenwards. 'Tell you what, love. I'll ask Vee to pop out for a cup of cyanide and we can both escape. You've brought me right down now. Let's cry together.'

19

Friday 8.10 a.m.

'Stand by!' The commercial break was ending and Vincent composed his face as the floor manager counted down the seconds above the *Daybreak* jingle.

'Welcome back.' Carol beamed at the camera and then at Vincent, sitting beside her on the settee. 'Well, as I said before the break, we have Vincent here with us again today. Aren't we lucky!' She turned to throw to Barry, beaming at him as though he was her best friend.

'Yes,' Barry said, obeying the autocue where his words were rolling up. 'To have him for one day would have been something! To have him for two days is miraculous. But before we talk to Vincent about his new charity project we have some more film of it to show you. And of course, at the end of today's show, we'll have an exclusive – *exclusive* – chance to hear his latest single. What's it called, Vincent? "Ceiling in the Sky". But first, Bermondsey . . .' They all sat back as the VT rolled.

Vincent watched, seeing himself clamber aboard the hoist and ascend the side of the building, follow the site manager from level to level, inspect the progress of each stage of the reconstruction. It was a good piece of film and he relaxed. This Daybreak thing had taken a lot of time but it was going to be worth it. Already they'd had phone calls and letters to the studio. The nice woman with the tired eyes, Liz, had told him that when he was in make-up and promised to sort it all out with Dave. 'Let me know how I can help,' she'd said, and, unless he was a bad judge of character, she'd meant it.

Last night he had woken at 2.15, thinking of what Dave had said about bad vibes. Now, it didn't seem to matter. An hour or two more and he could be out with Juno. It would be good to be out in the open air . . . He realised the VT was ending and gave Barry and Carol his full attention.

The elderly couple were sitting in the green room when Chris entered and he saw that they were holding hands as they watched the early stages of the show unfold on one of the large television sets. They turned at his entry, looking excited and tremulous. 'Is it time?'

Chris felt his throat constrict. How could he tell him they'd just been dumped? He moved to sit opposite them, grateful that there was no one else in the room to overhear their humiliation. 'I'm terribly sorry,' he said. 'Things have gone wrong – the timings are all out. I'm afraid we're going to have to drop your item.'

They neither of them spoke. Instead they turned to look at each other with questioning eyes. 'Well,' the man said at last. 'Well . . .'

Go on, Chris urged silently. Get mad. Lash out. We fucking well deserve it!

But all they said was one sentence, spoken by her. 'Oh, well,' she said. 'We're not important.'

Impassioned, Chris knelt down beside her. 'You are important! Your story . . . it's lovely. It's kept me going all the week, thinking of something nice happening. I . . . we all hope you're going to be happy for years and years.'

He was spitting into the wind and he knew it. Nothing he could say or do would alter the fact that they weren't wanted. What was the phrase? 'Not wanted on voyage.' The good ship *Daybreak* would sail on, leaving them floating like so much jetsam.

'It's all right, lad.' The old man's face was no longer crestfallen, it was full of sympathy, which was really salt to his wound.

'I'm just so sorry,' Chris said. 'If it was up to me . . .' But it wasn't and it wouldn't be for years – never, probably.

He handed them the money he had wrested from Liz. 'This is to cover your expenses.' He waved aside their protestations that it was too much. 'It's the least we can do.'

When he had seen them into the car that would take them to Euston he felt like doing murder.

Amy was in the green room when he returned. 'I heard,' she said. 'It's shitty . . . have this coffee!' For a moment he contemplated hurling the cup at the wall but Amy's hand was on his arm, calming him. 'I'm going to send them all the photos we took of them – they're really nice. And some souvenirs – all the Daybreak trash. And Simon will send them a nice letter plus flowers and champagne for their big day. We'll make the best of it, Chris. It's not enough but it's better than nothing.'

'It's not enough!' His own sombreness shocked him and he could feel his eyes pricking but he didn't care if he was seen to cry. He felt like crying! 'It's fucking well not nearly enough!'

He was lifting the cup with trembling hands when Dilly came in. 'Bad luck,' she said, poking around the sandwiches. 'I heard from Theo. Hard luck when you'd spent so much time on setting it up. Still . . .' she looked closely at him. 'No need to be a cry-baby.'

It was Amy who spoke. 'Drop dead, Dilly. Or go away. Preferably the former.'

The 8.30 news bulletin was ending and Birgitta was standing in front of her weather chart. Liz put down her pen and gave her full attention to the screen. The girl was right, she did look awful! Ghastly! She picked up her pen and made a note to talk to make-up about it. If they couldn't fix her skin tones perhaps Birgitta would have to go. She'd get another job easily enough. She was good and it would be a shame to lose her. Still, they couldn't go on like this.

She was about to go in search of coffee when the phone rang. 'Simon's not with you, is he?' It was the switchboard.

'No. He's probably on the floor or in the box.'

'I've tried there. His wife's on the line . . . could you speak to her?'

'No,' Liz said. 'I can't think of anything I'd rather do less!'

As she put down the phone it rang again. She recognised the editor's voice even though he was spluttering with satisfaction. 'I've just got the overnights.'

'Oh?' Liz said. The overnight ratings were not official but they were a good indicator of success.

'They're fantastic. Brilliant. God bless Vincent.' We're ten per cent up . . . eat your heart out Michael Grade. Keep him sweet, Liz, whatever you do. If he can do this I want him back.'

When she had put down the phone she reflected that it was pleasing to think Vincent had such a following. He was a decent bloke — he deserved it.

She was picking up her pen to resume work when the phone rang again. 'Sorry,' the switchboard operator said. 'I've still got Simon's wife hanging on. I can't find him and she wants to talk to you.'

She wanted to wail 'Why me? It isn't fair' — but she couldn't do that. 'Put her through,' she said instead.

'Liz? How are you? We haven't seen you for ages . . .

well, *I* haven't. Where *is* that man of mine?' If Jane had sought through the dictionary she couldn't have chosen more hurtful words: 'That man of mine.' And the most hurtful part was that Jane had a right to say it.

There was only another fifteen minutes to go – the wine item, a news and weather update and a last chat with Vincent. Simon thought of the weekend. Two days free of this place. Two days with Jane which would probably be even trickier than Daybreak.

He left the studio, walking past the picture of Mandy Baker, which always reproached him, and went in search of Liz. If they got through Monday's forward planning perhaps he and Liz could get an hour together somewhere. Her place, maybe. The thought of taking her to bed was erotic but it must not happen. Never again.

Was she good in bed – extra good – or did he truly love her? Perhaps it was forbidden fruit that gave extramarital sex its fillip. He had been keen enough on Jane before they married, when sex had been snatched in the back seat of his father's car with a frantic search afterwards to make sure they had left no trace. Perhaps, if he had thrown in his lot with Liz, he'd have gone off her too. He would never know.

He pushed open the door of Liz's office.

'We have to talk,' he said.

Her voice, when she answered, was uncharacteristically sharp. 'Not here!' He was about to back out when she spoke again. 'Did your wife get you? She was ringing earlier.'

Your wife! That was what she had said. Not Jane.

'Are you mad at me?' he asked and, as she shook her head, he saw that her eyes were glittering with tears. He would have moved to comfort her but at that moment a researcher appeared.

'They want you in the gallery, Simon. Some trouble with the VT.'

Friday 8.50 a.m.

On the floor the wine expert was in full flow behind a table filled with bottles and jugs of fruit punch. 'Wine doesn't go with curry . . . well, that's the theory. But of course it's a load of nonsense.' She shook her curls merrily and looked around for anyone brave enough to contradict her. 'Nowadays, curries are subtle . . . delicate korma or a lovely rich Thai . . . find a fabulously fruity wine and you have the perfect combination. I'd go for a New World wine — Australian, South American . . .'

She poured wine into three glasses. 'Try this one. It's a Cape Afrika Rhine Riesling . . . South African . . . full-bodied . . .' She drank, rinsed the wine around her mouth and spat into the bowl. Carol and Barry followed suit, murmuring appreciation as they did so. 'A medium curry like a tikka masala . . . now that needs a *big* wine

. . . juicy. An Aussie red or a Chilean Cabernet.' They drank and spat again.

'If it's a hot vindaloo you fancy you need the biggest walloping red you can find. Try this South African Pinotage.'

As the wine tasting continued Daphne moved closer to Vincent, who was standing just out of camera range, ready for his final spot. As she came abreast of him he half turned and smiled at her. It was too much! She put out a hand and touched his arm. 'I have to talk to you. Now!' He looked a little startled but he responded to her hand and moved with her away from the cameras.

'I haven't much time,' he said and she nodded to show she understood.

They retreated to the semi-darkness of a corner and she plunged. 'The *Herald* are doing a piece on you tomorrow . . . nothing to do with me . . . they've got a photograph . . . of you and Harry Quinn.' She saw his eyes widen, his nostrils flare with shock. 'They're not pulling any punches. They'll say you were a rent boy. I can't stop them. I would if I could – but perhaps you can. I wanted you to know.'

She saw his lips tremble and then begin to form words but before he could speak they became aware of a sudden tension behind them, a stillness as though the whole studio was waiting for a pin to drop.

Daphne turned to see Birgitta standing at her weather chart. In front of her Barry and Carol stood with the wine expert. Carol was speaking, or rather trilling nervously. 'Well, tell us what's in store, Birgitta.'

'What did you mean, ". . . our own blonde weather bimbo"?' Birgitta's eyes were wide, her hands clasped over the godget that changed her choats as though it were a breastplate.

'Just a joke . . .' Carol was definitely uneasy now, putting up a red-tipped hand to smooth the back of her coiffure. It was a gesture that tipped the scale. Birgitta snatched off her blonde wig and stormed forward.

'I am a true brunette – which is more than can be said for you . . . you . . .' For a second she sought for words and, finding none, resorted to action, seizing the wine slops bowl. 'Try that for a rinse,' she said and upended it over Carol Cusack's head.

In the gallery Simon smote his forehead with the palm of his hand. 'Shit.' Wine was running down Carol's forehead, streaking her make-up, running down the sides of her nose. 'Cut to Barry! cut to Barry!' Simon yelled but even as the director switched shots Birgitta struck again.

'And don't you laugh, you . . . you baboon.' This time it was a jug of punch, sliced oranges and lemons floating on its surface, that she upended over Barry's toupee.

'Go to the sting, go to the sting,' Simon and the director screamed in unison. As music clanged out the director leaned back in his chair. 'That's her finished,' he said.

Simon shook his head. 'Oh no,' he said 'She's far from finished. She's made for life. She has that most precious of all titles, the word 'controversial' in front of her name. She'll guest on every chat show, land a top job and probably marry a captain of industry. That's what you get nowadays for behaving badly, my son. Instant stardom!'

In the cloakroom Daphne cupped water in her hand and patted her burning cheeks. There were coffee stains in the corners of her mouth and she wiped them away with a forefinger.

What have you done? she thought and winced at the answer. She ought to go and ring in a first-hand account of the contretemps on screen but somehow that drama had got lost in a much greater one. When she had turned back from the wine-throwing, Vincent was standing there, a thin white line around his mouth, his eyes bleak. And then he had turned on his heel and marched off the studio floor.

I'll be sacked, Daphne thought but it seemed not to matter. Except that there was nothing Vincent could do. The piece would run come hell or high water. All she had achieved by the loss of her job was an extra day's agony for Vincent. She turned from the basin to dry her hands and went in search of a phone.

'How is she?' Liz asked as Simon appeared in the editor's doorway. She had poured drinks for the assembled production team, who appeared to be suffering varying stages of shell-shock.

'I still can't believe it,' the director said, draining his glass in one gulp. 'Thank God we've got it on tape — it's fucking TV history.'

'How is she?' Liz asked again.

Simon shrugged. 'Having a nervous breakdown, as you might imagine. And Barry's wringing out his toupee.'

'Don't joke.' The editor was slumped in his chair, too weak even to reach for a food supplement. 'Who's going to face upstairs? Tell me that. Heads'll roll over this, Simon.' He put out his hands and gripped the table edge. 'We need to put out a statement. Could we say it was a stunt — a set-up?'

'No,' Simon and Liz spoke in unison.

'What then? Don't give me negatives. I need positives.'

'Ignore it,' Liz said, 'and when the press get onto us call it "creative tension".'

'The press are already onto it.' Simon's voice was flat.' I've put Delia in to help the press office. We can't avoid the headlines, Colin. The whole bloody world saw it. You can't keep it quiet.'

The Editor sighed and reached for his Beta-Carotene. 'Oh well,' he said, 'I expect it'll do wonders for the ratings.'

'It will,' Simon said sadly. 'God help us, it will.'

'She'll never be the same again,' Theo said dramatically. He paused and struck a pose. 'Personally, I loved every divine second of it — especially when the orange slice lodged on Barry's ear.'

'What'll happen to Birgitta?' Vera asked.

'She's gone. Liz put her in a taxi and sent her

home. Best thing ... I mean ... Carol was incandescent.'

'Will she lose her job?'

'If she sells her story, Vee, she'll never need to work again. Not like you and I.' He sighed heavily and drew on his fag.

For a moment Vera was tempted to tell him about her win but reason prevailed. She remembered what she'd heard one of the researchers say about Theo, something about his gob being better than the Internet, whatever that was, and it hadn't been a compliment. And if everyone here got to know it might get out. Might even make the papers. After all, she did work in television, which made her a bit special.

'I'll make a brew,' she said. 'What with all the drama, I could do with a break.'

Chris sat at his desk, head in hands, oblivious of the hubbub around him as everyone discussed the show's end. Sod Carol and Barry. Sod Birgitta too. All he could think of were the faces of the old couple, hurt but proud, keeping their dignity. There was no dignity in TV. It was all shit. He felt tears prick his eyes again and bit his lip to stem them.

Once upon a time he had wanted to be a social worker. It wasn't too late. And anything would be better than this ... this ... He sought for words and suddenly a phrase popped into his mind: 'shoddy compromise'. That about summed it up: 'this shoddy compromise'.

'Cheer up.' Amy was looking at him quizzically. 'I expect they're halfway home by now and not feeling nearly as bad as you do. I've wired them flowers and notified their local paper. I know someone there — he's going to do a nice little piece. Something for them to cut out and keep.'

'Better than telly,' Chris said bitterly. 'That's gone in a flash. Still, ta, Amy.' He sighed. 'Fancy a meal tonight by way of a thank-you? I need a friend. I don't feel like being on my own.' Amy understood him, the only one who did. The only one who'd helped.

But somehow, in some way, he'd said the wrong thing. She looked at him coldly. 'If you want a friend, Chris, get a dog. I'm going out tonight. Still . . . Dilly might be *available*.' There was an accent on the last word that left him in no doubt that Dilly had told Amy everything. About last night's sex, about his doglike devotion . . . and now he didn't even want Dilly. 'Life sucks,' he said but he said it under his breath.

In the mêlée that followed the wine incident it was easy enough for Vincent to escape, picking his way between cables and cameras towards the first exit sign that caught his eye. He felt sick, physically sick, so sick that he feared he might vomit at any moment.

He slipped through a door and found himself in a bleak uncarpeted corridor, obviously meant for the eyes of staff only. He saw a door ahead with the letters 'WC' on it. A moment later he was locked inside a tiled chamber which held a huge and stained toilet bowl and a toilet roll dispenser scarred by a thousand forgotten cigarette ends.

He put down the seat cover and sat on it to put his head in his hands, but, even as he waited for the blackness to descend, a kind of relief intervened. He need never again fear discovery. He was discovered and there was nothing else to be done but go along with it.

He started to laugh suddenly. What a turn-up. The thing he had dreaded for so long had happened and the sky hadn't fallen. Never would fall now. No one would want him – or his music. Dave would be off like a streak in search of a better prospect but there was money enough in the bank and the royalties might still roll in.

He tried to remember other composers who'd fallen from grace but whose music had survived, but couldn't come up with a single name. It seemed not to matter. As long as he could feed Juno and support his mother, none of it mattered and the sale of the lease on his flat should cover that.

He sat in the loo for as long as possible but in the end he had to emerge. To his relief, no one was looking for him, not even Dave. He moved cautiously towards the main corridor but suddenly the funny little cleaner was barring his way.

'Can I get you anything, Mr . . . Vincent?' She was smiling at him in a funny way, a mixture of curiosity and what looked suspiciously like gratitude. Surely she couldn't know? Not yet.

'Thanks . . . I'm fine,' he said.

She put out a hand and touched his arm. Gently. 'You'll never know what you've done for me. That's a fact. I can't thank you enough. You've changed my life.'

And then she was gone, leaving him to seek the comfort of the green room and the coffee machine. She had looked at him with such . . . almost devotion. Did his music mean that much to people?

As if on cue, the journalist reappeared. 'Are you OK?' she said. 'I didn't mean to upset you – I just thought you ought to know.'

'Thank you. I'm grateful.' He looked down at his cup. When he looked up again he felt himself smiling ruefully. 'So it's out. How about me telling the story? In my own words. The unexpurgated version.' He looked in the direction of Vera's retreat. 'I think I owe it to the people who like my music to tell them the truth.'

_____ *21* ___

Friday 10.00 a.m.

As she waited for Lou Bryan to pick up her
telephone, Daphne's heart thudded uncomfortably.
She was not handing Vincent's story on a plate to Lou
Bryan, but the features editor would resist any attempt
by Daphne to do the piece herself or to present Vincent's
account of his life in any but a sensational way.

The ringing tone ceased and a voice said, 'Lou's
phone.'

'I need Lou . . .' Daphne sounded desperate when she
meant to sound determined. 'Get her, wherever she is.
It's urgent. It's me, Daphne.' A moment later Lou Bryan
was there.

'What is it, Daphne? I'm in the middle of something
important —'

'This *is* important. It's Vincent. He knows about the
story coming out . . .'

'Who told him?'

'I don't know.' She was lying in a good cause and it troubled her not at all. 'But he does know . . . he says if we dump the exposé he'll give us the true story. An exclusive. Pictures, details, the lot.' There was a low whistle at the other end of the line. 'There's one catch, Lou. He'll only give it to me.'

'No way.' Lou's tone was definite. 'This needs Mike . . . you can sit in. Hold his hand, keep him sweet . . . I'll get Mike . . .'

'It's no good, Lou. It's me or nothing. He's adamant.'

'Why? What've you said. It's not up to him . . .'

'Of course it's up to him, Lou. It's his story, for God's sake.'

'He can stuff it then – we'll go with the piece as it is. He can't go anywhere else in time . . .' She was still talking as Daphne depressed the rest and redialled.

'Give me the editor's secretary. It's Daphne Bedford and I've got dynamite here.'

Five minutes later she had the authority to do the exclusive. One thousand words by 3 p.m. and the rest of the story in three double pages on Monday, Tuesday and Wednesday. 'I've done it,' she said when she went back to Vincent. 'I need to sit down with you now and drain you – but the only version we print will be yours.'

It was eleven o'clock before Simon could return Jane's call. 'Sorry I couldn't ring sooner. The shit hit the fan . . . oh, you saw.' She sounded scared at the other end of the line. 'No,' he said gently. 'I won't be fired. Tomorrow the ratings will soar. Don't give it a thought.'

By the time he put down the phone he felt weary, but Jane, at least, was reassured. He ran his hands through his hair and thought about Liz. The tension had grown between them in the last few days. He was nerving himself to seek her out when there was a knock at the door.

'Chris . . . what can I do for you?' The young man looked wary but determined, his eyes a bit hostile behind his spectacles.

'It's about dropping my item today . . . I don't think it was right. In fact I think it was bad editorial judgement —'

He got no further. All the pent-up agony of Simon's week found vent. 'You don't think it was right? And who the fuck are you to *think* at all. We don't hire you to think, laddie. We hire you to gofer. And as for the lovebirds . . . they are the least of our problems. They're yesterday's news. You work out how I play things on Monday. Do I pretend my weather girl didn't assault my main presenters? Do I open on her hanging from a scaffold? Do I bring in a conciliator and do mediation right there on the settee . . . or do I show a fucking replay? When you've solved those problems ask me about editorial judgement. Until then get out of my goddamned office before I do something we'll both regret.'

*　　*　　*

Liz had sought refuge in her own room from the general misery pervading the office. She wanted a drink badly. On the other hand she had never been in greater need of a clear head. She was trying to decide whether or not to have a shot of whisky when there was a knock at her door and Daphne Bedford came into the room.

'I'm sorry to bother you . . .' The journalist looked flustered but determined. 'And I can't really explain — there isn't time — but Vincent is in trouble. Big trouble. I'm trying to help him but we need somewhere we can talk in private — and for quite a while.'

Liz hesitated only for a second. 'You can have this office,' she said, standing up and collecting the things she might need in the next few hours.

'I'll get him,' Daphne said. A moment later she reappeared, Vincent in tow. He looked pale but not unhappy, less a man in trouble than a man who had seen the light.

'I'm just going,' Liz said but the singer put out a restraining hand.

'Unless you're needed desperately I'd appreciate it if you stayed. For a while at least. I need to think clearly . . . it would help if you were here. Don't ask me why, it just would.'

For the second time Liz hesitated only for a second. 'OK,' she said. 'I'll stay until they scream for me. But first I'm going to get us all some coffee. Then you can get down to work.'

'Before we start,' Daphne said, as soon as Liz had left the room, 'let me say one thing. I'm not proud of everything my profession does but, in the main, we want to print the truth. And I think we need the press — a free press —'

Vincent held up a hand to staunch her flow. 'We don't disagree on that. God help us if there wasn't some force to expose corruption. It was a reporter who finally put Harry Quinn out of harm's way. You'll get no argument from me. Let's just get it over with.'

A moment later Liz appeared with a pot and three mugs on a tray. There was milk and sugar there too and a half-bottle of Glenfiddich. 'Just in case your flask runs dry,' she said.

Vincent took his coffee black and sugarless, the women both took theirs white. All of them had a generous slew of the Glenfiddich.

'Right,' Vincent said when they were settled. 'Where do I begin? My father died when I was seven — almost seven — it all began then.'

Around Chris, the office was profoundly quiet, as though the drama in the studio floor earlier had sucked up everyone's energy. He toyed with papers and reference books, trying to make sense of his jumbled thoughts.

Simon's viciousness had stung him but the thing that was troubling him most, the picture he couldn't erase from his thoughts, was the look the elderly couple had exchanged, the look that said, 'We don't matter. It is right that we do not make it onto the TV screen because we are not important.' And rising out of that uncomfortable picture, a 64,000-dollar question. Did he want to go on working in a medium that had no place for an ordinary couple with their unimportant love story?

If he and Dilly had made it . . . and he knew now that they wouldn't, for the reality had extinguished desire in a way that he could not yet fathom but quite accepted. But if he and Dilly *had* truly loved and lasted and grown old together, would their love not have mattered to the media? Because it had lasted, it was deep and abiding. Would that rule it out as acceptable TV?

He put his head in his hands at last and thought about no more Daybreak. Could he live without this daily fix of excitement and anticipation and achievement and failure? When he lifted his head at last he knew that he could.

The story had flowed from Vincent's lips, at first haltingly, then with increasing fluency. But he backtracked often and sometimes leaped forward, which meant that Daphne's notes would take hours to decipher if she was to present a polished end product. And for Vincent's sake, as well as her own, she must do just that.

'So when you escaped from Harry Quinn's you went back to the streets?'

'Yes, at first. I went to St Martin's, behind there. There was another boy, not long down from Edinburgh. We slept back to back for a couple of nights . . .' He saw her bemused face and elaborated. 'If you're going to be attacked it'll come from the back so you find someone you trust and you sleep, sitting up, back to back like two bookends. You prop one another up like bookends.'

Daphne closed her eyes for a second, aghast at the picture of two boys — hardly more than children — sitting up all night leaning against each other for safety. 'How did you know you could trust him? You hardly knew him.'

She glanced towards Liz as she spoke and saw such a look of compassion on her face that she felt her own lips tremble. She looked back at Vincent.

'You're right. I hardly knew him. But he was young, like me, and he looked scared and I didn't have much option. I knew I couldn't fend off sleep for ever so I took a chance on him.'

'And it paid off?'

His smile was wry. 'It did the first night. The second, I woke up in the dawn to find he'd gone off with my shoes.' He leaned forward. 'But that was rare. There was a comradeship there, we supported one another.'

Before she could reply the telephone rang. 'I'll take it,' Liz said, but after a moment she held the receiver to her chest and mouthed at Daphne. 'It's for you — a Lou Bryan?' Daphne shook her head vigorously and Liz nodded to show she understood.

'I'm sorry, I'm not sure that Miss Bedford is still in the building.' Obviously Lou was giving vigorous protest at the other end of the line. 'Well, if you'll hold on, I'll check.' She depressed the receiver rest several times and when she spoke again it was to the Daybreak operator. 'Can you transfer this call to an outside desk. I'll take it there.' She listened for a moment and then replaced the receiver, smiling at Vincent and then at Daphne as she did so. 'I'll leave you two in peace and sort her out. I take it you don't want to talk to her?'

'Not at any price,' Daphne said and returned to her questioning as Liz left the room. At least she would have done if Vincent had not interrupted.

'Come back as soon as you can,' he said. 'It helps to have you here.'

'Do you believe in fate, Theo?' Vera asked. The dresser looked up, startled at Vera's unaccustomedly sombre tone. Behind him the racks of clothes looked like a medieval arras, ironing board to the left, cheval mirror to the right as accountrements.

'Believe in her, Vee? I've lived with the madam for years. Got it in for me, she has. When I got out of bed this morning I knew she had it in for me. "That's right," I told her, "have another go – I can take it." And look what she does – I'm limp with today's carry on. Limp. Carol's gone on like a whirling dervish. And I've had to pick the pips out of that astrakhan of his. Thank God for beta-blockers, Vee. My ticker's taken a pounding today. Of course I believe in fate. Sodding bitch that she is. Why d'you ask?'

He was curious now, so she would have to be careful. 'I think I've reached a crossroads, Theo.'

'Marriage problems?' He was sympathetic now. 'Hang on to him, Vee. Unless he gives you a fourpenny one. I wouldn't stand for that. But if he's not brutal I'd stick it out. It's lonely on your own, Vee.'

Suddenly he looked his age, the leathery face grown monkeylike under the white mane, the mouth — for once devoid of spite — oddly vulnerable. But she wasn't Theo. Mentally she squared her shoulders, conscious of her strength. She was younger for a start, and a woman, which meant she was streets ahead. Best of all, she had five thousand pounds. She could not only exist on her own, she could thrive.

When Liz finally put down the phone on the *Herald* features editor she had convinced her that, wherever Vincent and the *Herald* reporter were, they were not in the Daybreak building. She had been using a researcher's desk so she could pretend to fuss with papers while she collected her thoughts. And she needed to think. Listening to Vincent's tale, the bleakness of his childhood, the horror of his adolescence, had helped to put her own problems into perspective. She sighed and levered herself to her feet. She must go back in there and give whatever support she could.

'And that was it, really.' Vincent leaned back and stretched his arms above his head. 'I'll dig out the photographs tonight, and the diary I told you about.' For a moment his voice faltered and the relief that had come over him as he talked left his face.

'It'll be all right,' Daphne said. 'People can be amazing when they understand.'

'And they will understand.' Liz was holding his gaze, emphasising every word. 'They'll understand, just as I do.'

Daphne left them together and went in search of a private phone. 'This is for the front page,' she told copy. 'FAO the editor. Catchline Vincent. Byline Daphne Bedford. Rock megastar Vincent revealed today that he once was forced to serve as a rent boy in London. Stop. In a recent interview with the *Herald* the six-times gold-disc winner whose music has dominated the British charts tells of the tormented childhood which led to his falling into the hands of a pimp, who is now in jail.'

As she went on talking her mind raced. She had done it at last, landed the *big* story. For the next few days her byline would dominate the feature pages. Tomorrow she would make the front page. She imagined the straplines, headlines and subheads: ROCK STAR IN AMAZING REVELATIONS . . . I WAS A VICTIM . . . VINCENT TELLS THE HERALD . . .

I've made it, Daphne thought, thinking of Lou Bryan's chagrin. I've made it, so why do I feel so low?

22

Friday 5.30 p.m.

As the bus neared her stop Vera got to her feet. Her head was still full of the drama of the day. If she was on speaking terms with Fred, what a tale she'd have to tell him. She pictured his eyes round with shock. 'She never? Over her head? Carol Cusack?' For a moment she contemplated calling a truce, just for the evening, but pride prevailed. He had started it, with his moaning about the beef stew. She would finish it. And, if she carried out her intention, she would be finishing it with a vengeance.

It was starting to rain again as she got off the bus and she ran the block and a half to her door, fumbling for her key as she went. There was a strange smell as she pushed open the door, an exotic, spicy smell, and Fred was in the kitchen doorway, looking sheepish, a tea towel in his hand.

'I got off a bit early . . . I thought you might like a night off the cooking so I called in the Chinese.' It was there on the table, orange and yellow and red, in cartons, fragrant and mouthwatering. Just what she fancied. She slowly took off her coat and laid it over the back of a chair, trying all the while to sort out her feelings.

'Well?' he said, obviously expecting praise but scared he wasn't going to get it.

'Very nice,' she said. 'A bit of a surprise. I was going to make corned-beef fritters . . . but very nice all the same. Can you put it in the oven while I pop upstairs and get changed. This waistband's killing me.'

She was playing for time, time to assess his behaviour and her own reaction to it. What a swine to throw her into confusion like this when she'd made up her mind. What had come over him? Cups of tea and Chinese takeaways? Was he having an affair?

In her dressing table mirror she surveyed herself critically. There was a flush to her cheeks and a light in her eyes. No, that was daft. No one changed overnight. Could he know about the five thousand pounds? Was that the reason for all this attention? No. He couldn't know because no one knew. No one but her. For the first time in her life she had a secret.

She sat on the end of the bed for a while thinking about cruises. Dinner at the captain's table was fine but afterwards . . . A lonely bunk didn't seem so inviting. She lifted an arm and placed it, in imagination, around Fred's thickening waist. It was the best thing about

Fred, that feeling when you hung onto him that he
was solid as the rock of Gibraltar. With a sigh she
got to her feet and went downstairs.

He turned at her entry and reached for the oven
cloth. 'Just a moment,' she said. 'You'd better sit down
I've got something to tell you and you're in for a bit of
a shock.'

Chris pushed open the door of Liz's office. 'Could I see
you for a moment?' She looked up and he saw that she
looked weary.

'Is it urgent?'

'No.' He was backing out when she suddenly pushed
her work away from her.

'Come in, Chris. You look like I feel.' She pulled open
a drawer and produced a bottle. 'Pass some glasses . . .
they're on that cabinet.' She poured two glasses of wine
and handed one to him. 'Now, what's up? It's been a
hell of a day all round.'

'My item was dumped this morning.'

She nodded. 'I know. Tough, but it couldn't be
helped.'

'It could've been helped, Liz. They could've junked
some of the other stuff but no . . . let's not lose any trivia
. . . far easier to humiliate two supremely unimportant
old people and their silly little story.'

'You *are* bitter,' she said drily. 'Still, I know how
you feel. It's happened to me before.'

'That's just it,' he said. 'It happens all the time —
we pick people up and dump them as though they were

supermarket carrier bags. Well, I've decided I've had enough. Simon clinched it for me — he said like it or lump it. Well, I don't like it so I'm doing the other thing.'

'Don't blame Simon.' She raised her glass and sipped. 'It wasn't his decision, Chris. I'm not saying he wouldn't've made the same decision but in fact he didn't in this instance. And if he was unsympathetic I think you should remember he'd had a hell of a day. We all have.'

He shook his head stubbornly. 'I don't care. I can't stand it any more. After all, what happened today was typical — people just come to the end of their rope. Birgitta did. Now I've come to the end of mine.'

'I hope you haven't. I'm glad you spoke to me first because I'm going to suggest you go away and sleep on this.' Liz leaned forward. 'We need people like you, Chris. Not because you're a good film-maker, although you are, but because you care. You're upset and that's good. It's when you cease to be upset that you lose your usefulness. TV's what we make it. It's as good or as bad as the people who bring it to the screen. The trouble is, we work together, eat together, sleep together . . .' She sighed and clicked her glass against her teeth. 'In the end we lose touch with them — the audience, the reality. We think this crazy place *is* the world, and once we think that we're lost. If you dislike the way things are, stay and change them, Chris. Don't run away from the most powerful medium in the world. We can do more good — or more harm — in a minute than your old-style missionary did in a lifetime. Don't run away from that responsibility.'

Her words rang in Chris's head as he left the studio and he scowled as he thought of the night ahead, with Dilly and Clifford rehashing the morning and making puerile comments. The sun was sinking and that seemed to mirror his spirits.

He was searching for a taxi when Amy caught up with him. 'I'll stand you a pint on one condition.'

'What?'

'You cheer up. I've had enough of long faces to last me a lifetime.'

'Done,' he said, suddenly feeling immeasurably better. She put her arm in his as they turned towards the pub and he hugged her to him. 'Ta, Amy,' he said.

'For what?'

'Just ta for being around, I suppose.'

'Shut up, silly bugger,' she said as they pushed into the dim cosiness of the bar. 'I like you better your old ungrateful self.'

Liz had waited for as long as she could to convince herself that Simon was busy, that he meant to face her but was being prevented. In the end she was forced to acknowledge the truth: that Simon was going to do what he had done before, every time she had laid down a deadline, every time there had been a choice to make. He was going to ride it out, counting on her love for him, the sexual chemistry between them, to see him through. How could she expect him to understand that this time was different when she didn't know herself what had made it so.

The office was half empty as she walked between the desks. She pushed open his door without knocking and stood in the opening, hands by her side so that no treacherous body language should counteract her words. 'It's over, Simon,' she said. Quite quietly. And then again, 'It's over.'

She had expected him to counter, had pictured him rising from his desk, his head shaking in protest, his arms reaching out for her as they had done so many times before. Instead he simply sat there, his hands limp on the desk in front of him, his head bowed like that of an ox awaiting slaughter. 'I love you,' he said without raising his head.

'I know,' she said. 'And I love you and that's the pity of it.' She moved forward. 'But we both know we're going nowhere. If I tried, if I really exerted myself, I suppose I could make you leave and come to me. But there'd be so much of you left behind that it wouldn't work. And the funny thing is, I love you for that, for the very thing that means I can't have you. Isn't that crazy?'

He had lifted his head as he spoke. Now he smiled. 'I want you to be happy, Liz. Above all else, I want that.'

'I will be,' she said. 'One day I will be and so will you.' As she turned away she wondered if he believed her. And she wondered if what she had said had the slightest possibility of coming true.

*   *   *

In the taxi Daphne reran her piece in her mind. Yes, she had done the best she could in the time. It must have been good because she had been offered a rise and promotion on the strength of it. Deputy features editor.

Watch your back, Lou Bryan — I'm right behind you, she thought and chuckled. But it was a chuckle of amusement, not one of satisfaction. Whatever it was she wanted out of life it was not to be Lou's deputy. Nor did she want to spend her life charting the misery of the Vincents of this world. Once was enough.

She paid the driver and swung open the door of the pub. There was only a barmaid behind the bar and two customers in the corner. 'Brian's upstairs,' the woman said. 'You can go on up.'

She wasted no time when she reached his sitting room. The first feature was done, relating the juiciest details before the other tabloids could run spoilers, but the rest was screaming for her attention. She would have to work all weekend. First, though, there was something important to do. 'Brian,' she said. 'I've only one thing to ask. Will you marry me and if you say yes, can we afford for me to retire?'

Brian didn't answer for a moment and her euphoria trembled. 'Are you joking?' he said at last. She spat on her forefinger and drew it across her throat.

'Swelp me, it's the truth, guv.'

'OK,' he said slowly. 'Then the answer is yes to both questions. And now that's over come here and help me — I'm about to come over funny.' And then she was in his arms and her victory over Lou Bryan had paled into insignificance.

The dog thrust her head at Vincent's hand, where it lay flaccid on his knee. He felt drained, powerless to move, although he desperately wanted a drink. In the next room he could hear Dave on the telephone, scrabbling desperately to limit damage, fix up interviews, get in with the truth before the story was out. He had seen the colour drain from his manager's face as he told him, but Dave had rallied almost at once.

'I wish you'd told me, Vince. I could've handled it. Still, it can be fixed.' How did you fix the sordid truth? For a few months he had sold himself for money – too little . . . and lost too much in return – but the fact remained. He leaned his head back and closed his eyes, longing for sleep but knowing it would not come. The early euphoria had left him now and the implications of the whole affair were closing around him.

The thought alarmed him sufficiently to bring him to his feet. He had photographs to find for Daphne Bedford and a messenger to engage to get them to the *Herald* offices without delay.

He had dispatched the photographs and was getting ready to escape with Juno to the open air when the phone rang. He decided to risk answering it personally. Dave had other things on his mind. It was Liz and he relaxed. She already knew. There would be no searching questions, no need to fend off the impertinences the media could heap upon you when they had you on the run.

'Are you OK?' There was genuine concern in her voice and he felt himself relax. He had trusted her this morning and her quiet eyes had helped him through.

'Yes, I'm OK. I didn't really get a chance to thank you for your help today . . .'

'That's fine — think nothing of it. I was glad to help. I was ringing to thank you for yesterday . . . and Thursday. It made a brilliant item. I only hope it does some good for your scheme.'

'I'm sure it will.' He plucked up his courage. 'Would you like to have a look at it one day . . . just when you have time?'

'Yes, I would. That's the other reason I'm ringing. Did you mean what you said — about the possibility of a job?'

'I always mean what I say.' He tried to keep the mounting excitement out of his voice. 'When can we talk?'

Simon carried Rosie, pick-a-back style, to bed and looked in on Jake, bent over his computer. 'Don't work too late,' he said and ruffled his son's hair.

Jane had set the table and put flowers in a centre-piece. 'Nice,' he said to make her smile. There was a lump in the centre of his chest but his mind was more peaceful than it had been for a long time.

'I've been thinking,' he said as she served the meal. 'When all this blows over — this business with the presenters — we could get away for a few days. I've heaps of leave to come. Where would you like to go.'

'Anywhere.' She was smiling like the happy girl she had been when he married her, like the happy girl she could always be if he toed the line.

'There must be somewhere you'd like to go.'

'As long as it's with you and the kids it doesn't matter. We could stay at home — you promised to paint Rosie's room.' Suddenly he felt the warmth of family closing around him. They would be happy, they must be happy! He owed them that. He closed his eyes for a minute to think of Liz and wish her well. When he opened them again he was smiling.

'So I did,' he said. 'I did promise to paint Rosie's room. What colour should it be?'

When she put down the phone Liz reached out to recork the wine and put it back in the drawer. She would've liked another drink but that way madness lay. For a moment she contemplated ringing someone — anyone. David would jump at the chance to go out — but that wouldn't help either. She had to see it through alone, this pain that was as acute as if someone had torn a limb from her and left a gaping wound. She would never lie in Simon's arms again. Might never again lie with any man, come to that.

A producer appeared. 'Still here? I thought you'd've scarpered after this morning . . . everyone's talking about it. Have you seen the *Standard*? It's front page!

Well, thank God it's Friday, I say. Gives everyone time to cool off. See you Monday.'

If this had been another day she would have handed over to the night editor, who would monitor news as it came in through the night and arrange the morning appropriately. But it was Friday. No one would take over until Sunday. She thought of the long weekend ahead without even thoughts of Simon to sustain her. At least she was meeting Vincent. That should help. As long as she stayed at Daybreak, seeing Simon every day and all day, she would be settling for a single crumb, and the crumbs from another woman's table were not enough. She would have to ask for termination of her contract and until that came through she must take care to be alone with Simon as little as possible.

How would she live without the buzz of Daybreak? Of live television? She had meant what she said to Chris. It did have the greatest potential for good or evil and needed good men and women to drive it forward. Perhaps she might come back to it one day. She got out her bag and began to gather up her things. If she went to Bermondsey that would be a challenge. And perhaps she could help Vincent. Perhaps they could heal together.

She called 'Goodnight', as she went through security. The guard nodded acknowledgment.

'Have a nice weekend.' She smiled and nodded.

'And you.'

Somewhere, somehow, she would be happy. As she reached the street she decided to take it a day at a time. Get tonight over, then Saturday. She was having dinner with Vincent on Saturday. On Sunday, while he worked with Daphne Bedford, she could walk in the park and buy Kentucky Fried for dinner. And one day soon she would go to Bermondsey with Vincent, and who knew what might come of that?

As if on cue the streetlamps sprang to life, glowing faintly in the dusk but glowing just the same. Over her fried chicken she would rejig her CV ready to go after jobs if Bermondsey came to nothing. New job, new life. She wiped a stray tear from her eye and went on making plans, oblivious of passers-by, hurrying homewards as darkness grew.

Epilogue

So night falls on a city, gentling the outlines of buildings, hiding shabby paint and scarred brick, garlanding dingy streets with lamplight, so that they become once more enchanted thoroughfares.

Lights go out in offices and spring up in lonely bedsits. Lovers meet and kiss. Or part, wondering how to face the night alone, all of them clinging to one certainty. With daybreak, everything will be renewed.